A GIFT of GRACE

A GIFT of GRACE

Amy Clipston

BOOK ONE

ZONDERVAN®

ZONDERVAN.com/
AUTHORTRACKER
follow your favorite authors

Cli

ZONDERVAN

A Gift of Grace
Copyright © 2009 by Amy Clipston

Requests for information should be addressed to:
Zondervan, *Grand Rapids, Michigan 49530*

Library of Congress Cataloging-in-Publication Data

Clipston, Amy.
    A gift of grace / Amy Clipston.
       p. cm. — (Kauffman Amish bakery series ; bk. 1)
      ISBN 978-0-310-28983-8 (pbk.)
       1. Amish — Fiction. 2. Custody of children — Fiction. 3. Domestic fiction. I. Title.
    PS3603.L58G54 2009
    813'.6 — dc22

                                      2008046710

Interior design by Christine Orejuela-Winkelman

Printed in the United States of America

09 10 11 12 13 14 15 • 23 22 21 20 19 18 17 16 15 14 13 12 11 10 9 8 7 6 5 4 3 2 1

❀ ❀ ❀

For my mother, Lola Goebelbecker, my best friend, with all of my love. You are the glue that keeps our family together. You've been our rock through all of the health crises we've faced with Joe's recurring kidney failure. I never could have coped with the trips to the hospital without having you there for our boys. Knowing that our children have the stability of your care is a comfort, especially during those rough times. You are a blessing to our family, and we don't thank you enough. Thank you, Mom, for everything you do for us every day.

For my wonderful husband, Joe. How quickly ten years have flown by since we said "I do." We've traveled many rough roads together, but the tribulations have made our marriage solid. Who would've imagined we'd be facing a second kidney transplant for you? However, you've handled your health problems with grace and courage. My faith has been challenged time and time again as I've watched you struggle and suffer, but each time you overcome your trials, my faith grows and strengthens along with you. You're my hero and the greatest inspiration in my life. As I've told you many times—you're stuck with me. I love you. Always ...

To our beloved sons, Zachary and Matthew. Thank you for always bringing joy and laughter to our home and our hearts. Zac, you're a thoughtful and giving young man. You've been so brave and mature through all of the upheaval we've had due to Daddy's illness. You've come through like a superhero and never lost your faith. Matt, you're our comic relief. We never know what you'll say or do. Your humor is a light at the end of a tough day. Boys, I'm so proud of you and so blessed to be your mom.

❀ ❀ ❀

Acknowledgments

I'm thankful to many family members and friends who helped me along the way with this novel.

Several friends deserve special recognition. Thank you to Teresa Gigante for acting as a spiritual guide and helping me find my voice.

Andrea Christy-Glover, Lauran Rodriguez, and Margaret Halpin, your proofreading, editing, and suggestions strengthened the story. Thank you for taking time from your busy schedules to offer edits and ideas.

Pam McCarthy, thank you for your unending support and friendship. You're a blessing in my life.

Words cannot describe how much I appreciate Sue Mc-Klveen's and Ruth Meily's help with research. Ruth, thank you for opening your beautiful Lancaster home and your heart to my mother and me. And thank you for the wonderful Pennsylvania Dutch cookbook.

Many, many thanks to my special Amish friend who welcomed us into her home and answered numerous questions about her community.

I also want to recognize Beth Wiseman for her generous research assistance and her friendship.

I cannot thank my wonderful agent, Mary Sue Seymour, enough for believing in my writing and giving me the chance to propose this book series to Zondervan.

My editor, Sue Brower, is a blessing in my life. I appreciate your guidance and patience with me as I continue to polish my work and grow as a writer. I'm honored and proud to be a part of your team. I look forward to future projects with you. Thank you also to my developmental editor, Becky Philpott, for your friendship, patience, and suggestions. You're the best! I'm also grateful to the rest of the fabulous Zondervan team.

Thank you also to my in-laws, Joe and Sharon Clipston, for the love and support they've given during my road to publication. Pop, you know I'm looking forward to using that pen at my first book signing!

My aunt and godmother, Trudy Janitz, has been by cheerleader as I've worked toward publishing this book. Thank you for your love and for sharing those fabulous Amish recipes. Thank you also to my aunt Debbie Floyd for her encouragement. Love you both!

My husband, Joe, deserves a medal for patience. Thank you for enduring late nights while I clicked away on my keyboard as you were trying desperately to sleep. Love you.

To my parents, Bob and Lola Goebelbecker, and my brother, Eric, thank you for encouraging my writing. Love you all.

And thank you to our Lord Jesus Christ for giving me the words and inspiration for this book.

Note to the Reader

While this novel is set against the real backdrop of Lancaster County, Pennsylvania, the Amish community I've created is fictional. I've incorporated many rules and traditions common to the Faith; however, because there are differences among Amish communities, actions and dialogue in this novel may be different from the Amish culture you know.

A GIFT of GRACE

Rebecca Kauffman's pulse fluttered as the large SUV she was riding in rumbled down the narrow road past the rolling farmland and green pastures dotted by heifers. The cows chewed their cud and nodded their greeting as if welcoming her back. The serenity of the lush, open fields intersected only by clusters of white farmhouses filled her soul with a peace she hadn't felt since she'd left last month.

Pushing the cool metal button on the door, she cracked the passenger window open and breathed in the sweet, warm, moist air, free of exhaust from overcrowded city roads.

The SUV negotiated a sharp bend, and Rebecca's heart skipped a beat when the three-story farmhouse came into view. A smile crept across her lips.

Home.

The whitewashed, three-story, clapboard house stood humbly near the entrance to her family's forty acres. The newly painted white picket fence was a stark contrast to the house's green tin roof, speckled with brown rust that told of its age. The green window shades were halfway up, and the windows were cracked open to allow the springtime air to cool the house naturally.

A sweeping porch welcomed visitors entering the front, and a white barn, almost the size of the house, sat behind it. The large moving truck filled with the girls' belongings seemed out of place next to the plain farmhouse and barn.

"This is it," Rebecca said.

Running her fingers over the ties of her prayer *Kapp*, her mind swirled with thoughts on how her life had suddenly changed. She was finally a mother, or rather a guardian, of her two teenage nieces, her sister Grace's children. Children would again live in the large farmhouse for the first time since she and Grace had been young.

"It's beautiful," Trisha McCabe, her older niece's godmother, whispered from the seat behind Rebecca.

"Thank you." Rebecca sat up straight in the leather front seat and smoothed her apron. "I love it here. It's so quiet. If you listen close, you can actually hear the birds eating the seed in the feeder by my garden." She pointed to the area near the front door where a rainbow of flowers swayed in the gentle spring breeze. Four cylinder-shaped feeders dangled from iron poles above the flowers. "The birds love those feeders. I have to fill them at least twice a week."

Trisha's husband, Frank, nosed his large truck up to the side of the farmhouse and then killed the engine. Whispers erupted from the third seat of the truck, and Rebecca assumed her nieces were analyzing the home.

Wrenching open the door, Rebecca climbed from the truck. She inhaled a deep breath and hugged her arms to her chest. Birds chirped and a horse brayed in the distance. The familiar sounds were a welcome change from the roar of automobiles, blare of television sets, and electronic rings of cellular phones she had endured at her sister's home.

Trisha jumped out from the backseat, her eyes scanning the field. "You and Grace grew up here?"

A rush of grief flooded Rebecca at the sound of her sister's name. Unable to speak for a moment, she nodded. "This house has been in our family for generations. Grace and I were both born here and grew up here."

Trisha glanced toward the front door. "The land is just gorgeous. Can I go in and freshen up?"

"Of course," Rebecca said, folding her arms across her simple black apron covering her caped, Plain purple dress. "The washroom is to the right through the kitchen."

"I'll be right back," Trisha said before heading in the back door.

Rebecca glanced inside the truck through the open back door and spotted her nieces speaking to each other in hushed tones. Jessica Bedford was a portrait of Grace at fifteen, with her long, dark brown hair, deep brown eyes, high cheekbones, and clear, ivory skin. Lindsay Bedford, on the other hand, was fourteen, with auburn hair, striking emerald eyes, porcelain skin, and a smattering of freckles across her dainty nose.

Watching her precious nieces, Rebecca's heart swelled with love. She'd met the girls for the first time when she arrived in Virginia Beach after hearing the news of the accident that took the lives of Grace and her husband, Philip.

The girls gathered up their bags and climbed from the truck.

Lindsay gasped as her eyes roamed the scenery. "This looks like a painting." She turned to her sister. "Can you believe we're going to live here?"

"Whatever," Jessica deadpanned with a roll of her eyes. She chomped her bright pink bubble gum and adjusted her ear buds on the contraption she'd called an iPod. Her obsession with the electronic devices seemed to exemplify the Amish perspective that modern technology interfered with community and family relationships.

Lindsay pointed to the barn. "Do you have a lot of animals?"

"We have a few cats, chickens, goats, sheep, a cow, and a couple of horses," Rebecca said.

Lindsay's eyes lit up. "Cool!"

The gentle clip-clop of a horse pulled Rebecca's gaze toward the road. A smile turned up the corners of her mouth as Annie and Titus Esh's horse and buggy traveled past her home.

"It's so good to see horses and buggies again," Rebecca said, waving at her neighbors. "Such a nice change from the traffic jams."

"Yeah, but I bet it takes four hours to get to the grocery store," Jessica mumbled.

"It's a much more enjoyable ride, though," Rebecca quipped with a smile. "There's no loud radio to take away from the beautiful scenery around us." She turned her gaze to her garden. "That reminds me. I need to check my flowers."

Moving toward her garden, she found that more flowers had bloomed and vegetables had matured while she'd been gone. Daniel must have watered them for her as he'd promised. Stooping, she yanked a handful of weeds. The feeling of her hands on the green plants sent warmth to her soul. Nothing pleased her more than working in her garden.

It's so good to be home.

Jessica sidled up to Rebecca. Slipping her iPod into her bag, her hand brushed the front of her blue T-shirt revealing Grace's wedding ring hanging from a sparkling chain around Jessica's neck. "I've never seen so many different flowers."

"They're so colorful," Lindsay said, joining them.

Rebecca's smile deepened. Perhaps she'd found a common ground with her nieces—gardening. "My mother planted roses when I was about six," she said. "I helped trim and water them during the spring and summer."

"Your mother planted them?" Jessica turned toward her, her eyes wide with shock. "My grandmother?"

"Your mother helped in the garden too. It's sort of a tradition for children to help in the gardens, especially the girls." She touched her niece's arm. "Do you like to garden?"

"I guess." Jessica shrugged. "I did a little bit with my mom."

"I helped her weed," Lindsay chimed in.

"Maybe you both can help me sometime," Rebecca said.

"Yeah. Maybe," Jessica whispered. "My mother loved to take care of her roses. I had no idea it was something she did when she was Amish."

Rebecca chuckled. "Well, gardening isn't just an Amish thing, but it is part of our culture. We love the outdoors. It's a way to praise God and celebrate His glory."

Jessica nodded. "That makes sense."

"Becky, *mei Fraa. Wie geht's?*" a voice behind Rebecca asked.

Turning, she found her husband, Daniel, pushing back his straw hat to wipe the sweat from his blond brow. He flashed his dimpled smile and her heart skipped a beat. Oh, how she'd missed him during their month apart.

It was so good to be home!

"Daniel!" Standing on her tiptoes, she hugged him. "Daniel, I'm doing great now. Oh how I've missed you."

"I'm glad you're home," his voice vibrated against her throat, sending heat through her veins.

Stepping back, Rebecca motioned toward the girls. "Daniel, these are our nieces I've told you so much about on the phone. This is Jessica, and this is Lindsay. Girls, meet your uncle Daniel."

"Welcome." He tipped his straw hat.

"Thanks," Jessica said, shifting her weight on her feet and glancing around the property.

"It's nice to meet you," Lindsay said.

"I hope you'll be comfortable here with us," he said. "The movers and I have almost gotten all of your boxes in."

"Great." Jessica's smile seemed to be forced.

Taking his hand, Rebecca smiled up at Daniel. Yes, it was so good to be home.

Shoo-Fly Pie

Crumb mixture:

1 – 1/2 cups flour
1 tsp baking powder
1/2 cup sugar
1/8 cup shortening
Pinch of cinnamon

Liquid:

1/2 cup hot water
1 tsp soda
1/2 cup corn syrup molasses

Combine the five ingredients of the crumb mixture, using hands to work into crumbs. Set aside 2 – 3 tablespoons of the crumb mixture. Line a 9-inch pie pan with pastry.

Combine the three ingredients of the liquid mixture, and fold the crumb mixture into the liquid. Pour into the pie shell and sprinkle the set aside crumbs over the top of the batter. Bake in moderate oven (350 degrees) for approximately 35 minutes.

2

S cowling, Jessica glanced around the property.
    What a nightmare.

As if it weren't bad enough that she and her sister lost their parents, now they were banished from their home and their friends, forced to live on a place that looked like the set from those *Little House on the Prairie* reruns they used to watch when they were kids.

Daniel draped his arm around Rebecca's shoulders and steered her across the dirt driveway toward the barn. Jessica shook her head while examining their clothing, reminding her of the costumes she and her classmates would wear during their yearly elementary school Thanksgiving play. Rebecca wore a long, purple caped dress covered by a black apron and a small white prayer *Kapp* on her head. Jessica wondered how she managed to keep from passing out in the warm sun.

Daniel was clad in a straw hat, dark trousers, and a long-sleeved dark blue shirt with suspenders. She also wondered how he beat the heat with the dark-colored clothes. They seemed to be stuck in the 1800s.

"I guess they're speaking in Pennsylvania Dutch, huh?" Lindsay asked, her gaze following their aunt and uncle.

"Probably. I wonder if they're talking about us." Taking in a deep breath, Jessica clapped a hand to her mouth and gasped at the foul odor. "What is that stink?"

"Maybe the horses?" Lindsay asked. "I think I remember that smell from when Aunt Trisha took us riding at Hunt Club Farm that one time."

"It's awful." Jessica's eyes scanned the pasture behind the house, following the line of the split-rail fence. A cluster of farm buildings dotted the horizon in the distance. "We're in the middle of nowhere, Linds. No neighbors. I bet we're the only teenagers for miles."

"There have to be kids somewhere." Lindsay dropped her backpack onto the ground at her feet. "I saw a little convenience store up on that main highway. Maybe kids gather there and hang out like they did back home."

"Maybe. What else would kids do around here anyway — go cow tipping?" Jessica shook her head in disgust. "I bet there isn't a movie theater for miles. Besides, it would take a week to get anywhere by horse and buggy."

"It can't be too bad, Jess. Mom survived here somehow."

Mom. Jessica sighed. She missed her parents so badly that her heart ached. How would she and Lindsay make it without them?

"Do you think it's true that they don't have electricity or TV?" Lindsay's question broke through Jessica's thoughts.

Jessica fetched her iPod from her pocket and examined it. "That's what I hear. I don't know how I'm going to charge my phone or my iPod. I brought the cord for it, but I can't plug it in if they don't have electricity."

"What about basic things we need, like lights? I guess we'll have to use candles like they did in those Old West movies Dad liked." Lindsay sighed and brushed a lock of hair back from her face.

"Oh no." Jessica ran a hand through her own hair. "I can't live without my hair dryer. The humidity makes my hair frizzy.

I'll never be able to leave the house." She groaned. "I wonder if they even have hot water. Will we have to take cold showers?"

Lindsay scrunched up her nose. "Why would someone want to live that way? It seems so ridiculous today."

"I agree." Jessica shook her head. "Maybe we'll wake up tomorrow and realize this is all a bad dream."

Lindsay frowned. "Then we're having the same dream. I don't think that's possible."

The back door slammed and Aunt Trisha ambled through the grass toward them. "Hey girls," she sang as she approached. "You've got to see the inside of the house."

"Why? Are there chickens and goats roaming around on the inside?" Jessica deadpanned.

Trisha wagged a finger at her. "Remember your manners, Jess."

Jessica rolled her eyes and folded her arms in response.

"The house is really quaint," Trisha continued. "The furniture is lovely, but there are no knickknacks. They don't even have carpet. It's like they only allow the bare essentials."

"No carpet?" Jessica's eyes widened with horror. "You've got to be kidding me. We'll freeze in the winter."

"Do they even heat their houses?" Lindsay asked, her eyes wide with worry.

Jessica turned her gaze to the large farmhouse. "The house looks old. Check out the rust on the roof. I wonder if it leaks."

"Rebecca said the house has been in her family for years," Trisha said. "It was probably built at the turn of the century."

"Sheesh." Jessica shook her head. "Our house back home was only five years old, and it was brick. I can't imagine living in a place as old as this."

Scanning the pasture, Jessica couldn't help comparing it to the house where she and her family had lived for the past five years. The wooden, split-rail fence that bordered the pasture looked as if it hadn't been painted in several years. A shiny, white plastic split-rail fence lined Jessica's backyard, as mandated by the homeowners' association.

Although Jessica's family's yard back home had been tiny, they had a deck where Dad barbecued burgers and steaks in the warm weather. Aunt Trisha and Uncle Frank would come over and sit on the deck for hours, eating and laughing until late at night. She'd give anything to sit on that deck now and be able to talk and laugh with her parents one more time.

But now life was completely different. She was stuck in a strange old farmhouse with two guardians whom she didn't know. She wondered if Aunt Rebecca and Uncle Daniel ever hosted barbecues. Did they have friends who liked to come over and laugh and eat? A chilling emptiness filled her gut.

"The house can't be too bad," Lindsay said, snapping Jessica back to the present. "Mom lived here." Her soft voice quavered.

Jessica glanced at her sister and found tears brewing in her sister's eyes. Swallowing her own tears, she looped her arm around her slight shoulders. "I miss her too," she whispered.

"I can't believe she's gone," Lindsay said. "It seems like just yesterday she was modeling her dress she got for their anniversary dinner. How could they go out to eat and not come back? It's just not fair!" Her voice choked on a sob, and Jessica pulled her into her arms.

Jessica rubbed her sister's back. She held her breath while trying to suppress her own tears.

"It'll be all right," Trisha said, circling the girls with her arms. "I miss your mom too, but we'll all be okay. Somehow."

Jessica gnawed her bottom lip. She wanted to believe Trisha's words, but somehow she couldn't believe she'd ever be okay again.

"Is everything okay?" a voice behind them asked.

Turning, Jessica found Rebecca watching them with concern shining in her eyes.

"We'll be okay," Trisha said while rubbing Jessica and Lindsay's backs. "The girls and I were just thinking about their parents and feeling a little sad, right girls?"

"Uh-huh," Lindsay mumbled, swiping her hand across her wet cheek.

Jessica nodded and cleared her throat, wishing the lump that was lodged in it would subside.

"I know this must be so difficult for you," Rebecca said in a soft yet reassuring voice. "It may seem impossible now, but the grief will get a little easier as time goes on. I remember when my mother died. I thought my heart would never heal. I still miss her, but the pain did get easier after a while. I held on to my faith in God, and my faith got me through it over time."

Standing with a sad expression on her face, Rebecca resembled Mom and reminded Jessica of their last conversation. The disappointment in Mom's eyes had made Jessica cringe. Regret mixed with grief surged through her soul and caused more tears to fill her eyes.

When her vision blurred, Jessica cut her gaze down to her shoes in hopes of hiding her tears. She couldn't cry here. Holding her breath, she willed herself to stop.

"Would you like to come inside?" Rebecca offered.

"Sure," Lindsay whispered.

Taking a deep breath, Jessica stayed back and followed Aunt Trisha toward the front of the house.

3

Let's go in the front door," Rebecca said. She led Trisha and the girls up the steps of the front porch. She absently wondered if her nieces would eventually come to like sitting there with her and Daniel during nice weather.

Stepping through the front door, they entered into a large, open room, sparsely decorated with simple furniture.

"This is our living room." Rebecca pointed to the plain blue sofa. The Bible from which Daniel read every night sat on a small table by his favorite easy chair. She smiled to herself. She looked forward to sitting with Daniel and the girls while they listened to the Word together. She hoped that the girls would join them.

"The kitchen is this way." Rebecca padded across the hardwood floor into the kitchen. She idly noticed how different her plain kitchen was from the elegant one in her sister's Virginia home. Rebecca's kitchen housed a long table with a bench on one side and four plain chairs on the other. The modest pegs on the wall contained a couple of straw hats and a black cloak. The counters were clear and clean with only a few canisters on them. A rack full of little spice bottles hung on the white wall.

Rebecca's kitchen was the definition of simplicity while her sister's had contained an elegant dining set and granite counters crammed with the latest cooking gadgets.

Rebecca scanned the room, finding her plain but comfortable gas-powered refrigerator and stove along with a pot-bellied stove, a far cry from the stainless steel appliances back in Virginia Beach. Her drying rack sat next to the sink awaiting her clean dishes. No fancy dishwasher like at her sister's house.

It's so good to be home.

Pushing aside her memories of her sister's English life, she walked to the refrigerator. "Would you like some iced tea?" She opened the door and fished out a pitcher. "Daniel always brews fresh tea in the mornings, so it's sure to be delicious."

"No thanks." Jessica clasped her hands together. "Would you mind showing us where our rooms will be?"

"Of course." Rebecca replaced the pitcher in the refrigerator.

"I'm going to go see what Frank is doing," Trisha said. "I'll meet you upstairs later."

Rebecca motioned for the girls to follow her. She pointed out more of the house on their way. "Over here we have another sitting room and a large pantry. We do a lot of canning, so it's full."

"Canning?" Jessica asked.

"You know, like canned vegetables."

"Oh." She shook her head with disbelief as if she'd never met anyone who canned before.

Rebecca could see she had a lot to teach her nieces about living on a farm. They climbed the steep stairs to the second floor and entered a long hallway with several doors.

"My room is here," Rebecca said, motioning to a door on the right. "It was my parents' room."

The girls glanced into Rebecca and Daniel's room. Rebecca could only imagine what they thought of it, since it was much plainer than Grace's room. While Grace and Philip had beautiful modern furniture, Rebecca and Daniel had a simple double bed and dresser.

"Did you know your father's parents?" Rebecca asked.

Facing Rebecca, Lindsay shook her head. "No, we've only seen pictures of them. His mom died before we were born, and his dad died when I was an infant."

"Oh." Rebecca shook her head and frowned. "That's sad that you didn't know any of your grandparents."

Jessica turned to her. "Can I see which room used to be our mother's?"

"Of course," Rebecca said with a smile.

Two movers slipped past them carrying boxes. Once they were gone, Rebecca and the girls padded down the hallway. They stepped into a bedroom at the end of the hall near the back staircase, and Rebecca turned to Jessica.

"This was your *mamm's* room. I thought you might like it." Rebecca crossed the small room and sank onto Jessica's bed.

Jessica scanned the empty white walls. "My mom grew up in this room."

"*Ya.*" Rebecca paused. "I mean, yes, she did. My childhood room was across the hall." She met Lindsay's gaze. "I thought you might want that room. Your boxes should be in there if you want to go see."

"Thanks." Lindsay disappeared through the doorway.

Rebecca scanned the room while reflecting on the history of the room. "Most Amish children share their rooms and even their beds, but your mother and I didn't have to. Since our parents only had two children, we were able to have our own rooms. Our *mamm* died young of cancer, so we were the only children she could have."

Nodding, Jessica glanced around the room.

"I know it's small, but you'll adjust." Rebecca wished Jessica would express her thoughts aloud since she seemed to be analyzing the situation. She worried that the child kept her emotions too close to her heart, and she might wind up depressed.

Rebecca wondered how her niece would adjust to this Plain life after leaving her worldly existence. The room was a stark contrast to what Jessica had in Virginia Beach. In her former home, Jessica's room contained loud lavender walls cluttered with posters and photographs along with fancy furniture, including a vanity, desk, bookshelves, and a frilly canopy bed. Lacy, tie-back curtains had decorated her large windows.

Here, the walls were plain white. Most of Jessica's and Lindsay's furniture had been put into a shed at the back of Rebecca's property since only a bed and two dressers would fit in the girls' new rooms. No photos or even a mirror hung on the wall. Plain green shades covered the windows.

Jessica brushed her hand over the wall and then frowned. "I forgot. No electricity, so no light switch."

"You'll get used to it. The kerosene lanterns work really well."

"It's pretty in a simple sort of way. You inherited this house?" Jessica stepped over and looked out the window at the large, green field.

"That's right," Rebecca said. "Grace and I were the only children in our family, as you know, and she left when she was nineteen. I was the only one left, so I got the house. It's been in our family for generations. Daniel moved in when we married."

Jessica faced Rebecca, folding her arms across her chest. "Can I decorate it a bit? I know it's tradition to be plain, but I'm not exactly Amish."

Rebecca nodded. "I think it would be okay with Daniel, as long as you decorate it tastefully. We'll go over some rules tomorrow after Trisha and Frank leave."

"Okay." Her niece gazed toward the pile of boxes lining the far wall.

"I'll leave you to your unpacking." Rebecca headed for the door. "I'll go start on supper. If you need anything, just call me."

Trisha and Lindsay appeared in the doorway of Lindsay's room.

Trisha looped her arm around Lindsay's shoulder. "Do you want me to help you unpack?"

Lindsay shook her head. "I'm fine. You can go do something else."

Trisha glanced at Rebecca. "Can I help you in the kitchen?"

Rebecca shrugged. "If you'd like, but it's really not necessary."

"I'd be happy to," Trisha said.

Rebecca headed down the stairs with Trisha in tow. They nodded to the movers climbing the stairs with boxes. They stepped into the kitchen, and Rebecca fished through the refrigerator for ingredients.

"How does your refrigerator work since you don't have electricity?" Trisha asked.

"It runs on gas." She carried a handful of vegetables to the table. "Would you like to make a salad?"

"Sure." Trisha smiled.

"Please have a seat." Rebecca nodded toward the table. "I'll bring you the chopping block and a knife." She crossed to the cabinet and retrieved a block and then a knife from the holder on the counter. She then snatched a large bowl from the cabinet and brought all of the supplies to Trisha. "Thank you for helping me."

"Oh, don't be silly." Trisha arranged the vegetables on the table. "I appreciate all you're doing for the girls."

Rebecca glanced through the contents of the refrigerator again. "It's no trouble. I'm doing what Grace wanted. I wish I'd been a part of the girls' lives sooner. I just hope the girls won't resent being here. It must be hard on them. I show up and their world turns upside down." Pulling out a container of potato soup, Rebecca chuckled. "I guess this is a hint. Daniel must want potato soup for supper."

"Sounds good," Trisha said, slicing tomatoes.

"It's Daniel's favorite meal." She grinned while fetching more ingredients from the refrigerator. "I guess he missed me." She pulled out a pot to warm the soup.

"I would say so," Trisha said with a chuckle. "He seems really nice. I met him just a few minutes ago. He's been helping the movers."

"*Ya*. He's a hard worker." Rebecca grabbed bowls from the cabinet.

They continued preparing the meal for a few moments, silence filling the room. Rebecca wondered what Trisha was thinking and if she were analyzing the Amish lifestyle. It was different from her life in the large house on the oceanfront in Virginia Beach.

"I'm sure the girls will adjust to being here," Trisha said. "Just give them some patience and time."

"Oh, I will." Rebecca snatched utensils and set the table. "I hope Jessica will consider going to work with Daniel in the store. I think it will be good for her, and it will help her understand our culture."

"What do you have planned for Lindsay?" Trisha asked.

"I was hoping she'd go to work with me."

"You work in a bakery, right?" Trisha sliced cucumber and added it to the bowl with the tomato.

"*Ya*. Daniel's mother has owned it since she was first married." Rebecca leaned back against the counter. "For some reason, I can see her baking alongside of me. Lindsay is very quiet, and she expressed an interest in cooking while we were in Virginia. I think she might enjoy learning some new recipes and also being with the other Kauffman women."

Trisha nodded. "I think you're right. She's very sweet and loving. Jessie is too, but Lindsay is more open to change."

Rebecca sighed while facing the counter. *I just hope they'll both open their hearts and give us a chance.*

❄

"Supper's ready," Rebecca called up the stairs. Turning, she walked into Daniel, who stood behind her while wiping his brow. "I'm sorry. I didn't see you."

"No problem." He pulled her close and placed a light kiss on her lips.

Her pulse raced at the feel of his lips on hers. "Why did I deserve that?" she whispered.

"I'm happy you're home." He breathed a deep sigh and tossed his straw hat onto the peg by the door. "Everything's unloaded. The movers just left. Frank and Trisha are outside talking by their truck." His countenance brightened. "Did you make the potato soup?"

"*Ya.*" She chuckled and placed a hand on his chest. "I got your hint."

"*Danki.*" He kissed her again and then headed for the bathroom. "I'll go wash up."

Footsteps scampering down the stairs announced the arrival of her nieces.

"What's for supper?" Jessica asked.

"Potato soup," Rebecca said.

"Soup?" Jessica raised her eyebrows in question. "In the summer?"

"*Ya.*" Rebecca nodded. "It's your uncle's favorite."

"Oh." Jessica continued to scowl.

"Go wash up," Rebecca said. "Everything is ready."

❄

Once everyone was seated at the table, Rebecca and Daniel bowed their heads in silent prayer. After giving thanks for the meal, Rebecca cut her eyes upward, finding her nieces exchanging confused expressions. Rebecca idly wondered if Grace continued any Christian traditions in her home after leaving the community.

"How is unpacking going?" Rebecca asked the girls while passing the soup pot to Frank.

Jessica shrugged. "Okay, I guess."

Rebecca nodded while spooning soup into her bowl. The sound of spoons scraping bowls and lips slurping soup filled the air. Rebecca racked her brain for something that would inspire conversation. She shot Daniel a pleading glance, hoping he'd make conversation. He gave a slight shrug in response.

"The soup is delicious," Trisha said, breaking the uncomfortable silence. "You'll have to give me this recipe."

"Thank you," Rebecca said. Cutting her gaze across the table, she found the girls studying their bowls. They must miss their family suppers back home. Sorrow filled her heart at the thought of their loss. She wished she could reach over the table and hug them.

Frank asked Daniel a question about the farmland, and the men discussed the farm and woodworking during the rest of the meal.

When everyone was finished eating, Rebecca, Trisha, and the girls cleared the table, and the men took their conversation into the living room.

Rebecca and Trisha made idle conversation about recipes while they and the girls washed the dishes and cleaned up the kitchen. Rebecca wished the girls would contribute to the conversation, but she didn't want to push them.

When the kitchen was clean, Trisha took each of the girls by the hand and smiled. "How about you two chatterboxes come for a walk with me outside?"

Jessica raised an eyebrow in question. "Come for a walk with you?"

"That's right." Trisha yanked them toward the back door.

She pushed the door open and then turned back to Rebecca. "We'll be back in a little bit, okay?"

"*Ya.* Sure." Rebecca waved them off. "Take your time." She folded her arms and moved to the window where she watched Trisha loop her arms around the girls' shoulders and lead them toward the pasture. She wished she could reach out to the girls like Trisha could, and she worried she'd never get close to them.

A hand gently touched Rebecca's shoulder while she stared out the window.

"They'll be fine, Becky," Daniel whispered. "They just need time to say good-bye to Trisha."

She smiled up at her husband, wondering how he ever learned to read her thoughts so well.

"Just have faith and give them time." He ran a finger down her cheek. "You'll be a *gut* guardian. I know it."

Taking a deep breath, Rebecca hoped he was right.

❁

"Where are we going?" Jessica asked Trisha as she led Lindsay and her toward the pasture behind the house.

Trisha hugged them closer. "I wanted to talk to you before I leave tomorrow."

Jessica's stomach twisted at the thought of Trisha's leaving. "Don't leave."

Trisha sighed. "Unfortunately, Jessie, I have to. Uncle Frank and I both have to get back to work. Besides, if we stay longer, it will just be harder to go."

Lindsay sniffed and swiped her hand across her cheek.

"It's okay, honey," Trisha said. "You'll both be fine."

"No, we won't!" Lindsay's voice was thick with emotion. "We won't be fine ever again."

Jessica cleared her throat in hopes of stopping the sobs choking her. "Please don't go. We need you."

Trisha stopped and leaned against the fence. She frowned and took their hands in hers. "I know you feel lost and alone without your parents. Your mom was my best friend, the sister I never had, and I can't imagine life without her. But please believe me when I tell you that you're in good hands here."

Jessica scowled and wrenched her hand from Trisha's grip. "How can you say that? We don't know these people! They're strangers to us, and this place is crazy. We won't be okay. We're trapped on the set of *Little House*!"

Trisha's expression softened. "Jessie, please listen to me." She reached for Jessica, who stepped back and scowled in response. "Girls, your aunt loves you. She wants you here. Just give her a chance."

"How do you know she loves us?" Lindsay asked.

"I can tell. I talked to her earlier, and she's very concerned about making you both feel at home." Trisha glanced toward the house. "This place may seem like another planet, but you're in a loving home. You'll be okay."

Jessica shook her head and hugged her chest. "I don't understand why Mom wanted us here. We belong with you."

"This was your mom's choice. Your dad had no family left after his parents died, and your mom always loved her sister. She told me that she wished she could've brought you here to meet your aunt years ago."

"So, why didn't she?" Lindsay asked as she moved next to Trisha and leaned against the fence.

"Your father wouldn't let her." Trisha shook her head. "Every time she made plans to bring you here, he refused to let her go."

Stunned at the news, Jessica gasped and shook her head. "What?" She sidled up to Trisha. "Daddy wouldn't let us come? What do you mean?"

Trisha bit her bottom lip as if collecting her thoughts. "Your mom said your dad wasn't comfortable with her coming back here. She couldn't ever get him to tell her why, but she suspected your dad was afraid she'd come back here and want to stay."

"Why would she want to stay?" Lindsay said, wiping her eyes.

"He was afraid she'd want to return to this community and leave him behind." A sad smile spread on her lips. "My point is that your mom wanted you to come here and see what her life was like. I would suspect she knew that your aunt would love you and give you what you needed."

"But so can you, Trisha," Jessica said. "And we already know you."

"Girls, you're going to have to just trust your mom." She squeezed their hands in hers again. "I have no legal right to you."

"There's nothing you can do? Nothing at all?" Jessica held her breath, praying for a ray of hope.

Aunt Trisha sighed and paused. "I can contact a lawyer and see what I can do."

"Yes!" Grinning, Jessica jumped up and down.

Lindsay smiled.

"Now, wait a minute," Trisha said, frowning. "I'm not promising anything. Your parents made a will, and that's what the law will follow. Don't get your hopes up yet."

"Okay," Lindsay whispered.

"You have to make the best of it for now. I doubt I can get custody of you because I'm not a blood relative," Trisha said.

Jessica stared at her sandals and heaved a deep sigh.

"Jess?" Trisha asked. "Did you hear me?"

Jessica nodded and sucked in a breath, silently hoping she and her sister would somehow make it in this strange new home until Trisha could get custody of them.

Yawning, Rebecca cracked several eggs into a large bowl the following morning and then began scrambling them. She'd spent most of the night staring at the ceiling and dreading this morning.

After breakfast, Trisha and Frank planned to head back home, and the girls would be devastated. The longtime family friends had been the girls' security after their parents' death.

She had silently talked to God throughout the night, asking Him how to reach out to the girls and convince them to trust her as their guardian. A verse Daniel had read to her in the past came to her during the wee hours of the morning, "Therefore, as God's chosen people, holy and dearly loved, clothe yourselves with compassion, kindness, humility, gentleness and patience."

"Compassion, kindness, humility, gentleness, and patience," she whispered. "Yes, Lord. I hear You." She poured the scrambled eggs into a large cast-iron pan. After placing the pan on the stove, she ignited the burner.

Arms hugged her waist, and she gasped with a start.

"It smells *wunderbar*." Daniel's voice was husky against her neck.

"Daniel Kauffman!" she scolded while looking up at him. "You startled me."

"Sorry." He gave her a mischievous grin, then kissed her. "The animals are fed. Do you need help here?"

She gestured toward the table. "You can set the table and grab the bread from the counter. *Danki.*" Turning her attention back to the frying pan, she grabbed a spatula and stirred the eggs.

"Frank was carrying his and Trisha's bags out to the truck when I was coming in," Daniel said while placing plates and utensils on the table.

Rebecca nodded. "They said they would leave after breakfast."

"Do you think the girls are prepared for that?" he asked.

She shook her head. "*Nee.* It's going to be tough." She turned the burner down and snatched a large plate. "I thought we could sit them down and talk with them after Trisha and Frank leave. We can discuss the rules and tell them a little bit about our daily schedule. We'll let them know what their life will be like here with us."

"*Ya,* that's a good idea." He placed a loaf of homemade bread and a plate of butter on the table. "We just need to be sure they understand that they're welcome here but have to respect our ways too."

"Of course." Rebecca dumped the eggs onto the plate and then carried it to the table.

"Good morning," Trisha said as she entered the kitchen. "Everything smells delicious."

"Thank you," Rebecca said while placing the skillet onto the stove. "Are the girls on their way down to join us?"

Frowning, Trisha nodded. "We were just talking, and they were a little upset about our leaving."

Rebecca met Daniel's gaze, and he gave her a sad smile as if to say it would be okay. She was so thankful to have Daniel by her side. Just his subtle expression of encouragement gave her strength.

Glancing at Trisha, Rebecca nodded. "This is going to be difficult on them, but we'll do the best we can to make their transition easier."

Trisha sighed. "I know you will." Her expression brightened. "Can I help you with anything?"

"If you grab the juice from the refrigerator, I'll get the glasses," Rebecca said.

While Trisha and Rebecca served drinks, Frank and the girls joined them.

Once everyone was seated, Daniel and Rebecca bowed their heads in silent prayer. When Rebecca looked up, she began passing around the plates of eggs, bread, and butter.

Daniel and Frank made most of the conversation during breakfast as they had during supper last night.

Rebecca frequently glanced over at the girls and found them studying their plates and glasses. She tried to draw them out by asking questions about their unpacking efforts, receiving only one-word answers in response.

When breakfast was finished, the men disappeared outside while Rebecca, Trisha, and the girls cleaned up the kitchen. Trisha discussed the weather and how much she enjoyed breakfast. Although Trisha addressed the girls, they quietly washed and dried the dishes while Trisha and Rebecca cleaned up the table and put away the leftover food.

When they had completed their cleanup, Trisha stood before the girls and frowned. Rebecca's stomach tightened, knowing by Trisha's expression what was coming next.

"Well, I think it's about time to say good-bye," Trisha said, glancing at her wristwatch. "Uncle Frank wanted to leave by nine, and it's almost ten."

Jessica frowned, and Rebecca's heart twisted.

Trisha reached into her pocket and pulled something out. "Take this." She placed a cellular phone in Jessica's hand, wrapping her fingers around it. "Share it with Lindsay. I'll pay the bill."

Her eyes widening with surprise, Jessica studied her god-mother's face. "You're sure?"

"I'm hoping you can find a way to charge it. I promise I'll call you at least twice a week." Trisha rubbed Jessica's arm. "Everything is going to be fine."

Jessica wrapped her arms around Trisha's neck and buried her face in her shoulder.

Trisha gave Rebecca a sad smile, and Rebecca backed out of the kitchen and into the living room. She felt like an outsider, just like when they were in Virginia and the conversations seemed to swirl around Rebecca without including her. She headed out the front door to the driveway, where Frank and Daniel stood by the truck.

"I think it's about time to head out," Frank said, leaning back on the driver's door. "Unfortunately, I need to get back to work tomorrow."

"They're saying their good-byes now." Rebecca folded her arms across her apron.

Frank glanced around the yard. "You have a beautiful home."

"Thank you," Daniel said, grasping his suspenders. "It's a lot of work, but we love it."

The front door opened, and the girls and Trisha came down the porch stairs. Jessica's eyes were red and puffy while she held on to Trisha's arm. Lindsay frowned and pushed her hair back from her face.

Rebecca glanced at Daniel, who met her gaze with a bleak expression before he ran his hand over his beard and turned his gaze toward a buggy passing by on the road in front of the house.

Frank leaned over and patted Daniel's arm. "If you need anything for the girls, please have them give us a call."

"Thank you." Daniel shook Frank's hand. "You're very generous."

"I promise I'll call you," Trisha said, hugging Jessica. "Everything will be okay. You'll be fine here."

"Please take me with you," Jessica whispered between sniffs.

"Jessie, we talked about this." Trisha took the girl's face in her hands. "You need to be strong for your sister. Everything will be fine."

Jessica wiped her tears with the back of her hand.

"I love you," Trisha said.

"I love you too," Jessica whispered.

"I love you, Lindsay." Trisha hugged the younger girl.

Lindsay wrapped her arms around her neck. "Love you. We'll call you." Pulling back, she rubbed her eyes.

Trisha turned to Rebecca and gave her a quick hug. "Thank you for everything. If you need anything, let me know."

"*Ya,*" Rebecca said. "I'm sure we'll be fine, but I'll keep that in mind."

Trisha opened the door to the truck and then handed Jessica a cord she'd used to charge the cellular phone's battery during their trip to Lancaster.

Frank hugged the girls and told them to keep in touch. He and Trisha then climbed into the truck and waved before the SUV rumbled down the driveway toward the main road.

They stood in silence until the truck was out of sight then Rebecca took a deep breath and faced the girls. Jessica stood hugging her chest, her eyes red and puffy. Lindsay wiped her eyes with the back of her hand while her lip quivered.

Rebecca glanced at Daniel who nodded and then clapped his hands together. "So," he said. "Who wants some iced tea?"

Jessica raised a questioning eyebrow. "Didn't we just have breakfast?"

"*Ya,* but there's always room for iced tea." He looped his arms around the girls and steered them toward the house. "Let's head inside and have some iced tea."

Rebecca's lips curled in a tentative smile at the sight of her husband guiding their nieces like a father. She followed them into the kitchen and fetched the iced tea pitcher from the refrigerator and then snatched four glasses from the cabinet. She placed them on the table and sank onto the chair across from Daniel.

After pouring four glasses of tea, she passed one to each of them. Her nieces stared down at their glasses, avoiding eye contact. Rebecca met Daniel's gaze, and he raised eyebrows, prompting her to speak first.

The verse of Colossians echoed in her mind again. "Compassion, kindness, humility, gentleness, and patience."

Rebecca cleared her throat and licked her lips. "Girls, your uncle and I wanted to let you know that you're welcome here, and we'll do anything we can to make your transition easier."

Jessica ran her finger through the condensation on the glass without looking up.

Lindsay raked a finger through her hair and gnawed her bottom lip.

"What your aunt wants to say," Daniel said, cutting in, "is we want you to be comfortable here, but we also have some rules."

Jessica's eyes cut to his. "Rules? What do you mean?"

"Although you aren't members of the church, we still need you to respect our values," he said before meeting Rebecca's glance and nodding for her to continue.

The girls' questioning stares were trained on Rebecca.

"We don't allow music in our house," Rebecca said. "However, we'll allow you to listen to your music quietly in your rooms. Also, we'll allow you to decorate your rooms."

"As long as there isn't anything offensive on your walls," Daniel added as he lifted his glass.

"We have devotional time every night, and we'd like you to join us. We read the Bible together. It's our family time." Rebecca reached out and took the girls' hands in hers. "I know this adjustment will be very difficult for you, but remember, we're your family."

"Thank you," Lindsay whispered.

"What will we do all summer?" Jessica asked.

"That was the next subject I was going to touch on." Rebecca squeezed their hands. "We all work in this house. I thought Lindsay would go to work with me at the bakery, and Jessica would work with Daniel at the furniture store."

"Furniture store?" Jessica looked back and forth between Rebecca and Daniel, her pretty face twisted in a confused scowl. "I used to hang out in my dad's work shed, but I don't know the first thing about making furniture."

"We thought you'd like to do the books since you're so good at numbers," Daniel offered. "Becky told me how you were a math whiz and hoped to study accounting."

"Oh." Jessica's scowl softened slightly.

"I know you'll do a *wunderbar* job," Rebecca said, patting Jessica's hand. She then turned to Lindsay. "And you've told me that you loved to bake. I think you'll enjoy working with me and the rest of the Kauffman women."

"Okay," Lindsay whispered, lowering her eyes.

"But you won't start until next week," Rebecca added. "I want to give you some time to get settled." She pulled her hands back, and she noticed a look pass between the girls.

"If it's okay, can we go back to unpacking now?" Jessica asked.

"*Ya*, of course," Rebecca said with a nod.

"Thanks." Jessica popped up from the table.

Lindsay gave a slight smile and followed her sister out of the kitchen.

Rebecca turned to Daniel and blew out a deep sigh. The conversation had drained every ounce of emotion from her soul.

"Becky," Daniel said, leaning over and taking her hands in his. "They'll be fine as long as we guide them."

"*Ya*," she whispered. "I hope so."

Later that evening, a light knock on Jessica's door caused her to jump. Placing an empty box in the corner, she stepped over and opened the door, finding her sister standing in the hallway clad in a pink nightgown and hugging her teddy bear.

"Linds?" Jessica asked, studying her puffy eyes. "You okay?"

Lindsay wiped her eyes and gave a sad smile. "I found my old Mr. Bear tonight. It made me think of home and how safe I used to feel in my room. I know this sounds silly, but can I sleep in here?"

Jessica glanced at her twin bed and then shrugged. "Sure? Why not?"

Lindsay's eyes scanned the room. "You're still unpacking? It's almost midnight." She yawned and lowered herself onto the bed. "Aren't you tired?"

Jessica shook her head and grabbed her nightgown from an open suitcase on the floor. "Nervous energy I guess. I'm trying not to think about ... everything."

"Yeah. I know what you mean." Lindsay pulled back the covers and climbed into the bed. "I know it's been a month, but I can't believe they're gone."

"Yeah," Jessica said softly. She changed into her nightgown and then snuffed out the kerosene lantern before climbing into the bed next to her sister. Staring up at the ceiling through the dark, she contemplated the events of the day. Her life was so different now that she couldn't wrap her brain around it.

"So, what do you think about this place?" Lindsay asked.

Jessica hugged the blanket to her chest. "I don't know what to think. It's so different."

"The Bible readings tonight were nice," Lindsay said.

"Yeah. It was nice."

"That verse from Isaiah was kinda sad, though. It made me think of Mom. How did it go? Something like, 'As a mother comforts her child, so will I comfort you; and you will be comforted over Jerusalem.'" Lindsay shifted in the bed. "But it was neat to read from the Bible. It made me miss Sunday school."

"Yeah." Jessica cleared her throat, hoping that the mention of the Bible verse wouldn't cause her to tear up again. She, too, had thought of Mom when Daniel read it. She had to change the subject before she cried again. "It will take me a while to get used to the silent prayer before dinner."

"Yeah. That is different," Lindsay said. "But it's good, comforting really. The food isn't bad."

"I'd do anything for a burrito, though," Jessica muttered.

"We can ask Aunt Rebecca if there's such thing as an Amish burrito."

The girls chuckled and then a painful silence filled the room, hanging over the bed like a dense fog.

"Isn't it strange not to hear traffic outside?" Lindsay's voice was soft and unsure through the darkness. "It's too quiet, almost creepy."

Jessica closed her eyes and imagined the roar of traffic whizzing by on Princess Anne Road, outside their subdivision in Virginia Beach.

"Can you believe Mom slept in this room?" Lindsay asked. "I can't picture her dressed in Plain clothes, can you? That's just not Mom."

Opening her eyes, Jessica stared up at the ceiling. "No, I can't see Mom in clothes like Aunt Rebecca. I guess that's why she left. She wanted to go to college. She told me the Amish only let their kids go to school through eighth grade, and that wasn't enough for her."

"Do you think Aunt Rebecca will make us go back to school in the fall even though we're past eighth grade?"

A sick feeling rolled through Jessica's stomach. "Gosh, I hope so. I don't want to work in a furniture store forever. I want to go to college and travel like Dad did. I want to backpack across Europe and see Big Ben and the Eiffel Tower. I don't want to be stuck here in this farm country forever."

"I don't care about going back to school," Lindsay muttered while snuggling down in the pillow. "I hate school. I'm not good at it like you. I fail math tests even when I study for days. It's fine with me to work in the bakery."

Frustration surged through Jessica. "Don't say that!" She clicked her tongue. "Dad was right—you sell yourself short, Linds. You're much smarter than you think."

"Easy for you to say," her younger sister deadpanned. "You don't have to study, and you get straight A's. Not me. I struggle all the way. Working at a bakery will be fine for me."

Sighing, Jessica rolled onto her side. Dad was right when he said Lindsay was too hard on herself. Lindsay just didn't see how much potential she had.

Jessica opened her mouth to tell Lindsay how important school was but closed it after hearing Lindsay snore. Closing her eyes, Jessica wished she could fall asleep as quickly as her sister. However, her mind swirled of memories of her parents—birthdays, Christmases, summer evenings spent in their large, in-ground pool, trips to the Outer Banks of North Carolina, and barbecues on the deck with Trisha and Frank. She'd give anything to have those days back.

Anything.

Her thoughts turned to the night of the accident, and guilt washed down on her like a tsunami. She wished she could take the whole night back and relive it.

Despite her best efforts, she recalled her parents leaving for their anniversary dinner, the last time she saw them alive. Her mother was radiant, dressed in the cutest little black dress with her chestnut hair pulled up in a perfect French twist, and her father looked so handsome in his pinstriped charcoal suit.

Lindsay had hugged them at the door and told them to have a great time.

But not Jessica.

No, Jessica had remained up in her room, pouting and angry because Mom wouldn't allow Jessica to invite her boyfriend over that night. In retaliation, Jessica didn't say good-bye to her parents.

To make matters worse, she'd called her mother's cell phone, and they argued — mere minutes before the accident. Jessica never got to say "good-bye" or "I love you."

And now they were gone forever.

Why did they have to die?

Guilt mixed with regret slammed through Jessica as she wiped a tear from her hot cheeks. Closing her eyes, Jessica swallowed a sob.

The Bible verse Lindsay had quoted rang through her mind.

"As a mother comforts her child, so will I comfort you; and you will be comforted over Jerusalem."

But how could Jessica find comfort when she didn't understand why her parents had to die?

"Why, God? Why?" she whispered.

Closing her eyes, she hoped she could somehow fall asleep and let go of the grief gnawing at her soul.

❁

Rebecca pulled on her nightgown and snatched the brush on her dresser. Running it through her long hair, she wondered how the girls were sleeping.

She'd heard soft voices in Jessica's room when she went to check on them a little while ago. She hoped they were able to settle down and sleep despite saying good-bye to Frank and Trisha today. Guilt nipped at her while she pondered the pain and anxiety the girls were enduring in this new home.

The bedroom door softly opened with a squeak and then closed. Turning, she found Daniel crossing the bedroom while pulling off his shirt.

"What's on your mind?" he asked.

"Nothing," she said, sinking onto the bed. She ran the brush through her hair and stared down at the log cabin pattern quilt her mother had made long before Rebecca and Grace were born.

"Becky, I know you better than that." She heard the smile in his voice. "I can tell when something is eating at you on the inside." He sat down beside her, and the bed groaned under his weight. "What is it?"

Sighing, she looked up into his eyes, taking comfort in the warmth there. "I wonder if I made a mistake bringing the girls here."

His eyebrows cinched in question. "Why would you think that?"

"What do I know about raising teenage girls?" she asked, her voice trembling with uncertainty. "And what do they know about living here in our community?"

"*Mei Lieb*," he began, taking her hands in his. "We will make it through this. We just need to guide them. They will adjust. You have a lot of love to give them, and they need you."

Rebecca felt the love and reassurance in his face and wished she could believe him. "I don't know, Daniel. When the lawyer told me that Grace wanted me to be their guardian I was so honored and felt so blessed to be their mother in her place. When I called you and told you, I wanted to cry because I thought this would be my chance to be a mother to someone who needed me. I saw this huge opportunity to make the difference in the life of a child and get back the years that Grace and I missed through her children."

She paused, taking a deep breath. "When I was there with them for the month in Virginia, I thought I would bond with them while we took care of their parents' affairs and got the home in order. I thought my being with them would make them feel close to me and make the transition here easier."

Glancing around the room, she scowled with defeat. "But now I see I was kidding myself. I had this simplistic dream of the girls moving in and feeling a part of the family. When Trisha and Frank left this morning, I saw almost the same grief on their face as I saw the day of the funeral. They lost their parents all over again today when their parents' best friends left."

"You sell yourself short," he said, gently squeezing her hands. "You're a *gut*, strong, faithful woman. You will be a *gut mamm* to them. We need to help them feel comfortable here, but also make sure they respect our ways."

"I took on too much." Tugging her hands from his grasp, she stood and padded over to her dresser. Opening the top drawer, she snatched the letter the lawyer had given her the day he'd read the will. She unfolded it, and tears filled her eyes as she read Grace's words for what felt like the hundredth time.

Rebecca,

I know that many years have passed since we lived together in our farmhouse in Bird-in-Hand. However, I still remember our late-night conversations in my old room when we'd talk about our plans. While I dreamt of going to college and seeing the world, you wanted to stay in Bird-in-Hand and become a wife and mother.

Even though we lost touch for many years, I never stopped thinking of you daily. I see your smile and your face in my Jessica. I always wanted my girls to know you and to know about my heritage in Lancaster County, but Philip wasn't comfortable with the idea of taking the girls down the path of those memories. I don't think he ever forgave our father for shunning me as punishment for leaving. Although he hasn't admitted it, I think Philip is afraid I'll visit you and not return to my English life. As much as I want to visit my old home, I can't risk losing him. My life is with him now.

If you're reading this, it means that something has happened to Philip and me. My girls need a home, and I can't think of a better guardian than you. You are the most loving, understanding, and faithful Christian I've ever known. You will love my children as if they were your own and give them the patience and understanding that only a family member can provide.

Although my girls have never been to the community, I trust that you will make them feel at home. You'll teach them our heritage, and they'll experience the community where I was raised.

Please give my daughters the love they need in my place. I know it's a lot to ask, but you're my sister, my only family. Please accept my girls into your home and your heart in my absence. And please remind them of how much Philip and I love them.

Thank you, sister. May God continue to bless you and Daniel.

Love you,

Grace

Glancing up, Rebecca wiped her eyes. "I'm afraid I'm going to let Grace down," she whispered, her voice quavering with regret. "I can't be the mother they need; only she can."

A soft smile turned up the corners of Daniel's lips as he

stepped over to her. "Yes, you can." He wrapped his arms around her waist and pulled her close. "Have faith, Becky. You're stronger than you think. We need to guide them and give them boundaries in which they can grow."

Burying her face in her husband's chest, Rebecca closed her eyes and hoped she could give the girls the emotional support they needed.

Amish Friendship Bread

Starter (Do not refrigerate):

3 cups milk
3 cups sugar
3 cups flour

Day 1—Mix 1 cup milk, 1 cup sugar, and 1 cup flour.
Days 2 through 4—Stir each day.
Day 5—Add 1 cup milk, 1 cup sugar, and 1 cup flour.
Days 6 through 9—Stir each day.
Day 10—Add 1 cup milk, 1 cup sugar, 1 cup flour.
Into each of three containers, put 1 cup of the mixture. Give to 3 friends or keep one for yourself as a starter and give 2 away.
With remaining batter, make the bread:

Bread:

2/3 cup oil
2–1/4 cups flour
1 cup sugar
3 eggs
1–1/2 tsp baking soda
1–1/2 tsp cinnamon
1–1/2 tsp salt
1–1/2 tsp baking powder
1 tsp cinnamon

Add above ingredients to starter. Pour mixture into 2 loaf pans or 1 bundt cake pan that has been greased and floured. Bake at 350 degrees for 45 to 50 minutes. You can also add raisins, blueberries, nuts, apples, bananas, etc. if you desire. Yield: 2 loaves or 1 cake.

Rebecca climbed the stairs the following afternoon and headed down the hall to the girls' bedrooms. Jessica and Lindsay had been working hard to unpack all day, stopping only shortly for breakfast and lunch. She'd offered to help them numerous times, but they had insisted they could do it themselves.

Stepping into the doorway of Jessica's room, Rebecca surveyed the progress. While there were still boxes spread around the floor, the room was starting to look organized. A small bookshelf held books and CDs, and the open closet door showed a line of clothing. Photographs in frames lined the dresser and small desk.

Jessica sat cross-legged on the floor while sorting through a box of books. She hummed softly to herself, making Rebecca smile. She hoped it was a sign that her niece was starting to feel comfortable in her new home.

Jessica glanced toward Rebecca and gasped with a start. "I didn't see you there. How long have you been watching me?"

"Only a few minutes. I didn't mean to startle you." Rebecca looked over her shoulder into Lindsay's room and spotted her hanging clothes. "Lindsay, do you have a moment?" she called.

Lindsay stuck a blouse in the closet and then joined her in Jessica's doorway. "What's up?"

"I wanted to tell you I'm going to plan a family gathering for Saturday night so you can meet the rest of the Kauffman family. Daniel is going to spread the word at work today."

"That sounds like fun," Lindsay said.

Jessica nodded, her face expressionless.

"I think you'll enjoy meeting our other nieces and nephews," Rebecca said, hoping for some sort of acceptance from her older niece. "A few are your age."

"Oh good." Lindsay smiled at her sister, but Jessica's countenance still didn't crack.

Placing items back into the box, Jessica stood, facing Rebecca. "I wanted to ask you something. Where's our school?"

"What?" Rebecca asked, confused.

"Our school." Jessica looked surprised at Rebecca's response. "The school Lindsay and I will attend in the fall. I mean, it's May, so we can just forget this year and hopefully just pick up with the next grade in September. Or does school start in August here? I know some schools start—" She stopped speaking, her brows knitted together with concern. "Why aren't you answering my question?"

Feeling caught between a rock and a hard place, Rebecca took a deep breath. She wasn't expecting to address the education issue so soon after the girls' arrival, but she'd known the issue would come. After all, that was the issue that drove Grace away. However, Grace wanted the girls here; it was her last request.

She took a deep breath and clung to Daniel's belief that the girls needed her guidance in order to find their way.

Then the verse of Colossians sang through her mind again. "Compassion, kindness, humility, gentleness, and patience."

"I wasn't planning on enrolling you in school," Rebecca said, her voice calm and even.

"What?" Jessica stepped toward her. "No school? How can you do that? Legally, don't we have to attend school?"

"It's not our way." Rebecca smoothed her apron. "You're living in an Amish home now, and our scholars stop at eighth grade. You both are beyond that age, and you will be given responsibilities, which we already discussed last night. I hope you understand and respect that."

"It may not be *your* way, but it's our way." Jessica pointed to her chest. "It's *my way* to go to school and get my diploma. I want to go to college and become an accountant. And I want to get my own place and save money to take trips and see the world." Jessica focused her gaze on her sister. "Lindsay, don't you want to graduate from high school?"

Lindsay glanced between her sister and Rebecca, looking caught between them.

"Jessica," Rebecca reached for her, but she stepped back.

"But I need to go to school." Jessica's eyes shown with desperation. "I need to get an education. I'm not going to want to live here forever." Her voice rose. "Don't you understand that? You're not thinking of what I want. Besides, my mother got her GED and went to college. If my mother did it, then why can't I?"

Rebecca sighed with regret for the pain the rules were causing her niece. She briefly wondered again if being their guardian was a mistake and then shoved the thought away.

This is what Grace wanted.

This is God's will.

"I know that this is difficult for you," she began, "but you have to learn to respect the rules of this home."

"But my mother—" Jessica began.

"Your mother left the community to pursue her English life, but you're not in an English home anymore. It was your mother who chose this life for you and your sister." Rebecca shook her head, hating having to be so harsh with her niece. "Jessica, please just listen to me. The sooner you learn to respect our ways, the easier it will be for you."

Jessica shook her head in disbelief. "This is unreal."

Rebecca gave her a weak smile. "You said you wanted to be an accountant. You'll get experience balancing the ledger at the furniture store."

Jessica pursed her lips. "I don't exactly see the connection between my dream to be an accountant and working in your little *Amish* furniture store," her niece snipped.

"It's the best we can do for you," Rebecca said with as much patience as she could muster.

"Whatever." Jessica threw her hands up. "I guess I'll unpack my boxes and just forget my dream of having a decent education. Apparently when my parents died, I also lost all touch with reality." Jessica slammed the door, the force vibrating the wall around it.

Rebecca stared at the closed door in front of her, the sound of its slamming echoing in her head. Turning to Lindsay, she grimaced. "I guess she's really upset."

Her younger niece nodded. "Yeah, but she'll calm down soon. She's always had a short fuse."

"Like your mom."

Lindsay's eyes widened in surprise. "You remember that about Mom?"

Rebecca gave a soft laugh. "Oh yes. I remember it clearly."

"I'll try to talk to her for you. Maybe I can get her to calm down." Lindsay knocked on the door with her fist. "Jess, please open the door."

"Let her be." Rebecca touched her shoulder. "I'll try to talk to her later."

"You're not going to discipline her?" Lindsay's eyebrows knitted with confusion. "Mom and Dad never would've let her get away with that."

"It's okay. I can't expect her to welcome me into her life and accept me as her guardian in just a matter of a few weeks. This is difficult on you both." Rebecca folded her arms, studying Lindsay. "You're handling this much better than she is."

Lindsay's expression softened. "I was never very good at school. I worked hard but still got crummy grades. I think I kinda let my parents down because I never seemed to get ahead no matter how hard I tried. I'm honestly not heartbroken about not having to go back to school. I like to bake, so I think working with you will be fun."

Rebecca shook her head in amazement. The girls were night and day, just like she and Grace once were. She looped her arm around Lindsay's shoulder. "Would you like me to help you unpack?"

Lindsay shook her head. "It's okay. I'm fine."

"Well then, I'll be in my sewing room if you need me. I'm working on some new trousers for Daniel." Rebecca took one last look at Jessica's door and then started down the hall.

As she sat down in front of her sewing machine, she hoped Daniel was right about the girls. She prayed that giving the girls the proper guidance would lead them to find their place in the community and understand God's plan for them.

Suddenly a calm filled Rebecca, as one of her favorite verses, Romans 15:13, filled her heart and her mind: "May the God of hope fill you with all joy and peace as you trust in him, so that you may overflow with hope by the power of the Holy Spirit."

She smiled. Yes, she trusted the Lord. The girls would adjust. She just had to have faith.

❈

Lindsay knocked on her sister's door again. "Jess, let me in." She blew out a frustrated sigh. "Come on ... This is ridiculous! You're acting like a baby."

"Acting like a baby?" The door swung open, and Jessica glared at her. "How can you say that? You act like your life hasn't been turned upside down!"

Grinning, Lindsay folded her arms. "I knew that would get you."

Jessica rolled her eyes. "You know me too well." Shaking her head, she crossed the small room and flopped onto her bed, slouching with her gaze fixed on the ceiling.

"Can we talk?" Lindsay asked, leaning on the doorframe.

"Who's stopping you? Talk."

"How about we go sit on the porch?" Lindsay said. "I'm itching to get out of the house for some fresh air."

"Sure, if you like the smell of horses." Jessica dragged herself up and followed her sister down the stairs and out the front door.

Once outside, they sat side by side in the porch swing and gazed toward the long dirt driveway.

Lindsay clasped her hands and waited for her sister to say something. She could've cut the tension between them with a knife. She was nervous about saying the wrong thing and setting her off yet again.

Jessica had become so touchy since their parents' accident, and Lindsay dreaded another screaming match. Yet, she'd felt she had to say something to try to calm her sister down and to help make the transition a little easier on them both. Lindsay smiled to herself, wondering how she'd suddenly become the older sister.

"How come you didn't stick up for me earlier?" Jessica asked, breaking the thick, awkward silence.

Lindsay gave her a sideways glance. Her sister always got right to the heart of the issue. "Because I didn't agree with you completely. You already know my feelings about school. I'm not good at it."

"I know you don't like school, but how can you not want to graduate, Linds?" Jessica faced her, leaning back against the arm of the swing. "Don't you want to make something of yourself?"

"Of course I do, but—"

"But?" Her older sister sat up straight and gestured with her hands. "There's no 'but' when it comes to your education. Mom and Dad always said the only thing that mattered was finishing school. Without an education, we'll wind up flipping burgers or waiting tables."

Lindsay nodded in agreement. She remembered her parents echoing that lecture many times when her grades had slipped. "I know, but Mom and Dad are gone now. I never liked school much. I wasn't good at it like you. I can't say I'm sad that I don't have to go back."

"That doesn't change the fact that we need to finish school. Rebecca can't just show up and decide our futures for us."

"You're right, but you can't walk into our aunt's house and slam doors and talk back. How do you think Mom would feel if she knew you were nasty to her sister?" Knowing her comment about their mother would upset Jessica, Lindsay braced herself for an explosion.

"Don't throw Mom in my face," Jessica hissed through gritted teeth. "We both miss her, and we both know she'd never want this for us."

Lindsay folded her arms across her chest in disagreement. "So then why did she make Aunt Rebecca our guardian? Mom included that note with the will saying she wanted us to experience life in the Amish community. This was Mom's decision, not Aunt Rebecca's."

Jessica's expression softened as she sighed. "I don't want to fight with you."

"Well, I'd like you to stop fighting with Aunt Rebecca. Give her a chance." Lindsay patted Jessica's warm hand. "I talked to her a lot while we were packing up back home, and she's really sweet. In fact, she reminds me a lot of Mom."

Her older sister's eyes narrowed to a glare. "Don't say that."

"It's true." Lindsay glanced over toward the road as a horse and buggy clip-clopped by. "And who knows, Jess. Maybe we'll actually like it here."

"I just hope we aren't here long." Jessica sat back in the swing. "I hope Aunt Trisha can get custody of us somehow. She promised she'd try."

"Maybe we'll find out we love living with the Amish."

"Just what I wanted to do for the rest of my life, dress like a nun and work in a furniture store," Jessica deadpanned.

"You might like it here." Lindsay glared at her. "Just give it a chance. That's all I ask."

Her sister shook her head. "When did you suddenly become my big sister?"

"I was just thinking the same thing a little while ago." Lindsay gave her sister a quick hug. "Try not to be so negative, and go easy on Aunt Rebecca. We're her first and only kids."

Her sister sighed. "Fine. But I *will* go back to school somehow. Rebecca isn't going to hold me back. *Ever.*"

Lindsay nodded. She didn't expect any more than that from her stubborn older sister.

7

Saturday night, Rebecca yanked a chocolate oatmeal cake from the oven to serve for dessert after their roasted chicken meal. Voices speaking Pennsylvania Dutch swirled around her. She placed the cake on the counter to cool and spun to face the other female members of the Kauffman family fluttering around her kitchen.

Her mother-in-law sidled up next to her and examined the cake. "Oh, Rebecca, you've outdone yourself." Elizabeth inhaled deeply. "That smells heavenly."

"*Danki.*" Rebecca lifted her glass of iced tea and took a long gulp. "I guess the men are converging at the barn, *ya?*"

"Don't they always?" Kathryn, the oldest of Daniel's three sisters, asked while cutting a piece of chocolate cake. "They have their secret male talk away from our curious ears."

"I'm sure all they talk about are their horses and the weather," Beth Anne said, while placing a plate full of crullers on the counter.

"Beth Anne, why are you leaving the crullers over there?" Elizabeth asked her namesake. "Bring them here, so we can enjoy them with the rest of our lovely desserts." She gestured toward the goodies lining the table.

"I thought we'd give them to the men," Beth Anne said with

a grin. "They didn't come out quite right. The men can enjoy the dry crullers while we keep the moist cakes to ourselves."

The women burst into cackles. Seven of Rebecca's young nieces and nephews chased each other through the kitchen, grabbing handfuls of butterscotch cookies on their way out.

Elizabeth patted Rebecca's back. "If that isn't the highest compliment of your cooking, Rebecca, I don't know what is."

"*Ya*, it is." Rebecca smiled. She adored all of her nieces and nephews, but she always felt a pang of regret for not being able to give Daniel a child of his own.

Footsteps pounded down the hallway and Sarah Troyer, Daniel's youngest sister, burst into the kitchen. "*Mamm! Mamm!*" Sarah leaned on the counter, taking deep breaths.

"Sarah Rose!" Her mother rushed over and looped her arm around her youngest child's shoulders. "Are you okay?"

"*Ya*." The blonde beamed, her blue eyes sparking in the light of the kerosene lamps. "I'm wonderful *gut*!"

Rebecca wiped her hands on a rag. "*Wie geht's?*"

Sarah's eyes filled with tears. "Peter and I are going to have a baby!"

"Sarah Rose!" Elizabeth clapped her hands and then pulled her daughter into her arms. "Oh, Sarah Rose. You're going to be a *mutter*."

"*Ya!*" Sarah squeezed her eyes closed and bit her lip. "Can you believe it? The Lord has blessed Peter and me."

"Oh, daughter." Elizabeth framed Sarah's face in her hands. "My heart is bursting with joy for you!"

Rebecca swallowed, fighting tears of joy mixed with a stab of envy. Although she was happy for Sarah and Peter, the news meant that Rebecca and Daniel would be the only married Kauffman offspring without children. Perhaps not children of her own—but they now had Jessica and Lindsay. Their home would finally be blessed with children.

"Sarah Rose is going to have a baby!" Elizabeth swiped the

tears splattering her pink cheeks. "My baby's going to be a *mutter.*"

"Oh, sister!" Kathryn exclaimed.

"You're gonna be a *mamm!*" Beth Anne added.

While the sisters exchanged hugs, Rebecca forced a smile, wishing her twinge of jealousy would dissipate. She'd long ago accepted the doctors' assessment that she couldn't conceive. Yet, sometimes the knowledge nipped at her.

She mentally berated herself for her negativity. *Stop, Rebecca! The baby is a wonderful blessing to our family.*

Her mother-in-law squeezed Rebecca's hand as if reading her thoughts. "The Lord has plans for you and Daniel," she whispered. "You'll see. The Lord works in mysterious ways. Remember the Scripture Romans 12:12 — 'Be joyful in hope, patient in affliction, faithful in prayer.'"

"*Ya.*" Rebecca smiled. She loved when Elizabeth recited that verse. "I know."

While Sarah and her sisters continued to hug and cry joyful tears, Rebecca silently prayed Sarah would have a happy, healthy pregnancy.

Rebecca scanned the kitchen for her nieces. Lindsay had stopped in earlier to see what Rebecca was baking, but she'd disappeared soon after. She wondered if Jessica had ever left the confines of her room.

Rebecca stepped over to her mother-in-law and touched her hand. "I'm going to go check on the girls."

Elizabeth patted her hand. "Don't be too long."

"I promise I won't." Rebecca motioned toward the living room. "I just want to be sure they're okay. We have such a large family, and it's a huge adjustment getting to know them all."

Stepping into the living room, Rebecca spotted Lindsay on the floor surrounded by several of Rebecca's young nieces and nephews. A smile formed on Rebecca's lips. She, too, had loved playing with the little children in the community when she was a teenager. When she was growing up, the best part of friendly visits was spending time with the children.

Rebecca couldn't help but think that she and Lindsay were very much alike. Perhaps her younger niece would adjust to this life. She couldn't help but wonder if Grace also had seen this potential in Lindsay. Maybe that was part of the reason why Grace had wanted her girls to live with Rebecca and not Trisha.

Lindsay's gaze met Rebecca's, and the girl smiled, causing Rebecca's heart to swell with hope. Oh how she loved getting to know her nieces and having them with her.

If only she could get through to Jessica. She needed to find a way to get that girl to open up and give Rebecca a chance.

The front door creaked open, wrenching Rebecca from her thoughts. Daniel's older brother Robert and his family filed in.

"*Wie geht's?*" Rebecca greeted Robert and hugged his wife, Sadie.

"*Gut. Danki.*" Sadie smiled. "Do I smell *Blitzkuchen?*"

"*Ya.*" Rebecca laughed. "Please go help yourself. It should be cool enough to cut."

While Robert, Sadie, and their seven children headed into the kitchen, Rebecca gazed at fifteen-year-old Katie near the back of the line, and an idea flashed in her mind. Since Katie had always been such a sweet, thoughtful girl, maybe she would be able to get through to Jessica. Katie could be the friend Jessica craved.

"Katie!" she called.

"*Ya?*" Katie possessed the same Kauffman blue eyes and blonde hair as Daniel and the rest of his siblings.

"Would you like to meet your new cousin?" Rebecca asked. "She's your age."

"*Ya.*" Katie's eyes lit up.

Rebecca led her up the stairs and down the hall to Jessica's room, where they found her laying on her bed with her ear buds stuck in her ears and her feet bouncing in time to music only she could hear. Her eyes were closed and she hummed to herself.

Katie gave Rebecca a sideways glance, her eyes filled with surprise. "She's English?"

"*Ya.*" Rebecca nodded. "Her mother was my sister. She left our community many years ago and married an English man."

"Oh." Katie turned back to Jessica, her eyebrows knitted with suspicion.

Despite Katie's apprehension, Rebecca held on to a glimmer of hope that the girls could somehow become friends. Taking a deep breath, Rebecca touched Jessica's foot, and the girl jumped.

Popping up to a sitting position, Jessica yanked out the ear buds and stared at Rebecca, her brown eyes wide with surprise. "Oh, hi. I didn't hear you come in." She smoothed her hair and glanced at Katie.

"Hi." Katie gave a tentative wave.

"Jessica, this is my niece, Katie Kauffman. Her father is Daniel's older brother, Robert." Rebecca gestured between the girls. "And Katie, this is my niece Jessica Bedford. I thought you girls might like to chat, since you're the same age."

"Oh. Cool." Jessica crossed her legs and patted the thighs of her jeans. She gestured toward the end of bed. "Have a seat, Katie."

"Okay," Katie said, her voice soft and unsure. She glanced around the room, scanning the sea of photos. She pointed to a portrait of Jessica's parents on their wedding day. "Who's that?"

"My mom and dad on their wedding day." Jessica rose, dropping her iPod on the bed.

Rebecca smiled. The girls were at least talking. *Wunderbar!* She slowly backed out of the room, leaving the girls to get to know each other. While heading down the hall, she said a prayer that Katie would break down the wall Jessica had built around her heart the day her parents died.

❄

Jessica watched Katie stand by the dresser and examine her parents' wedding portrait. Clad in the same Plain garb as Rebecca, Katie was the opposite of Jessica, who wore her favorite low-rider jeans and two form-fitting T-shirts, one over the other. How on earth did Rebecca expect these two opposites to get along? What could they possibly find to talk about besides the weather?

"You look just like your *mamm*," Katie said.

Jessica fingered her mother's wedding ring hanging from the chain around her neck. "Thanks," she whispered.

"It's true." Katie met her gaze and smiled. "Your *mamm* is Rebecca's sister?"

"Yeah." Jessica sank onto the edge of the bed. "Her older sister."

Katie turned back to the photograph. "I see it. They have the same eyes and the same smile. Very beautiful."

Thoughts of her mother flooded Jessica, causing a lump to swell in her throat. She cleared her throat, hoping to suppress threatening tears.

"I heard your parents died in an accident," Katie said. "I'm so very sorry. I can't imagine the sadness you and your sister have endured by losing both of your parents."

The girl's voice was soft and full of compassion, wrenching something deep in Jessica's soul. Knowing she would dissolve in tears, she didn't want to discuss her parents and relive the memories of the night they died. Therefore, she needed to find a way to change the subject quickly.

"So, you're fifteen?" Jessica asked, her voice wavering with the remnants of the guilt brought on by the memories.

"*Ya*." Katie fingered the ties of her prayer *Kapp*.

Jessica leaned back against the headboard. "Rebecca said kids here don't go to school beyond age fourteen. What do you do all day?" She patted the edge of the bed, and Katie lowered herself onto it.

"Oh, I stay busy." Katie nodded with emphasis. "My *dat* runs our dairy farm, and there's plenty to do. I help my *mamm* tend to my five younger siblings, and I also help make quilts, which we sell at the market."

"Five younger siblings?" Jessica shook her head in disbelief. "Wow. I thought one younger sister was a lot."

"I'm the second oldest to my brother Samuel. Most families have between six and ten children."

"Ten?" Jessica gasped. "That's incredible."

Katie shrugged. "It's our way I guess. And what did you do before you came here? You went to school?"

"Yeah. I was a sophomore in high school." Jessica sighed. "I wanted to graduate with my class in two years and then go to college." She frowned. "But now I can't. I'm going to work in Daniel's furniture store as the bookkeeper."

"That's not so bad." Katie frowned in response. "It's better than being stuck at home doing laundry and taking care of kids. I love my family, of course, but sometimes I wish I could do some work outside the house."

Jessica nodded. She hadn't thought about it that way. It could be worse.

She studied Katie's pretty face. Her skin was flawless. Jessica would bet Katie would be photogenic. She'd love to fish out her makeup bag from the remaining unpacked boxes and experiment with colors to bring our Katie's gorgeous blue eyes.

Jessica pointed toward Katie. "You'd look fantastic with a little eyeliner and lipstick."

Katie blushed. "Oh, we're not allowed to wear makeup. Vanity is a sin."

"It's a shame. You have a fabulous complexion."

"Danki." Katie's gaze found the iPod. "What's that?"

"It's called an iPod." Jessica picked it up. "Kids use it to listen to music."

"Oh. Music is forbidden too. We only sing hymns, but no instruments are allowed at all." Katie bit her lip as if debating if she should touch it.

Even music is forbidden? Grimacing, Jessica wondered how on earth these kids put up with all of the rules. Their lives must've felt like a prison sentence. Jessica glanced at the quiet, formal girl sitting in front of her on the bed. Katie looked like she needed some fun. She doubted any harm could come from listening to a few rock songs on the iPod.

She glanced up to the door, and a smile tugged at the corners of her mouth.

"The door is closed." Jessica held the iPod out to Katie. "I won't tell if you don't."

A slow smile turned up the corners on Katie's lips. She took the small device from her. "How does it work?"

8

Sitting at the kitchen table, Rebecca chuckled while Beth Anne recounted a story of a funny English customer at the bakery who wanted to know how to get the papers on the cupcakes after baking them.

Rebecca glanced around at her sisters-in-law and mother-in-law and couldn't help but think how lucky she was to be a member of the Kauffman family. It was the only stable family she'd ever known. Sometimes she wondered what it would've been like if Grace had stayed and married a man in their community. Would she also have been present at the frequent Kauffman family gatherings?

Rebecca's thoughts turned to Grace and their last visit together. It had been more than ten years ago when their father had passed away. He was their only living parent, since their mother had died after a long, terrible battle with cancer when Rebecca was eight and Grace was eleven. *Dat* had never remarried, leaving Grace and Rebecca to grow up without a mother to guide them. He did the best he could fulfilling both roles.

After her *Rumspringa*, when Grace decided she couldn't stay in the church, *Dat* disowned her. It had broken Rebecca's heart to see her older sister, her best friend, pack up and leave Lancaster County to pursue a life with her English boyfriend,

Philip Bedford, whom Grace had met while he was in town on a business trip.

Since she didn't have a phone, Rebecca tried to keep in contact with her sister through letters. After she married Daniel and began working in his mother's bakery, she occasionally received calls from Grace on the bakery phone. Although she longed to visit Grace over the years, she never did. Now she regretted it with all her heart. She had missed so much!

Rebecca stared down at her glass of tea while contemplating her sister. Because her father refused to talk to her, Grace never came back to Lancaster County until she and Rebecca buried him. Their last meeting was such a sorrowful one, but they did continue to keep up with letters and infrequent calls after the funeral.

Rebecca took a long drink of tea. She wished *Dat* hadn't shunned Grace. She knew it had broken her sister's heart. However, their father was a stubborn man who would never change his mind after he'd made a decision. To him, Grace was dead, and he only had one daughter.

Rebecca always loved her father, but she lost respect for him after the way he'd treated Grace. She was thankful when the Kauffmans welcomed her with open arms. With them, she felt like more than an in-law; she felt like a blood relative.

As she lifted the glass to her lips again, an idea flashed through Rebecca's mind. Maybe Grace had left the girls to Rebecca because she'd always known that the Kauffmans would accept her girls as they had accepted Rebecca. Perhaps Grace knew the girls would be loved unconditionally in Rebecca's home and that Rebecca remembered what it was like to lose their mother at a young age. Her heart warmed at the thoughts.

So engrossed in her thoughts of Grace, Rebecca was startled when the back door opened and slammed against the house. Robert appeared, followed by five of his children. From his frown, Rebecca could tell he was unhappy. She idly wondered if he and Daniel had exchanged tense words yet again. It seemed the brothers were always disagreeing these days. Robert felt Daniel was too eager to make allowances and embrace the Englishers that lived nearby.

Robert's gaze met his wife's, and Sadie stood like a shot. "It's time to go home," he said.

"*Ya*." Sadie nodded. She turned to Rebecca. "Have you seen Katie?"

"I took her up to meet my niece about an hour ago. Did you want me to check on her?" Rebecca asked.

"*Nee*." Sadie patted Rebecca's arm. "I'll go."

"*Mamm!*" Gretchen, Sadie's youngest at age two, moaned and then started to sob.

Sadie hoisted Gretchen onto her lap and whispered in her ear. She gazed at Robert who started toward the door.

"I'll get Katie," he muttered. "You start loading up the *kinner*."

Rebecca touched her sister-in-law's arm. "I'll help you."

"*Danki*," Sadie said with a smile.

❦

Katie grinned and swayed back and forth in time to the music singing through the iPod ear buds. The ties to her prayer *Kapp* bounced along with her. "This music is really *wunderbar*."

Jessica grinned. "I'm so glad you like it."

"What's the name of this musical group again?"

"Puddle of Mudd." Jessica leaned back against the headboard. "I love alternative rock, and they're one of my favorite bands."

Katie tilted her head in question. "Alternative rock?"

"It's a type of rock music. It's kinda difficult to explain." Jessica popped up and crossed the room to her laptop sitting on her dresser. She carried the laptop back to the bed and lowered herself onto the edge. "There are different kinds of rock music."

"Oh." Katie nodded, but her eyes glittered with confusion.

Flipping the laptop open, Jessica hit the Power button. She knew it wouldn't be long before she'd have to figure out how to charge that too. "I'll show you this awesome website that explains the different kinds of—" She stopped speaking and laughed.

"What?"

"I just remembered." Jessica gave a sweeping gesture with her arms. "I don't have Internet access here. I'm in an *Amish* home."

"*Ya*. That would make it difficult." Katie touched her arm, and they laughed together.

Jessica's eyes widened in surprise at Katie's openness and welcome. For the first time since arriving in Lancaster, Jessica felt as if she had a friend.

The bedroom door suddenly whooshed open and slammed against the wall.

"Katie," a gruff voice enunciated the name.

Jessica glanced over to see a tall man bearing the same blue eyes, blond hair, and beard as Daniel. She deduced this was Daniel's older brother Robert glowering in the doorway. He scanned the room, his glare focusing on the iPod and then the laptop. The stern look of his eyes sent a chill skittering up Jessica's spine.

Katie gave a soft gasp, stood up straight, and smoothed her apron and dress. "*Dat*, I—"

Interrupting, he said something to her in Pennsylvania Dutch, and Katie dropped the iPod onto the bed and hurried out the door. She gave Jessica an apologetic expression before bolting down the hallway.

Jessica sighed and contemplated how sad it was to see Katie run off like a misbehaving child. She wondered what Katie could've possibly done to be treated this way.

A frown formed on Jessica's lips. It seemed that Katie

should've at least had a chance to say good-bye to Jessica. Jumping up, she started for the door, determined to say good-bye to Katie whether that man liked it or not.

Jessica reached the bottom of the stairs and found Katie standing silently next to her stoic father while he spoke to Daniel in Pennsylvania Dutch. Daniel's expression was stony as he listened.

"Katie," Jessica called.

Katie looked over at her, and her eyes widened in surprise. She shook her head as if to tell Jessica not to speak. Her gaze moved to her father, and her expression became stony.

Jessica's mouth gaped. What on earth could Katie have done to make her father so angry? The whole scene seemed ridiculous. Although she longed to say good-bye to Katie, Jessica bit her lip. She worried that speaking to Katie might make the situation worse, even though she wasn't sure exactly why the situation was bad already.

Robert continued to speak in Pennsylvania Dutch and then turned to go. Jessica stepped forward and reached for Katie's arm.

"Jessica," Daniel said, the word soft but deliberate.

She pulled her hand back and cut a sideways glance to him. His expression was blank, but she got the feeling he was silently scolding her. She shook her head in disbelief, wondering if she'd ever understand this culture. She turned to head upstairs and slammed into a young man who looked a couple of years older than she was. He was handsome with his hair and eyes mirroring the rest of the Kauffman family.

"I'm sorry." She stepped to the side. "I didn't see you coming toward me."

"My fault. In a rush." He smiled, revealing a dimple in his right cheek. He cut his eyes to something behind her, and his smile faded. "Pardon me," he muttered, heading for the door.

Studying the handsome man, Jessica wondered if he was a

member of Katie's family. When she looked toward the door, she found Robert staring at her, and she got her answer — the young man had to be the older brother Katie had mentioned upstairs.

Too bad she didn't have a chance to introduce herself to him. It would've been nice to know who he was. Instead, he was rushed out the door, and Jessica was treated like an outsider. She absently wondered if that was why her mother had left the community. Had she felt like an outsider in her own home? Jessica shuddered at the thought.

Shaking her head, Jessica trotted upstairs. *What a strange family. Trisha has to find a way to get us out of here.*

❀

Rebecca yawned while pulling her nightgown over her head. The evening had flown by, yet she felt as if she'd plowed the back field. She climbed into the bed, snuggling down under the quilt.

Daniel stepped into the room and sighed while pulling off his shirt. "It was a long evening."

Rebecca sat up. "I was just thinking the same thing. The gathering was nice, no?"

"*Ya.*" His tone betrayed the word.

"Is something wrong?" she asked.

He frowned, and her heart sank. She had the sneaking suspicion Robert had said something to upset her husband. She wished the brothers would work out their differences once and for all for the sake of the family.

"What is it?" she asked softly.

"It seems Jessica was giving worldly ideas to Katie tonight." He scowled while walking to the bed.

"Worldly ideas? What do you mean?"

"Robert found them listening to music, and Jessica was showing Katie her computer. He was not happy, to say the very least."

Rebecca blew out a sigh. She'd hoped introducing Katie to Jessica would simply foster a friendship, not cause a family problem.

"Robert doesn't want Jessica near his *kinner*," Daniel said. "He said he won't permit Jessica to impose her worldly views on his family."

Rebecca grimaced at the ridiculous statement. "It sounds like Robert is blowing it out of proportion. I'm sure she wasn't imposing anything on Katie. Jessica is a good girl."

Daniel sat on the edge of the bed. "I know she's a good girl, but keep in mind what I said about guidance. We need to remind her of our rules."

"Of course she needs our guidance, but she just lost her parents. I remember when my *mamm* died. Grace and I were completely devastated. I didn't know how I'd make it through a day without her." She touched his warm hand. "We need to give her a little bit of leeway and patience."

"I'm not sure everyone else would agree with you on that," he said, holding her hand. "Robert is always looking for something to argue about, and he won't give her the benefit of the doubt. We need to make her accountable for her actions and not make excuses. She's almost sixteen. She's been disrespectful to you, and she needs boundaries."

"She needs to respect us, but it won't happen overnight." Rebecca shook her head. "You're expecting too much of her in less than a week. The girls only just arrived, and they're still getting accustomed to us. Jessica is disrespectful because she's scared. Grace and I felt lost and alone after our *mamm* died, and we still had our *dat*. These girls lost both of their parents at once. I can't imagine how much that must hurt. They're orphans, Daniel. Think about that for a moment."

"I understand what you're saying," he began, his eyes studying hers with an intensity that caused her nerves to stand on end. "But we need to keep reminding her that her actions have consequences. We have one family gathering in our home, and Jessica brings out her electronic devices and already causes problems between my brother and me. I have enough issues with Robert without her meddling. Robert has always been jealous of me for working with *Dat* in the shop while he was forced to take over Sadie's parents' farm. I don't need our nieces making this delicate situation worse. Robert wouldn't think twice about reporting Jessica's behavior to the bishop."

Rebecca felt her expression soften. He was taking the blame for something that wasn't his fault, and she wished she could make him see that. "Daniel, you've done nothing wrong. Jessica isn't baptized into the church, so the bishop has no authority over her."

"You know it's more complicated than that." He raked a hand through his hair with frustration. "The bishop has power over me and our household."

A pang of discouragement nipped at her. She knew Daniel was right. The situation was more involved than she'd imagined when she brought the girls to the farm. She only wanted to help her nieces adjust to this new life; she didn't want to have to fight for their acceptance in the community.

"*Mei Fraa,*" Daniel said, running his finger gently down her cheek, a gesture that always warmed her soul. "Becky, I only want what's best for this household. You know that."

"You need to realize the position I'm in," she said softly, pleading for his support. "Grace wanted the girls to be with me, and I have to respect her wishes. Her letter said she wanted her daughters to experience her heritage."

"I know," he said, taking her hands in his and heaving a deep sigh. "We need to keep reminding the girls of the rules in our community and ask them to abide by them. We don't need a reprimand from the bishop."

"I believe in my heart the girls will adjust as long as we support and guide them." Tears welled in her eyes as she stared into his. "And I need you by my side for this, Daniel. I need you to believe that this is God's plan for us and for the girls. They're a gift to us. They're the children I could never have."

Standing, he pulled off his trousers. He then sank back onto the bed and crawled under the quilt without a word.

"I keep thinking of that verse you read from Colossians," she continued. "It said, 'Therefore, as God's chosen people, holy and dearly loved, clothe yourselves with compassion, kindness, humility, gentleness, and patience.'" She pushed a lock of her hair back as she studied his eyes. "The girls need our guidance but also our kindness, humility, gentleness, and patience. Don't you agree, Daniel?"

He nodded, and his serious expression softened. "Come here, *mei Fraa.*"

Nodding, she snuggled under the quilt, and he snuffed the kerosene lamp. He pulled her close, wrapping his warm, sinewy arms around her. While his lips caressed her neck, Rebecca said a silent prayer that the girls would adjust and that the rest of the community would accept them.

9

Rebecca climbed the stairs Sunday afternoon. The girls' voices carried from down the hall, causing her to smile. She was getting used to the idea of having her nieces in the house, and she loved finally having her own family nearby.

Although Jessica had rarely smiled since moving in, she had helped out in the kitchen this morning and even made some small talk about the weather. Rebecca had given Jessica her space and not asked any questions about what happened with Katie last night.

She hoped Jessica would open up and not retreat back into her shell. However, if she did, Rebecca planned to be patient and let the girl come to her when she was ready. She knew she couldn't win her over by pushing her.

The voices grew louder as Rebecca padded down the hallway to where Lindsay stood in the doorway of Jessica's room.

"I really think it looks nice," Lindsay said. "It looks homey with those photos there."

"Hi," Rebecca said, sidling up to Lindsay.

"Hey." Lindsay smiled. "Jessica's hanging some photos and wanted my opinion."

Rebecca peeked into the room and spotted Grace and Philip's wedding portrait hanging on the wall facing the door. Her eyes welled with tears at the thought of her sister missing the chance to see her beautiful daughters growing up. She studied her sister's smile, Grace's best feature. "Oh, it looks lovely."

"I hope it's okay that we're putting holes in your walls." Jessica gave a weak smile. "I found a hammer and some nails and just took it upon myself to start hanging stuff."

"That's fine." Rebecca nodded. "I told you to make yourself at home, and I think it's perfectly fine for you to remember your parents."

"Even though you don't believe in photographs?" Lindsay asked from her doorway.

"*Ya.*" Rebecca nodded. "We can make an exception since this is your room."

"Thanks." Jessica's lips formed a sincere smile, and Rebecca stifled a gasp of delight. Her niece had a beautiful smile, just like Grace's. Rebecca hoped to see it more often.

"You're welcome." Rebecca scanned Jessica's room. Most of the boxes were unpacked, and her dresser was covered in framed photographs of her friends back home. The room did look homey, and she hoped Jessica felt at home too. "Your room looks very nice."

"Thanks." Jessica tossed an empty box into the pile in the corner. "It's coming along."

Rebecca glanced in Lindsay's room and also found it well organized. She, too, had photographs of friends and her parents displayed on the walls and on her furniture. A line of stuffed animals sat on her bed along with decorative pillows.

"You've been working hard too," Rebecca said. "It looks *wunderbar.*"

"Thanks," Lindsay said with a smile before stepping back into her room.

Rebecca turned to Jessica and took a deep breath. Remembering her conversation with Daniel from the night before, she knew she had to talk to Jessica and remind her to respect their ways and not share her worldly views with Katie or any other Kauffman niece or nephew.

"I was wondering if we could talk for a minute," Rebecca said.

Jessica shrugged. "Sure. What's up?"

"Last night, when you were talking to Katie, you let her use your iPod and you showed her your computer."

Jessica nodded. "Yeah. So?"

"Well, her dad wasn't very happy, and he said something to Daniel about it."

Jessica rolled her eyes. "You've got to be kidding me. Is that why he left in such a huff?"

Rebecca sighed and frowned. "That was part of it. I know it may seem ridiculous to you, but not everyone in our community is as open-minded as we are. We really need you to not share your music and technology with the other Kauffman children. Their parents may get upset about it, and it creates an uncomfortable situation for everyone. So, please just keep your music to you and Lindsay. Does that sound reasonable?"

Jessica nodded. "Yeah, I guess so." She then gave Rebecca an unsure expression and cleared her throat. "It would be nice if I could meet some kids like me. I saw a little convenience store up on Route 340 on our way here last week. I was wondering if I could walk up there today and see if there were any other kids hanging out since I have to start working tomorrow."

Rebecca's stomach tightened. Going out on a Sunday was not permitted, unless they were visiting family. Besides, it wouldn't be proper to let Jessica wander around alone. "I don't think that's a good idea."

"Why?" Jessica raised an eyebrow in question. "My room is clean and picked up. I think I deserve a break."

"Today's Sunday. Since we don't have service, we have devotional time without a formal service again until next week. We usually visit family members and friends, but we chose to stay home today so you two could get settled."

"That's not fair!" Jessica gestured wildly as her voice shook with anger. "I'm not a member of your church, so why does it apply to me?"

"Because you live here under our roof." Rebecca kept her voice calm. "I know this is a difficult adjustment for you, but you need to respect our rules."

"This stinks!" Jessica stomped out of the room and toward the stairs.

"Where are you going?" Rebecca called after her.

"For a walk around the pasture since I'm not permitted to leave the property on a Sunday," Jessica yelled over her shoulder while clomping down the stairs.

Rebecca stared down the empty hallway. She considered going after her, but wanted to give Jessica her space.

Sorrow and disappointment gripped her. She wished she had the magic words that would ease Jessica's mind and heart. How would she ever get through to this child? Being a guardian was so much more difficult than she'd ever imagined in her wildest dreams.

Closing her eyes, she thought of Grace. She wanted the girls here.

God sent me these children to replace the ones I couldn't have.

Warmth filled her, replacing the disappointment.

Jessica needs patience. She's hurting.

Elizabeth's favorite verse echoed in Rebecca's mind — "Be joyful in hope, patient in affliction, faithful in prayer."

"She doesn't mean her hateful words," Lindsay said, cutting into her thoughts. "We both miss our parents so much that we say things we don't mean."

Rebecca stared down at Lindsay. "I still remember how difficult it was when I lost my mother." She wrapped her arms around her. "Let's give Jessica some time alone to calm down. We'll check on her after a bit."

Lindsay sniffed and swiped her cheek. Then her eyes were wide and eager. "I'd like to join you and Uncle Daniel for your devotionals. I miss my church back home, and I enjoy hearing the Scriptures when Daniel reads them."

Hopefulness soared in Rebecca's heart at the light she found in Lindsay's pretty face. Grace had in fact instilled a Christian faith in her girls. They may not have been Amish, but they did believe in Christ.

Oh, how she missed her dear sister. She ached with her and her nieces' loss.

"I'd love for you to join us," Rebecca said softly, her voice thick with emotion. "We're going to start our Bible reading as soon as Daniel comes in from feeding the animals."

Lindsay gnawed her bottom lip as if deep in thought.

"What's on your mind?" Rebecca reached out and pushed a lock of hair back from Lindsay's face. "You can talk to me. I'll always listen."

Her niece met her gaze, her expression unsure. "Would you tell me more about my mom and her life here?"

"Let's go have some iced tea and talk." Taking her hand, Rebecca led her down the stairs.

❖

Lindsay stared at her half-full glass of iced tea and pursed her lips. "I know my mom grew up here with you. She told Jess and me a few years ago. But I still can't imagine my mom in Plain clothes. I guess I just can't see her as anything other than my mom in her favorite jeans and a striped, button-down shirt."

Rebecca nodded while memories crashed over her. It was ironic how she still imagined her sister as Amish, even though it had been twenty years since Grace had worn her prayer *Kapp*.

Her niece met her gaze, and the intensity in her eyes caught

Rebecca off guard. "Why did she leave? What made her decide that she didn't want to be Amish?"

Rebecca took a deep breath, debating what to reveal about Grace's past. "Your *mamm* wanted more than what the People could offer."

"What do you mean?" Lindsay rested her chin on her hand, her gaze unmoving.

"When we turn sixteen, we go through something called *Rumspringa*."

"What's that?"

"It means 'running around.' It's a time when we're permitted to experience the world and decide for ourselves if we want to be baptized and join the church or live among the English." Rebecca stood and snatched a plate of cookies from the counter while she silently debated how much to tell Lindsay. "Your mom was working in the market one day selling vegetables when she met a couple of college students who were working on a paper about the Amish. They wanted to interview her, and she wound up interviewing them about their lives at school."

Lindsay snatched a chocolate chip cookie from the plate. "So, she decided she wanted to go to college?"

"Yes and no." Rebecca lifted a cookie and broke it in half. "She knew she wanted to go to college, but our *dat* pressured her to join the church with her peers. She joined and was very unhappy."

"So she left?" Lindsay bit into the cookie.

"Not right away. She tried to hang on for a couple of years, and a few young men wanted to court her. But Grace was never happy. Her dissatisfaction became worse until she finally couldn't take it anymore."

"What happened?"

"She became obsessed with college. She went to the local library and took out college catalogs and studied them late at night in her room." Rebecca took a bite of the cookie. "She wrote letters to the college boards asking about scholarships. She wanted to have a job beyond our farm and the market. Once she met your father, her fate was sealed. They fell in love, and he promised her a good life back in Virginia. He said he'd help her get her GED and then go to college."

"Why is college bad?"

Rebecca met her gaze. "We believe that education causes pride, and pride is a sin. Our community doesn't educate our children past the eighth grade because we believe an eighth-grade education is enough to prepare them for our lifestyle."

The girl tilted her head, considering the statement. "I don't know if I agree with that. Education opens the mind to new ideas." She wagged her finger. "My dad always said education is the most important thing we do. He said school was our job, and he'd get upset if I didn't bring home at least a B." She grimaced. "That's why he was frequently upset with me. I had trouble bringing home C's, let alone B's. Jessica is so much smarter than me."

Then Lindsay brightened. "I may not be good at school, but I do agree it's important for getting ahead in life. Without an education, you can't go very far in the business world. That's what Dad always said."

Rebecca nodded with understanding of the differences in their culture. "I respect what your dad said, but those are our beliefs." She pursed her lips at Lindsay. "And you aren't stupid, Lindsay. Jessica may be a better student, but I can tell you're a very smart girl. You have a wealth of common sense. Don't ever let me hear you say you aren't smart."

Lindsay ate another cookie. The intensity in her eyes illustrated she was deep in thought, mulling over the conversation. "I heard Mom met Dad in a market." A smile formed on her pink lips. "She told a story involving lettuce or tomatoes or something."

Rebecca smiled. "Ya. She had gone to the market to deliver

some eggs and produce, and your *dat* was there. Apparently, it was love at first sight."

"And she knew then she belonged in the English world." Lindsay grabbed another cookie from the plate.

"It wasn't quite that simple. Your father wanted your mother to go with him back to Virginia right away, but she was afraid at first. It took him a few months to convince her to go. He went back to Virginia a week after they met, and he wrote her letters. He even came up and met her in secret a few times."

"Really?" Lindsay's eyes glittered with awe. "How romantic! It sounds like a love story from a movie or book."

Rebecca chuckled at her excitement. She was so innocent and so sweet. "Your dad pursued your mom and refused to take no for an answer. It took him about six months, but he finally convinced her to go with him. It was a very difficult decision for her to make, since her only immediate family left was your grandfather and me."

"How did my grandfather react?"

Rebecca shook her head as the memories replayed in her mind's eye as if it were only yesterday. She could still see *Dat's* face turning as red as a tomato and his brown eyes smoldering when he told her that if she walked through that door to go with the Englisher, she was never welcome in his house again. He said if Grace left the church, she would be dead to him and would no longer be his daughter.

A frown overtook Rebecca's lips. She couldn't tell Lindsay those words; they would hurt her too much.

"He was furious," Rebecca whispered. "Your poor mother tried to explain she felt like she belonged somewhere else. She believed God had a different plan for her than He did for me. But *Dat* wouldn't listen. He told her she was no longer his child."

Lindsay's eyes filled with tears. "How could he treat his daughter that way?"

Rebecca sighed. "He was a tough man. I think he believed he was doing the right thing. Our community believes in shunning a member out of love in order to encourage them to come back into the Faith. But it didn't work with Grace. Her mind was made up. She left and didn't come back until *Dat's* funeral."

A lump formed in her throat at the memory of the loss she experienced the day her sister left. The wound was still fresh in her heart even twenty years later.

"How did you and Daniel meet?" Lindsay asked, wrenching Rebecca back to the present.

Rebecca wiped her eyes and cleared her throat before she spoke. "We knew each other our whole lives."

"So how did you start dating?"

"At a singing."

"A what?" Lindsay tilted her head in question.

"A singing is a social gathering young people have on weekends. They gather in a barn and sing hymns and talk and laugh. It's a lot of fun. Daniel invited me to ride home in his courting buggy one night, and we started seeing each other."

Lindsay smiled. "That's romantic too."

Rebecca gave a little laugh. "That's how our young people date."

"It sounds more romantic than going to the movies or going to a dance. If you're alone in a buggy, you can really talk and get to know each other."

Rebecca nodded. She'd never thought about it that way. However, the girl was right. Riding around with Daniel was romantic back then. She thought he was the most wonderful man in the world, and she was so happy and humbled he'd picked her.

Her niece looked down at Rebecca's hands. "You don't wear a wedding ring." She studied Rebecca. "You don't wear any jewelry, do you?"

Rebecca shook her head. "No, we don't. It causes pride. Men grow beards when they marry."

"Jessica wears Mom's wedding ring on a chain around her neck."

Rebecca nodded. "I saw that."

"I have Dad's in a box in my room." Lindsay ate another cookie and drank more iced tea. She suddenly looked over at Rebecca and her eyes filled with tears. "I miss them so much I can't breathe sometimes."

Rebecca swallowed a lump in her throat and took Lindsay's hands in hers. "When my *mamm* died, I thought I'd never make it through another day without her. But somehow, I went through my daily routine and every day it got a tiny bit easier. Over time, hurt slowly transformed from a deep chasm in my heart to a small wound. You'll always miss your mom and dad, but someday the grief won't hurt as much as it does now."

Lindsay squeezed her hands. "Thank you for having us, Aunt Rebecca."

Rebecca bit back tears. "No," she whispered, her voice quavering with love. "Thank you."

❁

Rebecca watched Lindsay's face brighten while Daniel read from the book of John. The excitement in her niece's pretty face warmed her heart. Grace and Philip must have taken the girls to church and taught them about God's love. Rebecca hoped their faith would comfort them during this difficult time.

Once Daniel finished reading the Scripture, they bowed their heads in silent prayer.

After praying, Rebecca caught Lindsay's glance. "I'm going to go check on your sister."

Lindsay pushed out her chair and stood. "I'll come too."

They found Jessica leaning on the pasture fence and staring out at the Esh farm in the distance. Rebecca sidled up by her, and Jessica cleared her throat and swiped her glistening cheeks.

"I remember being blinded by grief when my mother died," Rebecca whispered, looping her arm around Jessica's shoulders. Her niece started to pull away, and Rebecca pulled her closer. "Some days I thought I couldn't get out of bed, but I pushed on. It may seem impossible, but the pain in your heart will ease. You will get through this."

Jessica faced her, fresh tears flooding her eyes and streaming down her pink cheeks. "I miss them so much." Her voice croaked. She fell into Rebecca's arms and sobbed on her shoulder.

"I know, Jessica, I know," Rebecca whispered into her hair. "But I'm here. I'll help you as much as you let me."

Lindsay took Rebecca's hand in hers and squeezed it while big round tears shimmered on her cheeks.

Closing her eyes, Rebecca held her breath and hoped she could be the strength that these poor, lost souls craved so desperately.

Hickory Nut Kisses

2 cups sugar
2 cups finely chopped hickory nuts
6 egg whites
3 – 1/4 Tbsp flour

Beat egg whites lightly, add sugar, nut kernels, and four. Drop on greased tins and bake at 350 degrees for 12 – 15 minutes or until lightly brown.

Jessica, it's time to get up," a voice in the distance said. "Jessica, you have ten minutes to get dressed and eat breakfast before Barry Holden picks us up."

Jessica moaned and rolled over. It couldn't be time to get up. She'd just fallen asleep only a few minutes ago after spending hours staring at the ceiling and wiping her tears. She missed her parents so much that her body ached. Her grief had kept her awake for hours and haunted her with nightmares. Through her dreams she'd relived the night they died over and over again.

No, it couldn't possibly be time to get up. She pulled the quilt over her head. It was so nice and warm under the covers. Although it was May, the morning was still a bit chilly.

"Jessica, please," the voice said again. "You must get up and get ready for work."

"Work?" Jessica's eyes flew open, revealing Rebecca's face smiling down at her. "What time is it?" She rubbed her eyes, which burned from lack of sleep.

"Six." Rebecca pushed a lock of hair back from Jessica's face. "Your sister is downstairs eating."

"Why do I have to go to work?" Jessica folded her arms across the quilt. "I'm not Amish."

"You're a member of this household, and we all work. We have allowed you some of your English ways, now it is time for you to try some of our ways." Her aunt stood. "Now, please get up. Daniel will be ready to leave very soon, and he doesn't like to wait."

Jessica rolled her eyes.

"Please, Jessica." Her aunt frowned. "I know you aren't happy to be here, but I hope you'll make the best of it. We're trying very hard to make you and Lindsay feel welcome."

With guilt filtering through her, Jessica sighed and sat up. She had to make the best of this until Trisha could get custody of her and her sister. "Fine. I'll get dressed."

"Thank you." Her aunt started for the door and then stopped, facing her. "If you don't want to go to the furniture store then you can come with Lindsay and me to the bakery. Those are your only options."

Wow, what a choice, she thought with sarcasm. "It's fine," Jessica said, climbing from the bed. "I really have no interest in baking your Amish stuff, whatever it is."

Rebecca smiled, as if she hadn't heard the sarcastic comment. "You'd be surprised. In fact, I think you'd rather like the pastries if you gave them a chance."

Yeah. Right. Jessica opened the closet. "I'll be down in a minute."

"Would you like something to eat?"

Jessica yanked a pair of jeans from a hanger while she considered the question. Her stomach was still sour from the sleepless night of nightmares. "No, thanks. I'm not hungry."

"What should I pack you for lunch?" Rebecca asked.

"Nothing." Jessica waved her off. "I have some cash. I can find a place to eat."

Rebecca folded her arms. "It's wasteful to buy lunch when we have a refrigerator full of food."

Jessica scowled. "I think I can spend five bucks on lunch without feeling guilty."

"That's your choice. I'll tell Daniel that you're on your way."

Rebecca disappeared through the door, gently closing it behind her.

Jessica shook her head while pulling on her favorite low-rider jeans. She then layered on two knit shirts. She couldn't believe she was getting dressed to go to work in a furniture store. Never in her life had she imagined she'd wind up in Lancaster County.

Well, I better make the best of it.

Sighing, she combed her hair up into a ponytail and then checked it with a mirror from her compact. She missed her vanity and its large mirror. She then put on makeup, taking time to apply foundation, powder, blush, and eye makeup, including eye shadow, eyeliner, and mascara.

I might as well look my best.

Opening up her jewelry box, she picked out her favorite gold hoop earrings, cross necklace, and a handful of bangle bracelets. She then slid on her favorite black ankle boots. After brushing her teeth, she grabbed her purse and hurried downstairs.

Reaching the bottom step, she found Rebecca, Daniel, and Lindsay waiting, all three of them frowning.

"I'm ready," Jessica sang, ignoring their frosty glares.

Daniel's stare hardened and then he spouted off in Pennsylvania Dutch to Rebecca, who sighed and nodded.

He then turned back to Jessica and pointed at her clothing. "Please go remove the jewelry and take off some of your eye makeup," he said.

"What?" Jessica asked with a gasp.

"I can't have you showing up at my father's store wearing all of that jewelry and eye makeup." He shook his head again. "It wouldn't be proper."

"Are you serious?" Jessica's voice rose to a screech.

"*Ya.*" He nodded with emphasis. "Very serious." He glanced at the clock on the wall and then tapped his foot with impatience. "Barry will be here any minute. We must hurry."

Jessica looked to Rebecca and shot her a look pleading for her support. "Do I really have to change?"

Scowling, Rebecca nodded. "Please do as Daniel asked."

"This is ridiculous!" Jessica threw her hands up with frustration. "I'm not Amish!"

"Jessica, please," Rebecca said.

"This is outrageous!" Jessica's voice rose an octave as she stomped up the stairs. She tossed all of her jewelry back into the jewelry box, except for her mother's wedding ring that she wore on the chain around her neck. She then grabbed a tissue and wiped off the eye makeup before stomping back down the stairs.

Her uncle, aunt, and sister were all waiting for her and still frowning.

"Let's roll," Jessica muttered before heading out the front door and walking down the stairs. An old white Ford van sat in the driveway, and she assumed it was their ride.

Daniel, Rebecca, and Lindsay filed down the front steps. Daniel opened the back door of the van and greeted the driver. He then climbed into the front passenger seat while Rebecca and Lindsay climbed in the back.

Jessica glowered while climbing all the way into the back. While she stared out the side window, Rebecca pointed out landmarks, such as homes of relatives or close friends. The terrain was hilly, and the roads were windy and rural. The scenery was the opposite of the flat, well-developed land Jessica was used to in Virginia Beach.

About two miles up the road, they came to a farm with a cluster of large houses set back off the road and surrounded by four barns, along with a beautiful lush, green pasture.

"Daniel's parents own that property," Rebecca said. "His brother Timothy lives in one of the houses, and his sister Sarah and her husband live in another. The bakery is the fourth house. It's the one closest to the road."

"Wow," Lindsay said.

"Daniel and his five siblings grew up in the biggest house, which is where his parents still are," Rebecca said as the van steered onto the long dirt road leading to the property.

The van stopped in front of a large, white clapboard farmhouse with a sweeping wrap-around porch. A large sign with "Kauffman Amish Bakery" in old-fashioned letters hung above the door.

Out behind the building was a fenced-in play area where a few of the Kauffman grandchildren ran around playing tag and climbing on a huge wooden swing set. Beyond it was a fenced pasture. The three other large farmhouses and four barns were set back beyond the pasture.

A large paved parking lot sat adjacent to the building.

"This is the bakery," Rebecca said.

"It's huge," Jessica muttered with awe.

"Believe it or not, that parking lot is packed at the height of the tourist season," Rebecca said as she wrenched open the door.

"We better head out," Rebecca said, glancing at Lindsay. "We're a couple of minutes late, and they're already baking for the day." She met Jessica's gaze. "Have a good day. I'll see you tonight."

"You too," Jessica mumbled.

After Rebecca climbed out, Lindsay leaned over the seat toward Jessica. "Be nice to Uncle Daniel."

Jessica rolled her eyes. "Get lost."

Rebecca and Daniel spoke in soft voices in Pennsylvania Dutch before sharing a quick kiss. Once Rebecca and Lindsay had disappeared up the stairs to the bakery, the van backed out of the parking lot and headed back down to the main road.

After turning onto Route 340, a one-story building with a sign declaring Kauffman & Yoder Amish Furniture came into view, about a mile from the large Kauffman farm.

"This is the store," Daniel said as the driver maneuvered into the parking lot.

"Kauffman and Yoder?" she asked.

The driver parked at the back of the store.

"My father built it with his best friend, Elmer Yoder, before I was born," Daniel said. "They'd grown up together and always dreamed of having a business. They both are master carpenters."

"Oh." Grabbing her purse, she climbed from the van.

Daniel thanked the driver, and the van motored back to the main road.

Glancing across the parking lot, Jessica spotted a late-model four-door Chevrolet pickup truck.

"Who owns the truck?" she asked Daniel while he sauntered back to her. "Is that another driver?"

"No, it's Jake Miller," he said. "Elmer's grandson."

"How come he gets a truck while the rest of you have to pay a driver?" She followed him to the back door of the shop.

"He's not Amish." He held the door open for her.

She stared at him. "How can that be?"

"Was your mother Amish?" he retorted, his gaze almost accusing.

"No." She padded through the door.

"Being Amish is our heritage. It's a very serious commitment to a way of life. It's not like picking out your shoes." Daniel stepped in and closed the door behind him. His tone had an edge to it, making her wonder where the resentment had come from. Was he going to hold a grudge against her due to the jewelry and makeup?

"Let me introduce you around," he said, gesturing into the building.

Jessica scanned the large shop, seeing several men building furniture. All wore the Plain clothes. She spotted beautifully designed dining room sets, bedroom suites, entertainment centers, hutches, end tables, desks, and coffee tables. She took in the craftsmanship and silently marveled at their talent. The pieces were works of art, not just furniture.

Hammers banged, saw blades whirled, and air compressors hummed. The sweet scent of wood and stain filled her nostrils.

A wave of grief washed over her. Dad would've loved seeing the shop and talking with the men. He'd enjoyed working with wood in his spare time. He had an elaborate woodshop set up in the garage with a sea of complicated tools.

Jessica had spent many weekends in the workshop behind the house chatting and watching Dad build furniture. They would talk for hours. He'd share stories of traveling around Europe and Africa and his exciting adventures. She loved listening to his stories, which were the inspiration for her dreams of world travels.

She'd give anything to talk to him again.

Why, oh, why did her parents have to die?

With tears threatening, she suppressed thoughts of her father and plastered a smile on her face while the men came over to meet her.

"This is my niece, Jessica," Daniel said, introducing her.

He rattled off the names of the men, and Jessica tried to commit their names to her memory. She met Daniel's brother-in-law Peter and his brother Timothy. She shook their hands and continued to smile. A man with weather-beaten skin in Plain clothes approached, and she immediately noticed that his eyes were the same blue as Daniel's.

"This is my father, Eli Kauffman," Daniel said. "*Dat*, this is Jessica. I don't think you had a chance to meet her the other night. It was a little bit chaotic at the house."

"It's very nice to meet you." Eli shook her hand.

"Thank you," she said. "It's nice to meet you, too, Mr. Kauffman."

Another older man approached. "Welcome to our shop. I'm Milton Yoder."

"Thank you, Mr. Yoder." She shook his hand.

"Let's take you up front so you can see your desk." Daniel placed his hand on her back, steering her through the shop. "It gets busy, but you can handle it."

They maneuvered through the shop to the front of the store, which consisted of large glass windows and samples of furniture. She ran her finger over a mirrored double dresser, silently marveling at the intricate detailed pattern in the wood.

"This is gorgeous," she whispered. "My dad would've loved this."

"Your *dat* was a carpenter?" he asked.

She nodded. "Not by trade, but he loved woodworking. He made my sister and me some really nice shelves for our rooms. He also made my mom a beautiful hope chest when they were first married. We saved them in your shed. When I have a house of my own someday, I'll use them in my room."

Daniel rubbed his beard as his expression softened. "I'm sure you must think of your parents often."

"All the time." Clearing her throat in order to suppress the swelling lump, she turned toward the front counter. A small desk covered in books and stacks of paper was located directly behind it. An old style push-button phone sat on the desk with a long, coiled cord. She guessed the long cord served to allow her to lean on the counter if a customer came in while she was on the phone. "I guess this is my station?"

"*Ya*, that's right." He patted the counter. "You'll sit here and answer the phone, take orders, file invoices, balance the ledger, and keep the books."

Jessica shrugged. "Shouldn't be too hard. I worked in my dad's office over the summer and school vacations."

"Oh, that's *gut*. You've had some experience with administrative work." Daniel nodded toward the chair, gesturing for her to sit.

He then explained the job to her, pointing out the phone, ledgers, order forms, and receipt books. Jessica knew she was capable of the job, since she'd served as administrative assistant to her father over school breaks, and she enjoyed the work. Dad had also let her dabble in the accounting, so she should be comfortable taking care of the ledger for the furniture store.

Her thoughts moved to her friends back home in Virginia. Jessica pushed those thoughts away and fingered her phone stuck in her jean pocket. She wondered why her best friend, Morgan, or her boyfriend, Brian, hadn't called to check on her. She'd given them Trisha's cellular phone number before she left for Lancaster County. Now that Jessica had a phone, her friends could call her any time. She assumed they would've gotten her number from Trisha. However, they hadn't called once. She wondered if they missed her.

"Does this job sound *gut* to you?" he asked, yanking her from her thoughts.

"Yeah," Jessica said. "I can handle it."

"*Gut.*" He nodded. "We open in thirty minutes. I'm going to check in the back, and you call me if you need anything."

"I'm sure I'll be just fine." Jessica opened the ledger and thumbed through it. The accounting system was basic and easy to understand. Grabbing a calculator, she ran through the last receipts, making sure they reconciled.

"Another Englisher," a voice behind her said. "I'm still outnumbered but at least I'm not alone anymore."

Glancing over her shoulder, Jessica spotted a young man clad in a gray T-shirt, jeans, and work boots. His dark brown hair was cut short, accentuating his bright, Caribbean blue eyes.

"Jake Miller." He extended his hand.

She stared into his eyes and swallowed a gasp. She shook

his warm hand, and her cheeks heated while her mind drew a blank. What was her name?

"You must be Jessica Bedford," Jake said.

"Right!" she said, a little too loudly. What a dunce. How could she forget her own name?

Glancing down, Jessica spotted her hand still clasping his. She yanked her hand back, and her cheeks felt like they were going to spontaneously combust.

"So, you're from Virginia?" Jake leaned on the desk.

"That's right. Virginia Beach." She settled back in the chair and wished her cheeks would cool down. She imagined her embarrassment ran a deep pink from her neck to her nose.

"Virginia Beach." He grinned. "I was there once with my folks for a church retreat. It's a nice place. I love that oceanfront. We rented bikes and rode from Rudee Inlet to the north end. It was fun."

"I like it there. I sure miss the beach." Glancing at the ceiling, she found strange, round glass light fixtures that hummed and emitted heat. "What's with the lights?" she asked, pointing toward the ceiling.

"They run on gas."

"Are they bright enough for intricate woodworking?" she asked.

He shrugged. "Yeah. Sometimes we use portable kerosene lamps if we need better lighting. We make do."

"What about air conditioning? It's pretty warm in here. I bet it gets really hot back there with all of the tools and compressors."

"We have fans that run through power inverters." He stood up straight and crossed his arms across his wide chest.

Man, he was handsome.

She pushed the thought away and glanced toward the walls finding no light switches, just like at Rebecca's house. "So there's no electricity in this building at all?"

"Nope." Jake grinned. "This is true Amish."

Jessica cinched her eyebrows with confusion. "Then how do the tools work? I heard air compressors and everything in there."

"The air compressors run off diesel generators. We use some electric tools, but the same diesel that powers the compressor also powers the generators." He gestured toward the shop. "So, there's still no electric bill."

She tilted her head while considering the process. "But isn't diesel like super expensive right now?"

He shrugged. "It depends on how you look at it. Utility costs are rising too."

"Hmm." She nodded. "That's very true. I guess everything is expensive these days." She contemplated the power inverter and thought of her iPod. She'd recently bought a charger for it. Maybe she could charge it here.

"Hey," she asked. "I have the power cord for my iPod. Would it be all right if charge through the power inverter here?"

He shrugged. "Sure. Why not?" He held out his hand. "I'll do it for you back in my work area."

"Cool." She fished the iPod and cord from her purse and handed it to him. "Thanks." Her gaze moved to the doorway, where Mr. Yoder stood. His stern expression gave her the same uneasy feeling as Daniel's cold comments earlier.

"Jake. There you are," Mr. Yoder said. "Can you come back here when you get a moment? I have a question for you on that wishing well you're building."

"Be right there." Jake held up a finger and turned back to Jessica. "Duty calls. I just wanted to introduce myself. Maybe we can go to lunch sometime. There's a great pizza place down the road that I like to eat at."

Was he asking her out? Jake was handsome, but she'd just met him. It seemed a bit forward. Jessica almost told him she wasn't interested in going to lunch or going anywhere with him, since she had a boyfriend.

However, Jake had a truck, which meant she could charge her phone in it. She'd stuck her phone charger in her purse just in case she had the opportunity to use it.

"Pizza?" Jessica asked. "That sounds good."

He winked when he stood. "Just yell if you have any questions. I used to work the front before my grandpa actually let me work with wood. I know it can get confusing sometimes."

"Thanks." She watched him go, and her eyes admired his broad shoulders. He sure was handsome, but she had a boyfriend.

Sighing, Jessica pulled out her phone and studied the display. No calls. No messages. She lifted it and punched up Brian's number. Before she hit Send, the shrill ring of the store phone rang out.

Placing her cell phone on the counter, Jessica lifted the receiver to her ear. "Kauffman and Yoder. May I help you?"

The customer spoke and Jessica leaned back in her chair. Her first day in the store had officially begun.

11

How's that pie coming?" a voice asked.

Lindsay turned to find Sarah Troyer, Uncle Daniel's youngest sister, leaning over her shoulder. "It's going great, thanks." She pushed the pan over so Sarah could see the Schnitz Pie she was creating.

"*Wunderbar.* You like to bake?" Sarah smiled, and her eyes twinkled in the light of the kerosene lamps. She was clad in a dark purple caped dress covered by a black apron with a prayer *Kapp* hiding her honey blonde hair.

"Love it." Lindsay smiled while cutting slits in the crust. "Me and my mom used to bake all the time. Lemon meringue pie is my favorite."

"You'll have to bake one for me." Sarah's smile faded, and she wiped her forehead.

"You okay?" Lindsay touched Sarah's arm.

"*Ya.*" Sarah's smile reappeared. "I'm just feeling hot and tired."

Lindsay lifted her eyebrows in question.

"I'm expecting my first baby." She lowered herself onto a stool in front of a fan plugged into a power inverter. She moved her hand back and forth in an attempt to cool her face. "Pretty soon my little one will be in there playing." She nodded to the small room off the kitchen where Beth Anne's and Kathryn's youngest children were playing. "We take turns throughout the day to watch them. We also take them outside to play on the playground. If you ever want a break, you can take them outside too."

"Congratulations on your baby. That's wonderful news! I love babies. I used to babysit for the little girls who lived across the street from us in Virginia." Lindsay rubbed Sarah's arm. "Congratulations. I guess I should say *wunderbar, ya?*" She giggled at her clumsy attempt at Pennsylvania Dutch.

"*Ya.*" Sarah chortled. "*Danki.* Peter and I are very happy. We're blessed with this baby."

Glancing around the kitchen she noted how different it was than the kitchen in Virginia. The walls were plain white, and keeping with their tradition, there was no electricity. The lights were gas-powered as were the row of ovens.

Rebecca had explained that the bulk of the baking for the day was done in the early morning in order to keep the heat to a minimum. Five fans ran through the power inverters and gave a gentle breeze. However, the kitchen was warm.

There were no fancy mixers or gadgets on the long counter. Their tools were plain pans and ordinary knives and cutlery.

Out front was a long counter covered in baked goods for sale. While the cash register ran on batteries, a push-button phone hung on the wall with a very long coiled cord.

A section of the store out front sold Amish mementos, such as books, postcards, key chains, candles, drawings, paintings, and country crafts.

The sweet smells of icing and cookies tickled Lindsay's senses and took her back in time to lazy Saturdays when she baked with her mother.

Sarah lifted a glass of water and took a long drink. "I guess this is very different from your life in Virginia, yes?"

"Yes, it's different." Lindsay opened the gas-powered oven

and slipped the pie onto the rack. She closed it again and set the timer for ten minutes.

"Rebecca is a wonderful woman," Sarah said. "She's a very caring and supportive wife to my brother."

Lindsay picked up a glass of tea. "She is wonderful. We're lucky to have her."

"I bet you miss your friends back home, though," Sarah said with a frown. "This is a very hard time for you."

"Yeah." Lindsay nodded. "We're having a hard time. My sister is really unhappy. She really misses our friends." Lindsay ran her fingers over the cool condensation on her glass.

"Don't you miss your friends too?"

"I do. Very much. But I'll make new friends. I bet Aunt Rebecca will let me go back to Virginia Beach to visit my friends."

"I'm sure she will." Sarah took another long drink.

Lindsay stepped over to the counter toward Rebecca. "Should I make another Schnitz Pie or start on some cookies? Or should I make some of those Fastnacht donuts?"

"How about some cookies?" Rebecca asked, crossing the kitchen. "Is everything going okay?"

"Going great." Lindsay gestured toward the oven. "I just put my sixth Schnitz Pie in the oven."

"*Wunderbar!*" Rebecca clapped. "Let's start on cookies. How about some peanut butter cookies? We're running low on the cookie rack out front."

Lindsay helped Rebecca mix up the cookies, combining the shortening, peanut butter, brown and white sugar, and eggs.

"So, how do you like the bakery so far?" Rebecca asked, rolling the mixed batter into balls.

"I'm having fun learning these cool new recipes." She wished she could've talked to her mom about the recipes she was learning. She wondered if her mom had ever missed the Amish foods she used to make when she was a girl.

While Lindsay rolled the dough into small balls, her thoughts moved to Trisha. She was surprised Trisha hadn't tried to call her at the bakery, but maybe she'd already spoken with Jessica.

"I'm glad because we like having you." Rebecca loaded the balls onto the baking sheet. "Elizabeth and my sisters-in-law already told me they enjoy having you here."

Lindsay smiled. "Thank you. They've made me feel very welcome." She grew thoughtful. Would she rather be with Trisha or with Aunt Rebecca? She wasn't sure, but she liked being with Aunt Rebecca. When she was with her, she felt closer to her mother somehow.

"I think you'll like these cookies." Rebecca slipped the baking sheet into the oven. "They're delicious and one of our biggest sellers."

"I think I want to stay here," Lindsay said before she could stop the words from escaping her mouth. "I want to be here, not with Trisha."

Rebecca stopped, and her smile faded. "What did you say?"

Lindsay hesitated, hoping she hadn't said something wrong. "I just said I want to stay here," she whispered.

"You mean that?" Rebecca asked.

"Yes, I do." Lindsay wiped her hands on her apron. "Aunt Trisha promised Jessica she'd get a lawyer to try to contest Mom and Dad's will and get custody of us."

"Oh?" her aunt asked, looking pained.

Guilt washed over Lindsay. *Good going. I said too much.*

"But I think this is where Jessica and I are supposed to be." Lindsay sucked in a breath. "I miss my friends, but this is starting to feel like home."

"Come here." Rebecca opened her arms, and Lindsay walked into her hug. Her aunt rubbed her back. "You have no idea how good it feels to hear you say that. Having you here feels natural. I think your mother knew I'd love you like you were my own daughter. I just wish Jessica could see how much love I have to give you girls."

Stepping back, Lindsay sniffed and wiped her eyes. "I think she'll figure that out. Dad always said she was stubborn."

Rebecca touched Lindsay's arm. "She's just like your *mamm*. Grace was never satisfied with our simple life, so she had to go out in the world and figure things out on her own."

"Did you miss her?" Lindsay asked.

"All the time." Her aunt smiled. "But if she hadn't left, I wouldn't have you and your sister to love." While humming, Rebecca wiped her hands on her apron and then continued rolling cookies.

Lindsay grabbed some dough and began to help her. Glancing at her watch, she realized it was after eleven. The morning had flown by at lightning speed.

She smiled while rolling out more dough. *Time flies when you're having fun. If only Mom could see me now.* She frowned as grief slammed through her.

Oh, how she missed her parents. She continued to roll the dough and hoped she was making her mother proud.

❁

Rebecca stepped through the doorway from the kitchen to the front counter of the bakery. Her gaze moved to the racks of pastries, jellies, postcards, key chains, dolls, books, and other souvenirs that the tourists loved to buy. She'd watched her mother-in-law's store grow from a small bakery to favorite tourist stop during her fifteen-year marriage to Daniel.

Elizabeth handed an English customer a bag and thanked her for coming to the bakery. She then turned to Rebecca and heaved a loud sigh. "Busy day, no? I think I've served twenty or so folks already, and it's only one o'clock."

"*Ya.* Busy." Rebecca leaned on the counter. "You going to eat your lunch now?"

"You can." Her mother-in-law gestured around the store. "It's quiet at the moment. You go and then I'll go." Her eyes studied Rebecca. *"Was iss letz?"*

"Nothing's wrong." Rebecca folded her arms across her apron. "Everything is fine. Lindsay's chatting and baking with Sarah."

"Ya, but something is *letz."* Elizabeth stepped toward her. "I can see it in your eyes."

Rebecca sighed and glanced toward the large glass windows at the front of the store. "I was wondering how Jessica's day was going. I'm worried about her."

"Oh, Jessica will be just fine. She just needs time to adjust to our ways."

"She was really upset last night. She was angry with me when I wouldn't let her walk up to try to meet some of the kids her age. She stomped outside before we had devotional time. Lindsay and I found her crying by the pasture fence. I told her that I understand her grief because I lost my *mamm.* She cried in my arms, but she never really spoke to me."

Rebecca absently wiped some crumbs from the counter into her hand. "I'm afraid I won't be able to get through to her. I want to be a good guardian for her. I feel like God is giving me a chance to finally be a *mamm* and I want to be the best *mamm* I can be for these girls. I don't want to let Him or them down."

"Oh, Rebecca," Elizabeth said with a smile. "You'll do fine. You have to be sensitive to how she's feeling and give her some time to adjust. This is a rough time for her. You need to just be patient and have faith that she'll accept our ways and open her heart to you." She placed her hand on Rebecca's arm. "You're loving and sweet. She'll open up to you and consider you her *mamm* soon enough."

Rebecca nodded even though Elizabeth made the situation sound much easier than it really was.

"What is it? You don't look convinced," her mother-in-law said, pulling her hand back.

Rebecca glanced toward the doorway to make sure Lindsay wasn't close enough to hear. "Daniel has been supportive, but he seemed to get frustrated with Jessica earlier," she whispered.

Her mother-in-law frowned. "What do you mean?"

"Jessica came downstairs this morning, wearing a lot of jewelry and makeup. Daniel made her take off the jewelry and some of the makeup before they left. He didn't raise his voice, but he seemed annoyed."

Elizabeth smiled. "Well, Jessica is just getting used to the rules. She's a teenager. Sometimes they have their own ideas about things. Remember the Scripture— 'Bear in mind that our Lord's patience means salvation.' The girls will adjust. Just be sure to listen with an open heart and be patient."

Rebecca nodded while she straightened a few boxes of assorted pastries. She hoped Jessica's day was going well and that both of the girls would enjoy their jobs.

12

Jessica breathed a sigh of relief when another customer headed out the front door of the store. She'd helped several since the open sign went up this morning. The flurry of customers and phone calls had given her a crash course in answering questions, taking orders, and balancing the ledger. So far, it wasn't so bad.

Glancing down, she spotted her cellular phone and recalled that it had vibrated a few times while she'd been taking an order for a desk earlier. The display read "1 voicemail."

She dialed the voicemail box and smiled when Brian's voice spoke into her ear.

"Hey, Jess," he said. "It's me. Sorry I haven't called, but I've been studying like crazy for finals. My dad told me I better pass chemistry, or I won't get to work at the oceanfront this summer."

Jessica leaned back in her chair and shook her head. Things hadn't changed. Brian was still flunking chemistry, and his dad was still on his case about it.

"I hope things are going all right in Amish world. I hope the horse smells aren't gettin' to you yet." He snickered, and Jessica rolled her eyes. "Well, give me a call when you can if they let you use a phone. Bye."

Her heart sank when he disconnected without saying he

missed her. Was he too embarrassed or hurried to say it? Did he still have feelings for her?

She stared down at the display and found only one bar left inside the battery display, indicating it was close to dead. If she dialed him without charging it, the phone would most likely turn itself off before the end of their conversation.

She cut her gaze to the phone sitting on the desk. She could call Brian from the shop phone. But what would happen when the phone bill came in? Would she have to pay the long distance charges? It seemed silly to run up a long distance bill when she had a cellular phone in her hand that had free long distance. However, it needed to be charged.

She remembered Jake's truck and began to think about how she could convince Jake to let her charge her phone.

"Hey, Jessica," a voice behind her said as if on cue.

She turned and found Jake standing in the doorway. Had he been reading her mind? "Jake. Hi." She sat up straighter and smoothed her shirt. She absently wondered why she should care how she looked. She didn't even know the guy.

"So, are you ready to quit yet?" He leaned back on the doorframe, folding his arms across his wide chest.

"No way." She waved off the thought. "This job is a breeze."

A grin tugged at the corners of his mouth. "A breeze, huh? Wait until July when folks are here ordering their lawn furniture. By then you'll be ready to either quit or get an assistant. Trust me."

"I can handle it." Her finger brushed her pocket holding her phone. Taking a deep breath, she worked up the nerve to ask him. "Jake, I was wondering if I could ask you a favor."

"Oh?" His eyes widened with curiosity.

"Could I possibly charge my phone in your truck? It's almost dead, and I wanted to call my boyfriend back. He left a voicemail earlier, and the battery barely has enough power for me to dial."

Still smiling, he rubbed his chin. "You want to charge your phone in my truck to call your boyfriend, huh?"

"It won't take long." She yanked the phone from her pocket and held it up. "It's one of those new ones, so it charges real fast. I'll get it back from you before I leave today. I promise."

"Hmm." He folded his arms again. "And what do I get from the deal?"

Jessica stared at him for a moment, wondering if he were joking or if he really expected something in return. How could a phone sitting on the console in his truck possibly inconvenience him?

"Well?" he asked. "I'm waiting for an answer."

"Look, Jake, I don't see how this is a big deal." She gestured with emphasis. "You're just letting me use a little bit of juice from your battery."

"And? What do I get? You get to use your cell phone." His grin was back.

She narrowed her eyes and folded her arms, giving him her best pouty look. "You get the satisfaction of knowing you helped someone out of the goodness of your heart."

"That's not enough." He stepped toward her. "Have you had lunch?"

"Not yet." She pointed to the desk. "It's been crazy busy. I was thinking about walking up the street to that little pizza parlor you mentioned if I can get someone to watch the front."

"I haven't eaten either. Have lunch with me."

She shook her head. "I don't think so."

"Why not? Your company would be sufficient payment for using my truck's battery."

"I don't think it's appropriate." She held up the phone. "I told you that I wanted to use my phone to call my *boyfriend*."

"I invited you to have a slice a pizza with me, not elope.

Loosen up a bit." He nodded toward the door. "We'll go have lunch, and your phone can charge."

"Loosen up?" Offended, she popped up from the chair. "I'm not stiff."

"Jessica, you look like you haven't laughed in years." He touched her arm. "It's almost one-thirty, and my stomach is growling. I'll tell my grandpa to cover the front, so you can get a break from this nuthouse for a while."

"But I need to—" she began.

"Let's go." He gently pulled her through the doorway to the shop. "We need to cut out before a customer comes in and ties you up for another thirty minutes."

As they made their way through the shop, Jessica couldn't help but smile. When Daniel's gaze met her, he frowned, causing her smile to fade and her stomach to twist with foreboding.

❀

Daniel shook his head while watching Jake holding Jessica's hand and yanking her through the back door of the shop. An alarm went off in his head. Did Jessica have any idea how it looked for her to go off alone with a young man she'd just met? The other men in the shop may assume things about her that weren't true. She might give herself a bad name merely by accident.

Jessica and Jake disappeared through the back door heading to the parking lot, while Daniel grimaced with concern. He was going to have to tell Rebecca to remind the girls of their rules and expectations again. Jessica should think long and hard about how her actions might look to other members of the community. She and Lindsay were English, but they had to respect the Plain ways. Going out alone with a boy could ruin Jessica's name before she even had a chance to prove herself as a good girl.

"Daniel?" his father asked, stepping over into his work area. "*Was iss letz?*"

"Nothing," Daniel muttered, lifting his hammer and turning his attention toward his current project, a bookshelf. "Nothing is wrong, *Dat*."

"You aren't being truthful." His father shook his head. "I can tell by the expression on your face that you're upset about something."

Sighing, Daniel motioned for his father to follow him out of the shop. They sauntered over to the far end of the parking lot and leaned on the fence. Daniel gazed over the large field beyond the fence.

"What's on your mind?" *Dat* asked. "You seemed upset last night at the gathering. Is it from changes in your home?"

"*Ya*. I guess you could say that." Daniel kept his gaze on the field in order to avoid his father's stare.

"I had my driver stop by Robert's farm on my way in this morning," *Dat* said. "I wanted to check in and see how he was doing."

Daniel held his breath, waiting to hear the complaints his brother had reported. If Robert had something negative to say about Daniel, it was always reported through *Dat*. Robert had expressed his criticisms of Daniel through their father since they were children. If Daniel hadn't finished his chores or had made some other mistake, Robert was always the first to run to *Dat* to ensure Daniel was properly punished. Irritation welled up inside him at the thought. He was certain that Robert had reported Jessica's behavior to *Dat*.

"Robert had mentioned Jessica was sharing her worldly music with Katie Saturday night," Dat said. "He was quite upset about it."

Daniel bit his lip to hold back his feelings regarding his brother telling tales.

"Robert said Jessica needs to be reminded to keep her worldly ideas to herself." *Dat* rested his foot on the bottom rung and leaned forward on the fence. "I saw her go off with Jake. The two of them alone will cause rumors. Jessica doesn't realize what she's doing to her reputation."

Daniel nodded. He knew how rampant rumors flowed through the community. Not only would the rumors affect Jessica's reputation, but they would also affect his and Rebecca's.

However, he could still hear her sweet voice repeating that verse from Colossians echoing through his mind like a hymn — "Clothe yourselves with compassion, kindness, humility, gentleness, and patience." He had to give the girls a chance — for Rebecca's sake.

"Jessica and Lindsay are still figuring out the rules," Daniel said. "I don't think it would be fair to charge her with the things Robert is accusing her of. She's a child, and she'll make mistakes."

"That's right, but you should remind her of the rules. The pressure is on you to make sure your household keeps our beliefs." His father's expression grew grim. "If the girls keep making mistakes, someone may go to the bishop."

Closing his eyes, a deep scowl grew on Daniel's lips. The last thing he needed was a visit from the bishop.

"You'd mentioned that the girls wanted to live with their friends, the McCabes," *Dat* said.

"*Ya*, they do." Daniel cut his eyes to the elder Kauffman.

"It would make sense to me. Why would they want to give up their worldly ways to live Plain like us?"

"I've wondered the same thing myself," Daniel said. "But Grace wanted them with us, and Rebecca also wants them here. We need to make the best of it. Rebecca loves them, and she loves her sister. I need to support her. She blames herself for not having children, and she sees this as God's gift to her. We need to try to make this work for her sake and to honor her sister."

Dat nodded. "That makes sense."

"Rebecca says we need to be patient with the girls, so I'm

giving them time," Daniel said. "I'll just give Jessica some pointers tonight at supper."

"*Dat!*" a voice bellowed. "We need your help with this bed frame."

Daniel spun to find his younger brother Timothy standing in the doorway with Peter Troyer, their brother-in-law. Both were motioning for *Dat* to come back in.

"I better get back to work," Eli said. "Duty calls."

Daniel nodded. "I'll be there in just a moment."

"Don't worry. Everything will be fine." *Dat* smacked Daniel on the shoulder before shuffling toward Peter.

Daniel waved at his brother-in-law and then turned toward the field. His thoughts turned to his youngest sister and her husband. In less than nine months, Sarah and Peter would welcome their first child, making Daniel the only married Kauffman child not to have children.

He knew it had broken Rebecca's heart when the doctor had said that she couldn't conceive. He wished they could have children of their own, but he'd given up on that hope a long time ago. It was God's will. It didn't change their marriage, and he'd gotten over the disappointment long ago. He still loved his wife as much as he did the day they were married. Perhaps more.

Sauntering back toward the shop, his father's words echoed through his mind. He had to remind the girls of the rules before the rumor mill began dissecting Jessica's behavior. But he also needed to keep in mind how important the girls were to his wife and respect her wishes with "compassion, kindness, humility, gentleness, and patience."

What do you think?" Jake asked while he sat across from Jessica in the booth at the pizza parlor.

"It's delicious." She lifted the slice of extra pepperoni from the plate. "Thank you."

"You're welcome." He lifted his cup as if toasting her and took a long gulp.

"So, how come your grandpa's Amish, and you're not?" She sipped her diet soda.

He placed his cup on the table and lifted his pizza. "Same reason your aunt is, and you're not."

"I'm guessing your mom left the community?"

"Bingo." He nodded while chewing.

"So, your mom was Amish and then decided she didn't want to be. How come?"

He wiped his mouth with his napkin. "She believed their teachings, but she wanted more freedom. She also fell in love with my dad, and he's Mennonite."

"Is that similar?" Jessica swirled her straw in her glass.

"They're real close." He gestured toward his clothes. "But we don't believe in the formal dress as you can see. There are some subtle differences."

"So, your mom left the church, but her family still accepts her?"

"That's right. She said it was rough in the beginning, and my grandpa was disappointed in my mom. However, he wanted to stay a part of my mom's life. When the grandchildren came along, there were no questions. My grandpa didn't want to be left out."

Stunned, Jessica shook her head. Her mom was treated like an outsider for leaving, yet Jake's mother was still a member of her family. That just didn't seem fair. *How is it Christian to shun your own child?*

"What's bugging you?" He leaned forward, his eyes full of concern.

"I just don't get it. My mom was treated like she didn't exist after she left the church, and yet here you are working in your grandfather's store." She sat back in her chair, disappointment and hurt overcoming her. "I feel like an outsider here, but you fit in like your mom never left."

"You're not an outsider," he said. "Well, you are to a certain degree, since you're not really Amish, but you're still welcome in the community."

"What made you want to work in the furniture store?" She took another bite of pizza.

"I enjoy working with wood." He shrugged. "I always wanted to be a carpenter, ever since I was a little kid. I took some classes in it and then started out as an apprentice in my grandfather's store. I just learned all I could and worked my way up."

"And your grandpa's okay with you being Mennonite and still working for him?"

He finished chewing and then took a drink. "Yeah, he's okay with it. I don't think he was happy when my mom left, but he got over it. He still wanted to be a part of her life and know her children."

"You have siblings?"

His smile faded. "I had a brother."

She studied his face. *He said "had."* She wondered what that meant, but she didn't feel comfortable asking him since they'd just met.

"I bet you miss your friends," he said.

Jessica lifted her glass. "Absolutely."

"Does your boyfriend go to school with you?" he asked.

"We're both sophomores." She nodded. "His name is Brian."

"It must be difficult to be away from him."

"It is, but hopefully I won't be here long." She lifted her pizza. "My godmother is going to get a lawyer and get custody of my sister and me. We want to finish school and go to college."

"But your aunt is guardian, isn't she?" he asked. "Isn't Rebecca the person your parents wanted you to live with?"

"Yeah, but we want to live with my godmother." She finished the slice.

"So, you don't like it here at all, huh?" he asked, swirling his straw in his cup.

"It's okay." She leaned her elbows on the table. "I just want to be in Virginia. That's my home. My sister and I have gone through school with the same kids. That's where we want to be."

"Makes sense. I guess you'll just have to see if that's what God has in store for you."

She bit her bottom lip. She hadn't thought about it that way. What was it that God wanted for her and Lindsay? How would they know?

He gave her a sympathetic frown. "I'm sorry about your parents. I can't imagine how it felt to lose them that way."

She rested her chin on her hands. "It was a shock. I never in a million years imagined they wouldn't come home that night." She swallowed the lump swelling in her throat, hoping she wouldn't break down in front of this guy she'd just met.

"I know exactly what you mean," he said, his voice much softer than it had been.

Jake stared down at his plate, and Jessica wished she could

read his thoughts. She had a feeling he really did know what she meant. She wondered if it had something to do with his brother. She wanted to ask, but she couldn't form the words. The question felt too personal, too intimate, even though she felt comfortable with him. What was it about him that made her feel so welcome, so accepted as a friend? She wondered if he felt it too.

He glanced over at her plate. "You about done?" he asked, breaking through her thoughts.

"I'm full." She rubbed her stomach. "It was delicious. Thank you."

"You're welcome," he said, smiling again. "We'd better head back soon. Grandpa is a slave driver."

She chuckled.

"Ah-ha!" He pointed to her face. "I knew there was a pretty smile in there somewhere."

Her cheeks heated. He thought her smile was pretty.

But why should she care what he thought? She had a boyfriend back home in Virginia Beach. Jake was just a friend.

"Let's head back before your uncle thinks I kidnapped ya." Jake cleared their dishes and then led her to the parking lot where they climbed into his truck.

"Thanks for lunch," she said while buckling her safety belt. "You didn't have to pay."

"My treat." He jammed the key in the ignition and cranked over the engine.

"Next time I pay."

"Next time?" He raised his eyebrows. "So that means you'll go to lunch with me again?"

"Maybe." She gave him a coy smile. "If you promise to keep my phone charged."

He grinned. "There's a price, huh?"

"Of course. You said so yourself." She settled back in the seat and smiled, happy to have found a friend in Lancaster County.

❋

"So, how was your first day?" Daniel asked while they headed down the road from the furniture store in the van.

"It went okay." Jessica stared out the side window at the beautiful farmland. "It was really busy, but I could handle it. I figured out a system with the ledger and the customer orders. I think I did okay."

"My father and Milton said they were very happy with your work." He glanced back at her. "They were pleased with how organized and thorough you are."

"Thank you. I was taught by the best—my dad." Jessica sighed. How she missed her parents.

"And you went to lunch with Jake?"

Jessica cut her eyes to Daniel. She couldn't help but wonder if he was implying anything. Her cheeks heated with embarrassment. "We went to the pizza parlor up the street, and it was delicious."

She hoped he'd drop the subject of Jake. She couldn't imagine what the big deal was. She had lunch with a friend. She needed to change the subject. "I hope Lindsay and Rebecca had a good day too," she said.

"*Ya*," he said. "I'm sure they did."

Daniel began to discuss the weather, and Jessica breathed a sigh of relief. She didn't want to talk about Jake. They were only friends, but she did look forward to seeing him again tomorrow. It was nice to finally have a friend.

❋

"Dinner was delicious," Lindsay said while clearing the plates. "I really like that chicken casserole. The cheese really adds flavor."

"I'm glad you liked it." Rebecca lifted her plate, along with Daniel's and started toward the sink. "You did a great job helping me."

Jessica stepped in front of her and snatched the plates from Rebecca's hand. "I got it. You go sit."

Rebecca studied her niece. "Are you sure?"

"Yeah." Jessica smiled. "You worked hard all day and then cooked us supper. Go put your feet up or do whatever it is you do after supper. Lindsay and I will do the dishes."

Rebecca glanced at Lindsay, who nodded.

"We got it, Aunt Rebecca," Lindsay said. "You go relax."

"Okay." Rebecca smiled. "Call me if you need me." She padded into the living room, where Daniel sat in his favorite wing chair while reading his Bible. He always read the Bible after supper and chose verses for their devotional time.

He looked over at her and tilted his head. "You all right, *mei Fraa*? You look perplexed."

"For the first time in probably thirty years, I don't have to do the dishes." She sank into a chair and sighed. "I don't know what to do."

Her husband chuckled. "The girls are giving you a much-needed break. Enjoy it."

"I don't know how." She smoothed her apron. "I guess Jessica had a good day. She was pleasant at supper."

"*Ya*, I think so." He placed the Bible on his lap. "She seemed to enjoy the work, and my father said she did a good job. She also had lunch with Jake Miller."

"Jake Miller?" Rebecca's eyes widened at the implication.

"The two of them went to the pizza parlor. She said he was very nice to her."

"Well, he's only a few years older than she is. Perhaps Jake can help her adjust to the move and missing her friends. I think he'll be a good influence. He has a very strong faith." She fiddled with the strings on her *Kapp* and contemplated Jake Miller.

Rebecca had known him since he was born, and he'd always been a good boy. She'd never once heard of him getting in trouble. His twin, however, was the one who'd often been in trouble. She'd heard there were rumors of foul play surrounding his death.

"I'm sure he's a nice boy, but it's not appropriate for her to go off alone with a boy. You know how people talk." His eyes studied her. "I think you need to talk to her again."

"I think we need to give her time to adjust. It was her first day on the job, and Jake is the only person at the shop who is close to her age. It only makes sense that she would befriend—"

Daniel leaned forward in the chair. "This is more than just a girl making a friend with a boy. Jessica has already introduced rock music and computers to Katie. Robert mentioned it to my *dat*, and he brought the subject up to me at work. Then she was seen being pulled through the shop by Jake. They left for lunch alone in his truck and were gone close to an hour. I would hate to see her get a reputation."

"I'm sure it was innocent," she whispered.

He frowned. "I know, but my father even mentioned her behavior."

She heaved another deep sigh. The rumors were starting already. She imagined the rest of the men in the shop would tell their wives about Jessica and then the gossip would continue, moving through the community like a brush fire.

"What if someone went to the bishop?" he asked, lowering his voice. "Do you realize the pressure he would put on this household?"

"No one will tell the bishop," she said, even though she knew she was wrong. There were members of the community who loved to tell the bishop every little rumor they overhead without going straight to the source for clarification. "Jessica isn't a baptized member of the church, so the bishop can't—"

"You know the bishop will go after the guardians of the misbehaving child." He pointed to his chest. "That would be me, as the head of this household. And they aren't even our children."

Her stomach twisted at the coldness of his words. So he did resent her for not giving him a child. The bitterness in his expression stole her breath, and for a moment she couldn't speak.

"They are our nieces," she finally said, her voice trembling with the pain caused by his words. "They're all I have left of my sister."

"But it may not be best for them here," he said. "You might want to consider that. If they aren't happy, then it may not be the best solution to keep them here."

"I think they belong here," she whispered. "It was Grace's wish, and I think it's God's will. They are the children I couldn't have, Daniel. Don't you see that? I couldn't give you children, so we have my nieces to care for."

He sighed, his eyes full of hurt. "I don't blame you for that, Becky. Don't you see that?" He gently touched her cheek, and she swallowed a lump that threatened to form in her throat.

"Just remind Jessica of our rules," he said, his voice warm and smooth like chocolate pudding. "That's all I ask."

"*Ya*," she whispered. "I'll speak with Jessica."

"She can't flaunt her worldly ways," he said, picking up the Bible. "Her inappropriate behavior reflects on our household, and we can't tolerate it." He turned his gaze back to the Bible.

Rebecca cleared her throat and made an attempt to change the subject. "Lindsay did great today," she said. "She's a natural in the kitchen and a fast learner. I think she enjoyed it too."

Daniel nodded without looking up from the Bible. "*Gut*. We can have our devotion and prayer time here after they're done with the dishes."

"*Ya*." Glancing toward the doorway to the kitchen, Rebecca sighed. She silently sent a plea up to God for guidance and patience with her nieces as well as a plea for understanding from her husband.

Peach Strudel

Line bottom of buttered baking dish with thick layer of peaches and sprinkle with mixed cinnamon, sugar, and dots of butter.

Sift into mixing bowl:
   1 – 1/4 cups of sugar
   3/4 tsp baking powder
   1 cup flour
   3/4 tsp of salt

Break 1 egg into above mixture; mix until crumbly. Put over peaches and bake at 350 degrees until crust is brown. Serve with whipped cream or ice cream.

14

So the furniture store wasn't so bad, huh?" Lindsay dried another dish and set it in the cabinet.

Jessica shrugged. "It was fine. At least it was busy, so the day went by quickly." She scrubbed the pot and then handed it to her sister to dry.

"That's good. The bakery was busy too." Lindsay swiped the pot with a towel. "But I liked learning the recipes. They eat some good food."

"You like it?" Jessica scrubbed the glasses.

"Yeah, I do." Her young sister smiled. "I think I might actually get to like it here. At least, it's better than I thought it would be."

Jessica stared down at the glasses. Had she just heard her sister correctly? She cut her eyes back up to Lindsay's. She checked to make sure the doorway was empty and then leaned over to her sister. "You like it here? You've got to be kidding me. Why would you want to stay here in this repressed culture? Don't you miss having a CD player and TV? And what about a computer and the Internet?"

Lindsay frowned. "There's more to life than electricity and music."

Jessica threw down the dishrag. "Don't you miss your friends?"

"Sure I do, but we'll make more friends here, Jess. And we can visit our friends. I'm sure Aunt Rebecca would let us take a bus down there to see them sometime. Maybe in a few months we can make a trip together. Since we have Trisha's cell phone, we can call them and arrange something."

Jessica nodded, and her thoughts turned to Brian. She gasped. *Oh no!* She'd forgotten to call him back.

"You okay?" Lindsay touched her arm. "You look upset."

"I just remembered I never called Brian back. He left me a voicemail earlier." She dried her hands on her jeans. "Can you finish up? I want to call him before it gets too late."

"Sure." Lindsay cinched her eyebrows in disbelief. "Your cell phone still works? I figured it would be dead by now."

"Yeah." Jessica snatched it from her purse on the counter. "Jake charged it for me in his truck."

"Who's Jake?" Lindsay asked, her eyes lifting with question.

"I work with him." Jessica started out of the kitchen toward the back stairs.

"He has a truck?" Her sister called after her. "Tell me more!"

"Maybe later." Jessica trotted up the stairs while flipping the phone open. She scrolled through to find Brian's number and then hit Send while hurrying down the hall. While it rang, she entered her room. While balancing the phone between her ear and her shoulder, she lit the kerosene lantern and flopped onto her bed.

"Hey, Jess," Brian said. "How are you?"

She smiled at the sound of his voice, warm and familiar. "Fine. How are you?"

"I'm okay," he said.

She heard a rustling sound and then his muffled words. "Who else is there?" she asked.

"Morgan and a few of my buddies are here," he said.

"Oh." Her stomach twisted with jealousy. Why was Morgan with him and his buddies? Were Morgan and Brian ... ? She pushed that thought away. No, they couldn't be.

"Hang on," he said. "Morgan wants to talk to you."

There was more rustling and then Morgan's voice sounded through the phone. "Hi, Jess! How are you?"

"Hi." Jessica rolled onto her back and stared up at the plain white ceiling. "I'm doing all right. What's new with you?"

"Not much. We're having a study group at Brian's." The sounds in the background faded, and Jessica imagined Morgan walking away from the group. "We're all cramming for the chemistry final on Wednesday. You know how Mr. Elkins' tests are."

"Yeah." Regret vibrated through Jessica. If her parents were still alive, she'd be cramming along with them. "How is everyone?"

"The same. You aren't missing much," Morgan said. "I got the voicemail you left last night. I've been meaning to call you. You mentioned that you were starting work today. How'd it go?"

"It went fine." Jessica rolled onto her side. "I'm running the front of the furniture store where my uncle works."

"Sounds exciting." Morgan's voice seeped sarcasm.

"Actually, it's not so bad. There's a nice guy who works there named Jake."

"Oh?" She heard the smile in Morgan's voice. "Is he hot?"

Yes! "I guess." Jessica tried not to sound too excited about him. She didn't want to give Morgan the wrong idea. "He took me to lunch and let me charge my phone in his truck."

"Wow! Do you like him?"

"As a friend—besides he's Mennonite, which is almost Amish. I think our lives are too different." Jessica closed her eyes, trying to remember the details of Brian's face. He was her boyfriend, not Jake.

"Does he like you?"

"Morgan, I'm dating Brian. Remember?" *At least I think we're still dating.*

"Yeah, but ..."

"But what?" Jessica sat up straight. "What are you implying?"

"I'm not implying anything." A voice sounded behind Morgan, and rustling noises filled the line again. "Hey, Jess," Morgan said. "Brian wants to talk to you. I'll talk to you later, okay? I miss you."

"Miss you too." Jessica leaned back on the headboard, and her lip trembled. She cleared her throat and pushed away thoughts of missing her friends.

"Hi again," Brian said. "So what's this about a hot guy at your new job?"

"What?" Jessica shook her head. "I didn't say anything about a hot guy at my job."

"I heard Morgan say something about a guy at your job who's hot or something. What's his name?"

"His name is Jake, and he's just a friend."

"Do you like him?"

"Brian, are you kidding me?" Jessica's voice rose with frustration. "I was forced to move against my will, and you think I'm dating other guys?"

"Are you?" he asked.

"No."

"Good."

She smiled. Maybe everything was okay between them. She'd only imagined that he'd moved on and forgotten her. "Do you miss me?" She held her breath, anticipating his answer.

"Of course. Do you miss me?" Brian asked.

"Like crazy." She grabbed a photo of her, Brian, and Morgan from her nightstand and studied it. She'd give anything to go back to that trip to the Outer Banks, sunning on the beach, the smell of suntan lotion and the sound of the waves crashing at their feet. She sighed.

More voices sounded in the background on the other end of the line.

"Look, I gotta go. I'll call you later, okay?" he asked.

She gnawed her bottom lip. Did he have to hang up so soon? "Yeah."

"Take care."

"You too," she said.

"Bye." The line went dead.

"I love you," Jessica whispered into the silent phone line.

She wondered why he had hung up so quickly. Did he really miss her or had he just said it to be nice?

Grief and regret sliced through her heart. She wished she were back in Virginia Beach and life was the way it used to be. She missed her parents, Brian, her friends, her house, and her school.

She snapped the phone shut, tossed it onto the bed, and dissolved into tears.

Jake's words echoed through her mind. Is this what God had in store for her — living a life in a strange place while her friends back home moved on without her? Why would God want her to be so unhappy? Closing her eyes, she continued to cry.

❁

Lindsay stood outside of Jessica's closed door and listened to the sounds of her sister's crying. She bit her lip, pondering if she should go in or mind her own business. Her sister was obviously upset. Something was wrong.

The sound of the sobs increased, and Lindsay couldn't take it any longer. She couldn't let her sister suffer alone. Pushing the door open, she entered her sister's room and found Jessica sprawled across her bed.

The phone sat at the end of the bed, and Lindsay wondered

if Brian said something to hurt her. Lindsay had long suspected he'd been cheating on her, especially after she'd spotted Morgan and Brian kissing one night when they came over to watch a movie with Jessica.

After that incident, Lindsay wanted to tell Jessica, but she was afraid of hurting her sister. Now she wondered if she'd made a mistake keeping it from Jessica.

"Hey." Lindsay lowered herself onto the bed and touched her sister's ponytail. "What happened?"

Jessica rolled onto her back and wiped her eyes with the back of her hand. "I just talked to Brian and Morgan."

"What did Brian do this time?" Lindsay frowned. She'd love to smack that boy for always hurting Jessica. Since they'd met, he'd broken up with Jessica twice, and her sister was always a fool and took that jerk back after he'd changed his mind. Lindsay wished her sister would realize that she was too good for that loser.

"I just get the feeling they've forgotten me and moved on with their lives." Jessica sat up and straightened her blouse. "And Brian has never really said he misses me. I just feel so alone."

"You're not alone." Lindsay hugged her. "You have me and Aunt Rebecca and Uncle Daniel. And what about your new friend Jake? What's he like?"

Jessica shrugged. "He's nice. I think he's a few years older than me. He's cute."

"Cute?" Lindsay grinned. Maybe Jessica had finally found someone nice and would forget that jerk Brian.

"Yeah. He's tall and has dark hair and blue eyes." Jessica's cheeks turned a bright pink. "He has a nice smile too."

"Oh really?" Lindsay touched her sister's arm. "He sounds more than just cute."

"We're just friends." Jessica frowned. "But I still love Brian even though I get the feeling he doesn't love me anymore."

"Mom always said we were too young to get serious about a boy. Maybe we should take Mom's advice."

Tears glistened in her older sister's eyes. "But Mom's gone, and I feel so alone."

Lindsay hugged her again. "You're not alone. Stop saying that. Aunt Rebecca says we have to have faith. Just have faith."

"How can I have faith when I don't understand why Mom and Dad had to die? Why did God have to take them from us?" she asked, her voice trembling.

"I don't know why they had to die. I wonder that all the time, but we'll make it through this together, okay?" Lindsay asked.

Jessica nodded and hugged her tighter. "I just miss them both so much, and I feel so lost without them."

"I know what you mean." Lindsay blew out a trembling breath. "Sometimes I have these dreams that our life is back to normal. We're living in our old house, and we're in the den eating popcorn and watching a movie with Mom and Dad. It's so real that I can smell Dad's aftershave and taste extra butter movie popcorn. Then I wake up in my room here, and it's like a cruel joke."

Jessica sniffed. "I have those dreams too. It's awful to wake up."

"I know." Lindsay pulled back and wiped an errant tear from her cheek. "But Aunt Rebecca says it will get easier. She says she felt the same way when she lost her mom. She says she held on to her faith in God, and He got her through."

Tears flowed from Jessica's cheek. "But we lost our mom and our dad at the same time. She only lost her mom. It's harder on us. We have no one."

Lindsay bit her bottom lip and swallowed her forming tears. "But we're not alone. We have each other and Aunt Rebecca and Uncle Daniel." Reaching out, she squeezed Jessica's hand. "Uncle Daniel is about to start devotions. Why don't you come downstairs? Aunt Rebecca sent me up for you. Maybe you'll feel better after you hear some verses and pray with us."

Jessica shook her head. "I'd rather be alone." She flopped down on her stomach on the bed.

Jessica studied her sister. "You used to like going to church. What happened?"

"That was different. I felt like I belonged there. Here I don't."

"But we're still worshiping God, Jess. We're just doing it a different way."

"It's not the same." She buried her face in her pillow.

"It makes me feel better when I hear the Word every night with Uncle Daniel and Aunt Rebecca. It gives me hope that we're going to be okay."

"Good for you," Jessica muttered through the pillow. "Go say a prayer for me."

Scowling, Lindsay stood. "Fine. Suit yourself. Stay here alone in your room if that's what you want."

Jessica grunted in reply without looking up at her.

Shaking her head, Lindsay exited the room and closed the door. She knew her sister missed their parents as much as she did, but she wished Jessica would open her heart to Aunt Rebecca and see how much she loved them both.

15

Rebecca stepped into the kitchen. Finding the counter clean and tidy, she couldn't help but smile. It was nice to have help. The fact that the girls were so thorough made it even better.

Too bad Daniel wasn't sure they should stay.

"Is it time for devotions?" Lindsay asked, appearing in the kitchen doorway.

Turning, Rebecca gazed at her niece. "I think Daniel's ready."

Daniel sauntered into the kitchen and sank into his usual chair.

Rebecca and Lindsay joined him, sitting across from each other. Lindsay listened, her eyes intent and focused, while Daniel read from the book of Job.

His message of hope filled Rebecca's heart. She again thought of Daniel's words, and she frowned at the thought of losing the girls.

She had to find a way to show Daniel they did belong in the family. They were Rebecca's flesh and blood. They were family, her sister's daughters. If she could get Jessica to tone down her worldliness, maybe then Daniel would admit that this could work.

When Daniel finished reading, they all bowed their heads

in prayer. Daniel then stood and carried his Bible back into the living room.

"I enjoy our evening devotion time," Lindsay said.

Rebecca smiled, marveling at the girl's strong faith. "Jessica didn't want to join us?"

Lindsay frowned. "I tried to get her to come, but she wanted to be alone in her room."

Pushing back her chair, Rebecca rose. "I'll go talk to her."

Rebecca climbed the back staircase and padded to Jessica's closed door. She took a deep breath to gather her thoughts and tapped on the door. After a moment, she heard Jessica's slippers slap across the floor and the door creak open, revealing Jessica frowning with her ear buds stuck in her ears.

"May I come in?" Rebecca asked.

Jessica yanked the ear buds out and shrugged. "Why not? It's your house." She schlepped back to her bed and flopped onto her stomach on top of it.

Rebecca stepped into the room and folded her arms. "Can we talk?"

Her niece gestured toward the end of the bed. "What's on your mind?"

Rebecca sank onto the bed. "I was wondering if we could talk about how things are going for you."

"What do you mean?" Jessica sat up and crossed her legs under her.

Rebecca paused and wondered how she was going to tell Jessica to adhere to the household rules without upsetting her.

Glancing across the room, her gaze fell on her sister's wedding portrait. Grace's electric smile grinned back at her, tugging at her heart. She was doing this for Grace. Closing her eyes, she prayed for her lips to form the right words.

"Rebecca?" Jessica asked. "What is it?"

"I wanted to talk to you about a few things Daniel has been

concerned about." Rebecca ran her finger over her apron. "I was wondering if you would do a few things for him."

Jessica's eyebrows careened toward her hairline with surprise. "Do something for Daniel?"

"*Ya.*" Rebecca straightened her back. "Daniel is concerned about your behavior."

Jessica grimaced. "We already talked about what happened with Katie. I get it—don't share my music and my computer. Can we move on now?"

Rebecca ignored the snide comment. "Daniel is concerned about your clothing."

Jessica's eyes flashed with anger. She pointed to Rebecca's dress with a disgusted expression. "I'm not going to wear that. I'll keep my music to myself, but I refuse to wear *that!*"

"I didn't say you have to dress like me." Rebecca reached for the girl's hand, but Jessica pulled it away. "I just would like you to be more conscious of your clothes. Just be more . . . modest."

"Modest?" Jessica shook her head with disbelief. "What are you getting at? It's not like I went to the shop with body parts hanging out."

"I know." Rebecca sighed. How could she get Jessica to listen and respond without using the sarcastic comebacks? "If you could tone down the makeup and the jewelry, Daniel would be more comfortable."

"But I took off some of my makeup this morning and I put almost all of my jewelry back in my box this morning."

"I know," Rebecca said, keeping her tone even. "Just keep that in mind tomorrow morning, and we won't have a repeat of what happened today."

Jessica sighed and shook her head. "Unbelievable."

"Also, he said that you went to lunch with Jake Miller alone."

"So?" Her niece scowled. "I thought you wanted me to make friends here."

"Yes, I do, Jessica." Rebecca clasped her hands together, hoping to get her message across without the girl losing her temper. "But going off alone with a young man you just met sends the wrong message to others."

"You've got to be kidding!" Jessica jumped up from the bed. "Did everyone think I was making out with him on our lunch hour?" She shook her head and waved her arms for emphasis. "We went to a pizza parlor to have lunch, and that's all we did—eat and talk. And I had a good time."

"I believe you." Rebecca grabbed her niece's hand, pulled her back toward the bed, and motioned for her to sit. "It's just the perception. There's a lot of talk in this community."

"There's nothing I can do about gossip." Her niece lowered herself onto the bed and continued to frown. "I am who I am and that's it."

"Jessica, it's more complicated than that. If the People feel you're a bad influence on our community, the bishop will censure Daniel and take him to task for not being the proper leader in his family."

Her niece lifted an eyebrow in disbelief. "Are you serious?"

"I need your support on this. If you just keep your worldly ideas and attire to yourself, then things will go much more smoothly." She took her niece's hands in hers. "You and Lindsay are very important to me. I want to be a good support and guardian to you girls. Your mother wanted you here, and I will do my best to keep you both happy and safe."

Jessica was silent for a moment while her eyes studied Rebecca. "Why are you brainwashing my sister?"

Taken by surprise, Rebecca gasped. "What are you talking about?"

Her niece yanked her hands back. "Lindsay loves your little

devotion time at night. She's really getting into your religion. Why are you trying to turn her into one of your kind?"

"One of my kind?" Appalled, Rebecca shook her head and gasped. "We're Christians just like your parents. We just choose to worship in our homes instead of in a church. I find it disrespectful that you insult our culture."

Jessica folded her arms and scowled, her pretty face twisted into an angry grimace. "Lindsay thinks we belong here, but I don't. We belong in Virginia with our friends and school and electricity and ... all the normal things a teenager has. That's where my mom wanted to be. She didn't want to be Amish, and she didn't want to be here."

"I think you should give us more of a chance and also respect our ways. You're a child, and you have no right to insult my home." Feeling that the conversation wasn't going to be resolved, Rebecca stood. "Please follow our rules—at least outside of this room. That's all we ask." She started toward the door.

"Aunt Rebecca?" Jessica said.

Rebecca faced her niece. "*Ya?*"

"I still don't think I did anything wrong. If they don't accept me, then it's all the more reason I should leave." She nodded toward her parents' portrait. "I think we belong with Trisha, and she's trying to get custody of us."

Rebecca sighed. They were back to square one. "I know. Lindsay told me."

"I'm not going to let you convert my sister."

Shaking her head, Rebecca grasped the doorknob. She closed her eyes and took a deep breath while silently repeating the verse from Colossians—"Compassion, kindness, humility, gentleness, and patience."

"I know you're trying to pick a fight with me," Rebecca began, "but it's not going to work. I'm not trying to convert anyone. I'm only trying to do my best as your guardian. If you choose to fight me on it, then I can't stop you. But my only hope is you'll realize I love you and want the best for you." She wrenched open the door. "Good night."

Rebecca held her breath and shook her head. The discussion with Jessica had gone much worse than she'd imagined. Instead of reaching an understanding with Jessica, her niece had accused her of trying to influence Lindsay.

She groaned and covered her face with her hands. She had no idea how to get through to this girl. Going from no children to two teenage daughters was much more difficult than Rebecca had ever imagined.

But she reminded herself that somehow this was a part of God's plan. They were meant to be here; they were the children Rebecca had always prayed to have. It also was what Grace wanted for her girls.

She checked on Lindsay and found her ready for bed. After saying good night, Rebecca continued down the hallway.

While walking toward her bedroom, Elizabeth's words echoed through her mind—"Bear in mind that our Lord's patience means salvation."

She needed to pray for patience and have faith. There was a reason why Grace had sent the girls here to experience her heritage.

All Rebecca could do was hold on to the belief that the girls belonged here. She loved them no matter what, and she had to show them how much she loved them. The best way to prove her love was to keep her heart open to them.

She had to understand and believe in them, since Grace believed in her.

She stepped into her bedroom. Changing into her nightgown, she wondered what she could've said differently to get Jessica to listen to her words instead of giving sarcastic, defensive replies.

"You're ready for bed early tonight, *mei Fraa*," a voice said.

Rebecca jumped at Daniel's words. She was so engrossed in

her thoughts that she hadn't heard him enter the bedroom. She turned to see Daniel cross to the bed.

"It has been a long day," she said. "I thought I'd turn in early."

"Are the girls settled?" he asked.

"*Ya*," she said.

"Did you speak with Jessica?" he asked while pulling off his suspenders.

"*Ya*," she said, releasing her hair from the bun.

"And?" he asked.

Rebecca sighed, silently debating how much to tell him. She didn't want to upset him too. She'd had enough cross words this evening. "I explained to her that her behavior has been inappropriate and asked her to be more mindful of our ways."

"How did she take it?" Daniel removed his shirt and sank onto the edge of the bed.

"She said she hadn't done anything to deliberately disobey the house rules." Rebecca ran the brush through her long hair. "I explained that her dress and her going out to lunch with Jake Miller alone had caused some concern."

"Did she say she would change her ways?" he asked.

"She said she'd try," Rebecca whispered, knowing she wasn't being truthful, but wanting to avoid another discussion about how the girls may not belong here.

"*Gut*." Daniel stepped over to her and took her hands in his. "*Danki, mei Fraa*."

Rebecca nodded, staring into the eyes she'd admired for nearly eighteen years. She'd fallen in love with her husband the first time he'd asked her to ride in his courting buggy.

In the fifteen years they'd been married, she'd never doubted their relationship or his love for her. He'd always been loving and respectful. Even when they learned she couldn't bear a child, he was her strength and comfort. He told her he'd love her no matter what. He said that even without children in their marriage, he'd never blame her or feel resentment toward her.

However, when he said that maybe the girls didn't belong with them, she'd wondered if she really knew her husband. She had never imagined the man who could live without children of his own would reject her two nieces who so desperately needed parents. She now looked into his eyes and wondered if he truly was the loving man she'd always thought he'd be. Doubting him caused a deep ache in her heart.

"I love you," he said, touching her hair.

A lump swelled in her throat. She pushed her disappointment aside and forced a smile on her face. "I love you too."

He traced her cheek with his finger while his orbs studied hers. "Something is bothering you, *mei Lieb*."

Rebecca held her breath trying not to cry at the sound of his voice calling her "my love." That pet name always sent her insides into a wild swirl.

"Talk to me, Becky." He cupped her face in his hands. "*Bitte*."

"I just hope that the girls find their way with us," she said, praying he'd understand.

"Let's not discuss the girls." Mischief glowed in his handsome face. He took her hands in his and tugged her toward the bed. "Let's turn in for the night."

As they stepped toward the bed, she sent up a silent prayer that Jessica and Daniel would both release their stubbornness and find common ground.

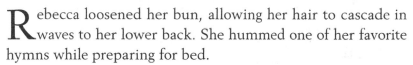
R ebecca loosened her bun, allowing her hair to cascade in waves to her lower back. She hummed one of her favorite hymns while preparing for bed.

The past couple of weeks had blown by in a blur. With the beginning of June came the start of the tourist season, and business at the bakery boomed. Lindsay continued to excel with her cooking. She picked up recipes as if she'd been born to make them, and she helped Kathryn and Beth Anne care for the younger nieces and nephews who stayed at the bakery during the day.

While running a brush through her long brown locks, Rebecca smiled. Lindsay seemed to fit in so well, and it warmed her heart to have her niece with her every day. The girl continued to ask question after question about the Faith. Her eyes lit up while they discussed the Amish beliefs and what life was like living in the Faith.

Rebecca longed to know if Lindsay had any interest in being baptized and joining the church, but she hesitated asking since Jessica had accused her of influencing her little sister.

She frowned at the memory of that conversation with her older niece. The words still stung two weeks after they were spoken. Jessica had become more withdrawn since that night. She rarely spoke to Rebecca, but she had changed her behavior.

She wore shirts that didn't cling to her body, she didn't wear much makeup or jewelry, except for the chain with her mother's ring, and she stayed in her room during family visits.

Rebecca was disappointed to see Jessica so withdrawn from the family, but she held on to Elizabeth's advice to be patient. She prayed Jessica would soon make more of an effort to be a part of the family. Rebecca believed that in due time, Jessica would come out of her shell and accept Rebecca into her heart.

Rebecca placed the brush on the dresser and padded to her bed. She was turning down her quilt when a faint knock sounded on the door. "Come in," Rebecca called.

The door opened with a creak, revealing Lindsay standing in the doorway with her arms folded across her pink nightgown and her eyes round with uncertainty.

"Lindsay." Rebecca sank down onto the bed and motioned for her to enter the room. "Please, come in. Is something wrong?"

Biting her bottom lip, her niece stepped across the threshold and scanned the room. "Are you alone?"

"*Ya.*" Rebecca patted the quilt next to her. "Daniel sometimes likes to stay up late reading downstairs. Join me here."

Lindsay crossed the room and lowered herself onto the bed next to Rebecca. "I was wondering if I could ask you a question."

"Of course." Rebecca smiled at her niece's wide-eyed innocence. "You know you can ask me anything."

"I was wondering ..." The girl ran her finger over the stitching on the log cabin-design quilt that had belonged to Rebecca's parents. "I was wondering if it would be okay if I went to the service with you on Sunday."

Rebecca cupped her hand to her mouth and stifled a gasp. She'd hoped the girls would open their minds and hearts to the idea of joining her at Sunday services, but she'd never dreamt it would happen so soon. Lindsay continued to amaze her with her interest in their way of life.

"Are you certain that you want to go?" Rebecca asked.

"*Ya.*" Lindsay giggled after saying the word. "I thought I'd try a little Pennsylvania Dutch."

"*Gut!*" Rebecca said with a smile. "Now, honestly, Lindsay, are you sure you want to go to service?"

"Well, yeah." Her niece's brows knitted together with confusion. "Why would I ask to go if I didn't mean it?"

"I just want to be sure that you don't feel pressured." Rebecca took her niece's warm hands in hers. "If you ever feel pressured by me to follow our ways, you'd tell me, yes?"

Lindsay's eyes studied hers. "Yes, of course I would. But you don't pressure me. I enjoy our daily devotions, and I miss going to church. Being with you and learning about your ways makes me feel closer to my mother. Is that crazy?"

"No." Rebecca pulled her into a warm hug. "It's not crazy at all. It makes perfect sense. Now you know that most of our service is in German and Dutch. You may feel a bit lost."

"I know," Lindsay said, still holding onto Rebecca. "But the more I practice, the more I'll understand."

Warmth and hope swelled within Rebecca while she held Lindsay close. It was her dream to share a service with her nieces. She hoped that Lindsay's interest would spark Jessica's.

"I have another question." Her niece pulled back from the hug. "Would you help me find something more appropriate to wear?"

Rebecca's eyebrows furrowed in question. "What do you mean?"

"You make your clothes, right?"

Rebecca nodded.

"Would you help me make a dress like yours?"

Rebecca's eyes widened in shock. "You want to dress Plain for service?"

"*Ya*," Lindsay whispered. "Would that be okay? Or would I get in trouble with the other members of the church?"

Rebecca shook her head. "I don't think you'd upset anyone."

"I know this is a big step, but I think I want to try. Well, you know," Lindsay's cheeks flushed a bright pink, "if you think it's okay."

"Of course I think it's okay." She took Lindsay's hands and stood. "Let's go down the hall to the sewing room."

❦

Early Friday morning, Rebecca stood by Elizabeth while they kneaded dough for sugar cookies. Her sisters-in-law and Lindsay were out back in the play area with the children.

"How are things going with the girls?" Elizabeth asked.

"Better," Rebecca said with a smile.

Elizabeth studied her. "You look happy. Things must be going *really* well."

"Lindsay wants to come to service on Sunday." Rebecca rolled out the dough.

"Really?" Elizabeth's eyes widened in surprise.

"*Ya.*" Rebecca began to cut out the cookies. "We've been making a dress for her. We work together in the sewing room every night."

"*Wunderbar.*" Elizabeth looped her arm around Elizabeth's shoulders and gave her a quick squeeze. "How is Jessica doing?"

Rebecca's smile faded. "She stays in her room alone most evenings. She doesn't participate in our devotions at all."

"She's not adjusting well." Elizabeth shook her head.

"She'll be okay," Rebecca said while placing the cookies on the sheet. "We just need to give her time and give her guidance. Like we read in 2 Peter 3:15: 'Bear in mind that our Lord's patience means salvation.'"

"Are you sure?"

Rebecca stopped placing the cookies on the pan and met her mother-in-law's frown. "What do you mean?"

"Are you sure that Jessica will adjust to our ways?"

Rebecca considered the question and a chill of doubt washed over her. "She has to adjust. There's no other way."

Elizabeth rolled out her dough. "Just be sure you're listening," she said without looking up.

"What do you mean?" Rebecca asked.

"Be sure you're listening." Elizabeth began to cut out the cookies.

"Listening to whom—Jessica?" Rebecca studied Elizabeth, trying to understand what she meant. "She's a child. How can she possibly know what she wants? She's a lost soul now that her parents are gone. Her mother wanted her with me."

Elizabeth finished cutting out the cookies and loaded them on the pan. Then she faced Rebecca and gave a knowing smile. "Just open your heart and make sure you're listening. That's all I meant."

"But this is what Grace wanted." She took a deep breath. "This is God's will. These girls are the children I could never have."

Elizabeth took Rebecca's hands in hers. "Just open your heart and listen." She squeezed her hands and let go. "Let's get these cookies in the oven."

Rebecca slipped the cookie sheets into the oven while contemplating Elizabeth's advice.

Wasn't she listening to the girls? And Daniel?

Wasn't she listening to God?

A chill slithered through her veins despite the heat emanating from the row of ovens.

The door from the parking lot opened, revealing Sarah schlepping in while hugging her arms to her stomach. She groaned as she crossed to the nearest chair and sank onto it.

"Sarah Rose." Elizabeth rushed over to her, grabbing a cold glass of water on the way. "You look awful."

"I feel awful." Sarah took the glass and gulped. "I woke up sick, and I can't seem to shake it." After placing the glass on the counter, she swiped her hand across her forehead. "I'm burning up and my stomach is churning. Is this normal?"

"*Ya*, unfortunately." Elizabeth rubbed Sarah's back. "I was sick with all of my pregnancies, but it will get better after the first trimester."

Sarah glanced over at Rebecca. "I'm sorry I wasn't here to help bake this morning."

Rebecca shook her head. "Don't worry." She touched Sarah's shoulder. "You look a little green. You should take it easy. Maybe go home and lie down for a bit."

"*Nee.*" Sarah shook her head. "I'd go crazy at home alone." She turned to Elizabeth. "*Mamm*, was *Dat* different while you were pregnant?"

"How do you mean?" Elizabeth pulled up a chair and held Sarah's hands.

"Peter's been acting different lately. He's been really quiet. He hardly talks to me anymore." Tears filled her eyes. "I don't know if he loves me anymore, *Mamm*." Covering her face, she sobbed.

"Oh, Sarah Rose." Elizabeth pulled her youngest child close and rubbed her back as she cried. "Of course he loves you. Your hormones are just getting the best of you."

Rebecca smiled and hugged her chest. She knew Sarah would make a wonderful mother. Rebecca just hoped she could too.

❁

Later that afternoon, Lindsay pulled a sheet of Dutch almond cookies from the oven. She inhaled the sweet aroma as she scooped the cookies onto the cooling rack.

A smile overtook her lips while she contemplated how much she enjoyed learning the recipes. Mom would be so proud!

"What have you got there?" Elizabeth asked as she examined the cookies lining the rack.

"I thought I'd try a new recipe. The bakery was quiet, and the ovens weren't on." Lindsay placed the rack in the sink. "I hope it's okay."

"Of course it's fine." Elizabeth smiled. "The cookies are perfect." She looped an arm around Lindsay's shoulder. "You're a wonderful addition to our bakery. I'm so glad you're working with us."

"Thank you." Lindsay felt her cheeks heat with embarrassment at the compliment. "I enjoy learning these new recipes. My mom and I used to bake together." She sighed. "I really miss her."

"I'm sure you do." Elizabeth rubbed her shoulders. "I knew Grace when she was young."

Lindsay's eyes widened with surprise. "You did?"

"*Ya.*" The older woman's smile looked a little sad. "She was a lovely girl. You and your sister resemble her. She wanted more than the community could offer her."

Lindsay nodded as she turned off the oven. "I know."

"Rebecca mentioned that you want to come to our service."

Lindsay bit her lip. Was Elizabeth going to say she wasn't welcome? "Would that be okay?"

Elizabeth laughed. "Of course it is. We'd love to have you worship with us." She rubbed Lindsay's arm again. "You're always welcome."

Lindsay smiled. "Thanks."

Elizabeth snatched her recipe book from the far counter. "Would you like to learn how to make walnut kisses?"

"Sure!" Lindsay grabbed a mixing bowl from the counter.

❀

Saturday night, Lindsay stood before Rebecca clad in a purple dress with a black apron and white prayer *Kapp*.

Rebecca cupped her hand over her mouth while tears stung her eyes.

"What do you think?" Lindsay asked, twisting her hips back and forth while running her hands over her the apron. "Do I look ridiculous? Does it look like a Halloween costume instead of normal Plain dress?"

"You look beautiful. The dress is perfect." Rebecca wiped her eyes. "In fact, you look like your mother only with red hair."

"You think so?" Her niece fingered the ties to the prayer *Kapp*. "I always thought Jessica looked just like Mom, and I looked more like the Bedford side."

Rebecca shook her head. "I definitely see Grace in you."

Lindsay grinned. "Cool." Her smile faded. "So, can I still go with you and Daniel tomorrow? And can I wear this?"

"*Ya.*" Rebecca nodded and cleared her throat, hoping to stop the threatening lump. "You most certainly can." Her thoughts moved to Jessica's accusation that Rebecca was influencing and trying to convert her. She didn't want to upset Jessica by encouraging Lindsay to dress Plain.

"But how will Jessica feel about this?" Rebecca asked.

Lindsay shrugged. "I really don't know what she thinks."

She began to remove the straight pins from the apron. "You didn't tell her that you were making a dress to wear to service?"

"No, I didn't tell her. I told her a few weeks ago that I enjoy our devotional time together, and she really didn't understand it."

"Well, you must do what feels right for you," Rebecca said. "Do whatever you feel in your heart."

"This definitely feels right," Lindsay said with a smile.

"*Gut.*" Rebecca finished removing the pins and then hugged her niece. "I look forward to having you at service with me tomorrow."

"Me too." Lindsay held on to Rebecca as if for dear life.

Once the dress was removed, Lindsay pulled on her nightgown, and they walked arm in arm to Lindsay's room.

"I'll wake you up early tomorrow," Rebecca said.

Lindsay hugged her again. "Thank you for everything."

"You're welcome." Rebecca gently closed the door and then tapped on Jessica's door.

She waited a few moments for a response and then opened it slowly. She spotted Jessica fast asleep sprawled across the bed in her plaid pajama pants and a short-sleeved gray shirt. Rebecca tiptoed across the room and covered her niece with the quilt.

She kissed Jessica's head, snuffed the kerosene lantern, and then quietly left.

When Rebecca entered her room, she found Daniel pulling on his nightclothes. He gave her a confused expression when their eyes met. "Where have you been, *mei Fraa?*" he asked.

"Lindsay and I were in the sewing room finishing up a project," she said while she crawled into the bed.

"What project?" He climbed into the bed beside her.

"She wanted a Plain dress, so we made one together." She snuggled down under the quilt and snuffed the lantern on her side of the bed. A faint light crept in past the edges of the window shades.

"Why would she want that?" He gave her a concerned expression.

"She wants to come to service with us tomorrow and she wants to dress appropriately." When his eyebrows careened to his hairline with confusion, she pressed a finger to his lips before he spoke in response. "Please listen to me before you pass judgment, Daniel. Lindsay is very interested in our faith and wants to learn more. She constantly asks me questions about our beliefs. She enjoys our nightly devotions."

"Our faith is not a passing fad for her to try, like their rock music and their Internet," he said, frowning.

"She knows that, and she respects it." Rebecca took his

hands in hers. "I believe she is opening her heart and mind to our faith, and she truly wants to know more about it. Daniel, please give her a chance. She feels that learning more about the Faith will bring her closer to Grace."

"That doesn't make any sense. Her mother left the Faith, and I believe she will do the same in time." He shook his head.

Rebecca sighed while disappointment washed over her. She wondered what it was going to take to get Daniel to understand. "It's a way for her to connect to her mother's past and connect to me. I'm the only family she has left."

"She can go with us, but don't expect her to join the Faith. She'll leave just as her mother did. I don't want to see you hurt again, the way Grace hurt you." He kissed her. "Good night."

Good night," she muttered. She bit her lip to stop the angry words that formed in her mind. She wanted to tell her husband to stop being so cynical and stop judging the girls. But she knew it wouldn't do any good. Arguing with Daniel never went well.

Closing her eyes, Rebecca prayed for guidance and faith as she did every night. She hoped that God was listening and heard her words.

Jessica rolled over and yawned. Rubbing her eyes, she glanced at her watch and gasped when she found it was after eleven in the morning.

She'd planned to rise early in order to complete her chores and spend the rest of the day relaxing while Daniel, Rebecca, and Lindsay went to service and then visiting. She wasn't thrilled when her sister told her that she was going to service, but Jessica didn't get upset with Lindsay. She assumed Lindsay would be bored out of her mind and not go to another one.

Instead of getting up early to get her chores done, Jessica had lost part of the day by sleeping in. She'd have to hurry if she wanted to salvage the rest of the day.

Leaping from the bed, she snatched her jeans and a T-shirt from the floor and yanked them on. She gathered her hair up into a ponytail and then ran down the stairs. Jessica fixed herself a few pieces of bread slathered with jam and ate them quickly. She headed outside.

She groaned when she spotted the forest of weeds tangled in both the vegetable and flower gardens. She scanned the rows of vegetables mixed in with the bright, healthy green weeds and frowned. This task would certainly take a good part of the day.

"Standing here staring at it won't get it done," she muttered, eyeing the offending vegetation. She padded to the barn, grabbed a large bucket and then returned to the vegetable garden. After dropping the bucket onto the ground, she grabbed a trash can from the side of the house and yanked it to the garden.

Squatting, she began ripping the weeds from the ground. She made her way through the vegetables, filling up the bucket with weeds and emptying it into the trash can as she weaved through the peas, onions, carrots, string beans, cucumbers, and tomatoes. The weeds seemed to take forever to dissipate.

Her arms, legs, and back ached, and perspiration trickled from every pore in her body. Sinking back onto her bottom, Jessica wiped her brow and closed her eyes. She needed to get out of her sweat-soaked clothes. She bit her lip and scanned the area. She was more than halfway done with the vegetables but still had the flowers to complete. She'd get changed and then return to the task of weeding.

She trotted into the house and up the back steps to her room. After shedding her jeans and T-shirt, Jessica slipped into her most comfortable jean shorts. She pulled a tank top from her dresser and shook her head. It was hot outside. Really humid and hot. That tank top would still cover too much skin.

Biting her bottom lip, Jessica pulled out her hot pink string bikini top. She knew wearing a skimpy top wouldn't win her any brownie points with Daniel, but maybe finishing the weeding would. He'd been so quiet with her lately that she could nearly cut the tension between them with a knife. He wasn't rude, but he'd been cold. Their conversations in the van on the way to and from work seemed strained. The only bright spot in her days lately was chatting with Jake. She could at least be herself around him.

Jessica hoped Trisha would call soon and report that she'd won custody of her and Lindsay. However, when they'd spoken a few weeks ago, Trisha hadn't made any headway finding a lawyer who would take the case. Jessica wondered if she was even trying very hard.

In the meantime, Jessica had to make the best of it. She hoped that by doing extra chores today she'd earn enough favor around the house that Daniel would smile and chat with her once in a while. She'd do her best to get the weeding completed quickly and then she could change into something more suitable before Daniel, Rebecca, and her sister returned.

She pulled on the bikini top, twirled her thick ponytail up into a bun secured with a few clips, stuffed her iPod into her pocket, and jogged down the back stairs and out to the garden.

She fished her iPod from her pocket, stuck the ear buds in her ears, and crouched down. While she continued weeding, she lost herself in the comforts of her favorite rock songs.

Even when Jessica thought she'd collapse from the pain and the grief of losing her parents, the songs seemed to give her the comfort she needed to make it through another lonely day in Lancaster County. The music dulled the constant pang of regret that pulsed through her all day and all night long.

Whenever she closed her eyes, Jessica could see the two police officers standing in the doorway of her home in Virginia Beach. She could hear the one officer saying the words "Your parents died in a car accident tonight. They were hit head-on by a drunk driver."

Even though nearly two months had passed since the accident, the pain was still sharp in her heart, and the guilt still haunted her.

Jessica sucked in a breath while emptying the bucket full of weeds into the large trash can. She'd wished so many times that she could relive that night.

Maybe her parents would still be alive if Jessica hadn't sulked in her room before they'd left for their dinner date. If she had talked to her mom instead of stomping off in a huff, she could've delayed the time that they'd left, and then the drunk may never have passed them on the road at all.

She shook her head while moving to the peppers. It was silly to play the "what if" game, but Jessica couldn't help but blame herself.

The last conversation she'd had with her mother was an angry one. She'd been furious that her mother wouldn't let her invite Brian over. Jessica knew she wasn't allowed to have him over when her parents weren't home, but she'd pushed the issue anyway, insisting she was trustworthy enough to have a boy in the house. But Jessica was too proud to let it go. She'd called her mother's phone and argued with her just moments before the accident.

Had the angry words she and her mother exchanged distracted her father's driving?

Jessica pushed the torturous thought away. She couldn't face the reality of her regrets. Not now when she was already so miserable being stuck in this household.

Her thoughts moved to Brian and Morgan as she dumped another bucket of weeds into the trash can. She hadn't spoken to them in a few days. They both had finished school for the year and started their summer jobs. Jessica wished she were working at the oceanfront with them. She longed to spend the summer at the beach, working by day and walking barefoot through the hot sand with her friends at night. On their days off, her friends would caravan down to the Outer Banks, driving out on the beach for a daylong picnic in the sweltering sun.

It was unfair that her friends were having all that fun without her. She wondered what she had done to deserve the fate of living and working here. When would Trisha save her from this nightmare?

She was so caught up in her thoughts of home that at first Jessica didn't hear the horse clip-clopping up the dirt drive. When she glanced over, she spotted the buggy rolling toward the barn. Jessica dumped another bucket of weeds and then wiped the palms of her hands on her shorts. She frowned at the dirt trapped under her long fingernails.

Turning toward the barn, she spotted her sister trotting toward her clad in a dark purple Plain dress, complete with a black apron and cape and a white prayer *Kapp* covering her bun.

Gasping, Jessica shook her head, hoping that she was imagining her sister dressed like that. However, as Lindsay approached, the image didn't fade.

"What are you doing?" Lindsay yelled, a frown creasing lines into her pretty face. "Don't you realize it's Sunday? We don't do chores on Sunday!"

"Whoa!" Jessica shook her head again, fury bubbling within her. "What are you wearing? Is today Halloween?"

"Very funny." Lindsay gestured toward Jessica's clothes. "It's more than you have on! This isn't a beach, you know. Daniel will flip when he sees you." She cut her eyes behind her to where another buggy crunched in the rocks toward the barn. "You better go change while you have the chance. He won't be happy when he sees this."

"Oh no." Jessica shook her head. "Don't change the subject. What were you thinking?" She grabbed her sister's arm and yanked her closer. "Lindsay, why are you letting her brainwash you? Remember that little church we went to back home? You know, the one we grew up in? It's not Amish or even Mennonite!"

Scowling, her younger sister wrenched her arm from Jessica's grasp. "No one is brainwashing me. I happen to feel comfortable dressed like this." She smoothed the apron, and her expression softened. "I think I look good in it. It makes me feel closer to Mom."

A wave of disappointment mixed with despair surged through Jessica. She had to fight to keep Lindsay on her side. "Lindsay, we're not going to stay here. Trisha is going to get custody of us, and we can go back home. We belong there, not here."

"This is my home now," her younger sister said, her expression hardening again.

"You don't mean that," Jessica whispered. "Your home is with Trisha and Frank and our friends. This is just a place to stay until Trisha can work something out. We can finish school and then go on to college. If we stay here, we'll suffocate."

"No." Lindsay shook her head. "I think you need to open your eyes and your heart to the truth. God has a plan for us, and He needs us here. You should've come to service today. You would've seen how wonderful this community is and how much they want us here. Although the service was mostly in German, I still felt a part of something bigger. I felt God's presence in my life. It gave me a peace I haven't felt since Mom and Dad died."

Jessica blew out a sigh. This nightmare was worse than she'd imagined. She was losing her sister, the only family she had left. As if it weren't bad enough to lose her parents, now her sister was going to join the Faith and leave her behind.

"What's going on here?" a voice boomed behind them.

Jessica turned to see Daniel staring at her wide-eyed. "Daniel," she said, her body trembling in response to his accusing stare. She folded her arms across her chest. "I wasn't expecting you back so soon. I was hoping to have the weeding—"

Daniel turned. "Rebecca!" he bellowed.

Rebecca gazed over from where she stood with Robert, Sadie, and their children. Jessica swallowed a groan when the group faced them, and their eyes rounded at the sight of her. She wished she could crawl into the trash can full of weeds and hide from the glares.

Daniel hollered something in Pennsylvania Dutch, and Rebecca rushed over. When Rebecca's eyes met Jessica, a surprised gasp escaped her lips. She then hurried over to Jessica, Lindsay, and Daniel.

Daniel prattled on in Pennsylvania Dutch, his face red with anger. He gestured wildly, and Rebecca nodded, whispering something under her breath. She then looped her arm around Jessica's shoulders and steered her toward the house.

Before reaching the stairs, Jessica cut her eyes to her sister and found her surrounded by Daniel and his family. Katie Kauffman sidled up to Lindsay and placed a hand on her shoulder. Lindsay and Katie looked so comfortable together, both dressed the same.

Lindsay looked like one of them, and an overwhelming emptiness consumed Jessica. She blinked back tears at the realization that she'd lost her sister.

"What are they doing here?" Jessica asked Rebecca as they stepped into the house.

"Robert and his family are here to visit," Rebecca said, her gentle voice a stark contrast to her husband's rant.

"I messed up, huh?" Jessica asked, swallowing her tears.

"You could say that," Rebecca said.

"I was only trying to—"

"Shh." Rebecca led her to the back staircase. "Just go and get changed. We'll talk later."

Jessica stared at Rebecca. She was tired of being corrected and ordered around like some stupid, irresponsible kid. She resented their judgmental stares and their ridiculous rules. She wanted to go home, and despite what her sister said, this wasn't home!

"What, Jessica?" Rebecca asked while pushing back a wisp of her hair that had fallen from beneath her prayer *Kapp*. "What is it?"

"Why don't we just get it over with now?" Jessica asked, folding her arms with impatience. "I know what you're going to say."

Rebecca gave a sigh of defeat. "And what is it that I'm going to say, Jessica?"

Jessica studied her brown eyes. She looked tired. Maybe she was as tired of Jessica as she was of her aunt. "You hate me, don't you?" Jessica asked, her voice trembling with a sorrow she hadn't expected.

"No." Rebecca's eyes softened as she reached for Jessica's hands. "I could never hate you."

Jessica stepped back from her reach, afraid of the comfort Rebecca seemed to want to offer. "You're sick of dealing with me. I'm the bad kid while my sister is the perfect one, running around in that long dress. She's the daughter you'd always dreamt of, but I'm just the problem child. I'm an unexpected bump in the road that has brought you nothing but headaches and heartache."

"No, that's not true." Rebecca shook her head. "I love you both. I just wish you would give us a chance instead of pushing us away and running around in clothes that deliberately upset Daniel."

"Deliberately upset Daniel?" Jessica winced as if she'd been smacked. "I didn't wear this to upset you or Daniel." She pointed to her clothes. "I wore this because the sweat was pouring off me while I was breaking my back weeding your stupid garden!"

Jessica's voice quavered as she continued. "I thought maybe, just maybe, if I did the weeding then Daniel would actually talk to me during our rides to and from the furniture store." She paused to take a deep breath, fighting threatening tears. "But no, it didn't work. Daniel ignored the fact that I spent all morning weeding and shouted because I was wearing a bikini top and shorts. He only focused on the fact that I wasn't wearing a dress that would probably make an Eskimo sweat in Antarctica!"

With a sympathetic expression, Rebecca reached for her again. "Jessica—"

"Save it." Jessica held her hands up. "I'll be in my room and away from the eyes of the community, so I won't embarrass you and Daniel any more today."

She started up the stairs and then stopped and faced Rebecca again. "Oh, and I'm sorry for working on Sundays. It seems I can't even get the days right when I try to do something nice."

Turning, Jessica stomped up the stairs. When she reached her room, she flopped onto the bed and sobbed into her pillow.

For what felt like the millionth time, she asked God why her parents had to die and why she and Lindsay had to come to this awful house.

"Where are you, God?" she whispered. "Have You forgotten me?"

Swiping away a tear, Rebecca watched Jessica stomp up the stairs. Her niece's words echoed in her mind. Poor Jessica had been trying to do something good. She wanted to finish the weeding so Daniel would realize she was truly trying to be helpful. However, the good intentions had blown up in her face. Now her niece's heart was broken, and Rebecca's heart was shredded.

Daniel's reaction had rattled Rebecca. Up until today, she hadn't seen him lose his temper about the girls. Now he was furious, and she wondered how she was going to make Daniel see that Jessica only wanted to impress him. All Daniel would see was an inappropriately dressed girl doing work on Sunday. To make matters worse, she had embarrassed him in front of his brother Robert yet again. Daniel would never believe that Jessica was trying to gain his approval.

How could she make him see the whole picture without getting him angrier than he already was? But if she didn't try to make Daniel see the truth, he would never know how hard Jessica was trying. It seemed Rebecca would never win in this situation. No matter what she did, she was bound to hurt some-one she loved.

Had God heard her prayers? Was He listening?

Sighing, Rebecca wiped another tear and cleared her throat.

She had to pull herself together before she went outside to greet her visitors.

"I guess that didn't go well, huh?" Lindsay asked, sidling up to Rebecca.

"No, not at all." Rebecca folded her arms across her chest. "She said she was trying to help. She thought that by doing the weeding she could win Daniel over."

"She picked the wrong day to do it, though. And that outfit was just about the worst possible." Lindsay shook her head and frowned. "I wish we had gotten home before Robert pulled up. I could've gotten her inside and avoided everyone seeing her."

"*Ya*," Rebecca said, studying her niece.

Rebecca had been so proud to have Lindsay with her today. Lindsay looked like she belonged, sitting with Katie and the other young women their age during the service. The community had embraced her during the service. Rebecca was still astounded by Lindsay's interest in the Faith and her desire to be a part of it. Unfortunately, she had no idea how to reach Jessica.

"Do you want me to check on her?" Lindsay asked, nodding toward the stairs.

"I don't know." Rebecca shook her head. "I think she may need to be alone."

Lindsay bit her bottom lip as if contemplating the situation.

"We'll check on her later," Rebecca said, looping her arm around Lindsay's shoulders. "I promise. Right now we need to be with our guests and act like nothing happened."

"*Ya*." Her niece nodded with emphasis. "Nothing happened. Got it."

Plastering a smile on her face despite her inner turmoil, Rebecca took Lindsay's hand and led her back out to the yard, where Daniel stood talking with Robert and Sadie.

The children were gathered around the fence by the horses. Katie met Lindsay's gaze and gestured for her to approach. Lindsay trotted over, joining the group at the fence.

"Is everything all right?" Sadie asked Rebecca.

"*Ya*," Rebecca said with a forced smile. "Everything is fine." Needing to change the subject quickly, she waved toward the door. "How about you go sit on the front porch and enjoy this beautiful day the Lord has given us? I'll get us some iced tea."

The men nodded and then made small talk about the weather and work.

"Iced tea sounds nice." Sadie stepped toward her. "Can I help you?"

"*Nee*. I can manage." Rebecca patted her sister-in-law's arm, hoping to deter her from coming to the kitchen.

Rebecca met Daniel's glance, and he scowled, causing her heart to sink. She knew she would endure another earful about Jessica this evening. Rebecca shook her head. They didn't need to air any more of their family troubles in front of his brother. She'd deal with her husband after the company was gone.

The men headed for the front of the house, and Rebecca started for the back door.

"Wait for me." Sadie rushed to catch up with her.

Rebecca squelched the urge to groan with irritation. The last thing Rebecca needed was her nosy, outspoken sister-in-law making conversation in the kitchen. "I'm fine, Sadie. *Danki*."

"Don't be silly." Sadie swatted her arm. "I'm happy to help."

Rebecca forced a smile. *Ya, and get more gossip about my niece to spread at your quilting bee.*

They stepped into the kitchen, and Rebecca pulled the container of freshly brewed iced tea from the refrigerator.

"Is Jessica doing okay?" Sadie asked, her voice overly timid as if she were trying to appear genuine.

"Jessica will be just fine." Rebecca snatched four glasses from the cabinet and placed them on a tray.

"Are you sure?" Her sister-in-law's expression was grim. "Robert says she needs guidance."

Rebecca felt her back stiffen in response to the criticism. "I would say she needs understanding more than anything right now, considering what she's been through with losing her parents and moving to an unfamiliar community."

Sadie placed a hand on Rebecca's sleeve. "She needs to learn respect for our ways. She forced her rock music and a computer on my sweet Katie."

Taking a deep breath to settle her frayed nerves, Rebecca paused before she spoke. "I don't think Jessica forced anything on Katie. I think they were just two girls getting to know each other. It was innocent."

Sadie shook her head, clicking her tongue. "I don't think so, Becky."

Rebecca bit her lip at the pet name that she only permitted Daniel to call her. Sadie was being condescending, and it made her angry. "Sadie, as I said, you must remember that the girls just lost their parents. They're trying to find their way in this world, and it's our calling to give them love and support."

"Oh, of course. But we also need to remind them that they're living in *our* community, *ya?*" Sadie's expression softened. "I see Lindsay is finding her way quite well. Perhaps her older sister should follow her lead."

"I think Jessica should go at her own pace." Rebecca placed the pitcher on the tray.

"I don't know." Her sister-in-law shook her head. "I think her pace is misled."

"We need to give the girls love and understanding. It's the Christian thing to do, *ya?*" Rebecca heaved the tray and started for the front door.

Sadie followed at her heels. "Well, her behavior has not been so Christian. I can't say she was dressed like a good Christian earlier, and according to Robert she gave my Samuel a seductive look the last time we were here."

Shocked by the words, Rebecca stopped dead in her tracks,

and the tray teetered in her hands. "What did you say about the last time you were here?"

"She gave my Samuel a suggestive look at the front door on their way out."

"Who said that?"

"Robert." Sadie gestured toward the front door. "They were leaving, and she turned and walked into Samuel. Then she gave him *the eye*." She dramatically pointed to her eye and winked.

"The eye? I'm not sure what you mean." Rebecca shook her head in disbelief.

"She looked at him like she wanted to ... you know!" Sadie gave a frustrated sigh. "She wanted to tempt him."

Rebecca silently counted to ten, hoping to curb her boiling fury. "Sadie, Jessica is a child. She's not going to try to seduce any young men. She's just a confused teenager who wants to fit in. I would appreciate it if these judgments about her were kept to yourself."

Sadie folded her arms across her apron. "I think you're naïve when it comes to your niece."

Rebecca's eyes narrowed in response. She willed herself to keep her temper in check. "Remember what Elizabeth always says, 'Be joyful in hope, patient in affliction, faithful in prayer.' Perhaps we should take that advice and keep my nieces in our prayers."

Her sister-in-law's brows knitted, her hazel eyes gleaming with irritation. "*Ya*. Perhaps we should."

Rebecca continued through the door, where she found the men sitting side by side and discussing the rising cost of lumber. She placed the tray on the ledge in front of the men and sank into the porch swing.

Rebecca's thoughts wandered while the men and Sadie chatted about idle things. Her mind kept replaying her conversations with Daniel and then with Jessica. She pondered how she was going to keep her husband happy and also get through to Jessica. How could she balance her role as wife with her role as guardian to two English girls?

Elizabeth had repeatedly told her to listen, pray, and have faith. She'd done so over and over in her mind, but none seemed to be leading her down the right path. No matter how hard she tried, she still found both Daniel and Jessica disappointed and angry with her. She needed to find the solution before she lost them both forever.

Closing her eyes, she prayed from the bottom of her heart:

Lord, tell me what to do. Please Lord, give me the knowledge I need to be a gut *wife and guardian.*

Much to Rebecca's dismay, Robert's family stayed and visited through supper and into the early evening.

Lindsay spent her time with Katie and her younger sister Nancy. It warmed Rebecca's heart to see the girls talk and laugh. However, she spotted Sadie and Daniel frequently watching Lindsay with an accusing eye. Rebecca yearned to tell them to give Lindsay the benefit of the doubt, but she knew it was no use. They'd both deny being suspicious of the girl even though it was written all over their faces.

Jessica spent the evening in her room and didn't even come down when Rebecca called her to supper. Rebecca had longed for the company to leave early, so she could talk with Jessica and try to get her to understand that she loved her and wanted the best for her.

When the guests finally left for the evening, Rebecca hurried up to Jessica's room and was heartbroken to find her asleep, sprawled across her bed clad in a pair of plaid boxer shorts and a short-sleeved T-shirt. Her phone was lying next to her one side and her iPod and ear buds were on the other.

A pang of guilt rang through Rebecca. If she were a good guardian and surrogate mother, she would've helped Jessica through this difficult day. But her duties as wife and hostess had kept her chained to her company. She should have snuck away and at least brought Jessica a meal. Grace would've been disappointed in Rebecca's neglect today.

Rebecca moved closer to the bed. Jessica looked angelic with her dark hair framing her face and her lips curving in a sweet smile. She touched her arm, and Jessica sighed in her sleep and rolled to her side.

Tiptoeing toward the door, Rebecca hoped she could talk to her alone tomorrow night and make her see that everything would be all right.

She gingerly shut the door and crossed the small hallway to Lindsay's room. She gave the door a light rap and then opened it, finding Lindsay sitting cross-legged on the bed while writing on a small lap desk.

Her niece looked up and smiled. "Hi."

"Hi." Rebecca leaned back on the door frame. "What are you doing?"

"Writing a letter to my friend Cindy." Lindsay pushed a lock of hair behind her ear and nodded toward the door. "Is she okay?"

"She's asleep." Rebecca sighed. "I wanted to break away earlier to talk to her, but I kept getting caught by Sadie. It was as if she knew I wanted to talk to Jessica."

Her niece nodded. "I'm sure she'll be okay."

"I'll talk to her in the morning. I just hope she isn't upset all day tomorrow." Rebecca stood up and smoothed her apron. "Thank you for coming to service with us today. I enjoyed having you with me."

"*Ya.*" Lindsay giggled. "I enjoyed it too."

"You know you don't need to feel obligated to come to service and be a part of the community, yes?"

"Yes." The girl nodded her head. "I know that. But it feels right."

Rebecca smiled. "You look beautiful in your Plain dress. I think your *mamm* would be proud."

Lindsay's porcelain cheeks glowed a light pink. "I have a feeling you're right."

"Well, good night." Rebecca stepped into the doorway. "I'll see you bright and early."

"Good night, Aunt Rebecca." She smiled as Rebecca closed the door.

Rebecca sighed while a myriad of emotions rioted within her. The day had been a mix of disappointment, frustration, and also happiness. She was happy to see Lindsay fitting in and excited about her new life. However, she was also disappointed in Daniel and frustrated with Jessica. She wondered how she was ever going to find a balance.

Stepping into her bedroom, Rebecca spotted her husband sitting on the side of the bed with his arms folded across his wide chest while waiting for her. Still fully clothed, his handsome face wore a stony scowl, sending a chill slithering up her spine. He rarely lost his temper, but when he did, it was like a storm rolling in during the heat of summer.

Rebecca pulled the door closed and stood in front of it, bracing herself for his tirade. She took a deep breath and willed herself to remain calm.

"I think it's time for you to make a choice, Rebecca." His voice was barely a whisper.

"What do you mean?" she asked, her body trembling in anticipation of his wrath.

"Are you going to be my wife or are you going to be the girls' mother?" He stood. "It's obvious to me that you can't be both."

"I disagree," she said. "I'm capable of being both. There's no need for me to choose."

"Ack, but there is." He stood facing her, his eyes flickering with fury in the light of the kerosene lamps. He gestured toward the hallway. "That girl's behavior can't be tolerated, and you can't handle her."

"Jessica needs our love and understanding. She's just lost her parents." She kept her voice calm and even, despite the frustration coursing through her veins.

He shook his head. "She needs *discipline*, and she needs to learn *respect*. She simply cannot run around half naked in my home, Rebecca!" His voice rose. "She's bringing disgrace on this household, and I will not allow it!"

"Daniel." She reached for him, but he stepped away from her, causing her to flinch with hurt. "Just give her time. She'll find her way. Lindsay is finding her way, so I know Jessica will get there."

"Jessica is just like Grace." He gritted his teeth as if her sister's name disgusted him. "She even looks like her. She'll never accept our ways here."

Rebecca gasped at the scorn in his eyes. She swallowed the disillusionment rising in her soul. "I loved my sister, and I love the girls. They are all I have left of Grace. If you're still the man I fell in love with eighteen years ago, I think you can find it in your heart to give them the love and patience they need and deserve."

He studied her for a moment, but the anger never left his eyes. "It's my duty to make sure that all of us in this household live within the bounds of our Plain life. The girls *must* obey. They have no choice."

Her body shook with anger and hurt. Never before had Rebecca and Daniel been at such odds. This impasse was new, terrifying territory.

"They belong here," she whispered, her voice quaking with the emotion battling within her. "It's God's will."

"Don't speak to me about God's will." He wagged a finger at her. "They belong with *their* kind. They belong with the English. They should be with Trisha."

She took a deep breath and mustered up her strength. "*Nee.*"

Stunned, he raised his eyebrows. "You're disagreeing with me?"

"I'm their guardian," she whispered, hugging her arms to her chest. "They belong with me."

He stared at her for what seemed like hours. She held her breath, wondering what he would do next. She'd never seen him so furious. She wondered if he would strike her as other men struck their wives when they didn't obey. Daniel had never been a violent man, and he had never raised a hand to her during their fifteen years of marriage. Yet the rage flickering in his eyes was unexpected, and it alarmed her.

However, he never raised his hand to her. Instead, he remained silent. After several minutes, he marched past her and left the room, quietly closing the door behind him.

Rebecca remained standing in the same spot, her feet stuck as if in cement, for several more minutes, awaiting his return.

When he didn't return, she changed into her nightclothes and climbed into bed. She contemplated their stressful and upsetting conversation over and over again while staring at the ceiling.

His side of the bed was still empty when she fell asleep. For the first time since before their wedding night, she slept alone.

If you don't talk to me, I'm going to fire you," a voice behind Rebecca said.

Rebecca turned to find her mother-in-law wagging a finger at her.

"I mean it," Elizabeth chided. "I don't pay employees who are quiet all morning and ignore me when I speak to them."

"I'm sorry." Rebecca sighed and placed a tray on the counter beside the bowl of filling she had prepared to spread inside the batch of Whoopie Pies. "I'm just tired this morning. I didn't sleep well last night."

"Tired?" Her mother-in-law raised a suspicious eyebrow. "I'd say it's more than just being tired."

Rebecca glanced around the kitchen, finding Beth Anne and Sarah engrossed in baking breads and cookies.

"We can step outside," Elizabeth whispered, as if reading her thoughts. "Kathryn is covering the front, and it's quiet right now. The lunch rush is over for the moment, and Lindsay is out back with the children." She took Rebecca's arm and led her toward the back door. "We'll be right back," she called over her shoulder.

They stepped into the gravel lot behind the bakery, and Rebecca glanced to her right, spotting Lindsay playing on the swing set with her nieces and nephews.

While watching the children, Rebecca silently debated how much to tell her mother-in-law. After all, Daniel was her son, and she wouldn't take kindly to criticism of him.

On the other hand, Rebecca had no one else in whom to confide. She needed a friend, and Elizabeth had been all that and more ever since she'd joined the Kauffman family.

Rebecca sighed, wishing she could turn back time and make things right with Jessica. If she'd only reached out to the girls when they were younger, maybe then Jessica would trust her more.

"Please tell me what's on your mind before it eats you alive," Elizabeth said, placing a hand on Rebecca's shoulder. "You're clearly troubled. You need to lift your burdens to God. He'll guide you and ease the trouble in your heart."

"That's just it," Rebecca whispered, her voice trembling and tears filling her eyes. "I've been praying and listening, but I still don't know what to do."

"Is it Jessica?" Her mother-in-law's eyes were soft with understanding.

"*Ya.*" Rebecca swiped her tears with the back of her hands. "She upset Daniel yesterday, and he's not taking it well at all."

Elizabeth shook her head. "He's a stubborn one for sure."

"You have no idea." Rebecca cleared her throat in hopes of stopping more tears. "He didn't sleep in our bed last night."

Elizabeth gasped, covering her mouth with her hand.

"He said I need to choose between being his wife and being their guardian." Rebecca kicked a stone with the toe of her shoe. "I told him I can be both, but he said I can't. I don't know what to do. I'm afraid I will lose both my husband and my nieces if I can't figure this out." Rebecca's voice shook as she succumbed to more tears.

"No, you won't." Elizabeth pulled her into a warm hug. "You'll never lose Daniel, and those girls love you. You must trust God. He will give you strength, and in the end, you and

Daniel will come out stronger than before. You two love each other, and you've made it through some difficult times. This is just another test of your faith, and you both shall pass it. I know it. I can feel it in my heart."

Rebecca sniffed and rested her cheek on her mother-in-law's shoulder. She prayed Elizabeth was right.

Her mother-in-law patted her back as she stepped out of the hug. "You're a strong woman, Rebecca. I know you can make it through this. Just keep giving Jessica the best guidance you can and listen to your husband. Daniel really does want the best for you and his household. He is not trying to cause you pain. It will work out."

"*Danki*." Rebecca patted her arm. "I don't know what I would do without you."

"Ack." Elizabeth smiled. "You'd figure it out. You're a smart girl. You married my Daniel, didn't you?"

Rebecca laughed and wiped her eyes. "That I did."

Sarah appeared in the doorway. "*Mamm*. Would you come see this apple bread? I'm not sure it's right, and Kathryn keeps saying it is. We really need your expert eye."

"*Ya*." Elizabeth gave Rebecca another smile. "You'll be fine. You'll see."

Rebecca squeezed the older woman's hand as she stepped past her. "I'll be there in a minute."

"Take your time," Elizabeth said.

Rebecca watched Lindsay dance with her smaller nieces while pondering Elizabeth's words. They made sense, but she couldn't shake the feeling of despair that had seeped into her soul last night when Daniel didn't come to bed.

She kept wondering if their marriage was falling apart. Divorce wasn't permitted, but that didn't mean that decaying marriages remained amicable. She'd heard of plenty of couples who lived in silence, simply moving through the daily motions without any love or intimacy.

She didn't want that for her and Daniel. They married for love, and she didn't want to lose her best friend. She needed to find a way to keep her marriage alive as well as care for her nieces.

"Aunt Rebecca?" a voice asked.

Rebecca spun to see Lindsay leaning on the fence that separated the parking lot from the playground. She twisted the ties on her prayer *Kapp* and gave a tentative smile. "Are you okay?" she asked.

Rebecca studied her niece. Lindsay looked as if she belonged in that prayer *Kapp* and dress. She resembled a redheaded Grace. Rebecca's eyes welled with tears. Oh, how she missed her older sister. Why did Grace have to leave? Why didn't Rebecca take the time to get to know her sister and what kind of mother she was when she had the chance?

Guilt rushed over her at a sudden revelation—Rebecca had been just as wrong as her father and the rest of the community to shun Grace. Why hadn't she accepted Grace's decision to leave and join the English? Why had she punished her sister instead of supporting her?

Pushing the thoughts aside, Rebecca stepped over to the fence.

"Aunt Rebecca?" Lindsay's eyes were full of concern. "You look really upset."

"I'm fine. *Danki.*" Rebecca wiped her eyes with the back of her hand.

"Is there anything I can do?" Her niece bit her bottom lip.

"*Nee.*" Rebecca touched her hands.

"It's about Jessica and me, right?" Lindsay frowned. "We've messed up your life."

"*Nee, nee.* It's not that." She pushed a stray wisp of hair back from Lindsay's face. "This has nothing to do with you."

"But it's Jessica. She's caused a lot of problems, and Uncle

Daniel is still upset, right?" Lindsay's frown transformed into a knowing expression. "I can see what's going on around me."

Rebecca sighed. "It's complicated." She placed her hands on Lindsay's shoulders. "But rest assured you've done nothing wrong."

"We should probably go live with Aunt Trisha. We've really botched things up here."

Rebecca shook her head and closed her eyes. She dug deep in her soul for the words to express how wrong her niece was.

"Lindsay," she said, opening her eyes and squeezing her niece's shoulders. "Please listen to me. You and Jessica do belong here. Your mother wanted you here, and I vow to keep that wish alive. You need to understand that this is a huge adjustment for Daniel and me. But that doesn't mean we don't want you."

Lindsay nodded, her eyes glistening with bewilderment.

Rebecca paused and took a deep breath. "I mean it when I say that I love you and your sister. I want to be the best guardian I can be, but you have to be patient with me. And that means Daniel and everyone else need to be patient with you and Jessica too."

Her voice trembled as she continued. "Unfortunately, Uncle Daniel has exhausted all of his patience, so now we need to encourage Jessica to try a little harder. You and I are caught in the middle, and there isn't much more that we can do."

"So, we need to get Jessica to change?"

Rebecca nodded. "Maybe we can ask her to remember she's responsible for her own actions and her decisions."

Lindsay scowled. "I don't know if it will work, but we can try."

"Thank you." Rebecca pulled her into a hug.

"I love you, Aunt Rebecca," Lindsay whispered while holding onto her.

"Thank you," Rebecca said softly as tears spilled down her hot cheeks.

❊

Jessica sighed and stared down at the ledger on the desk. Leaning back, the chair squeaked. She glanced at her watch and found it was nearly six. Daniel had left earlier saying he had to make a supply run for lumber, but she couldn't help but wonder if he'd left early to avoid talking to her.

His silence made the ride to the shop seem longer than usual this morning. However, she'd expected as much after the disaster yesterday. She still couldn't figure out how they had arrived home so early after the Sunday service.

It seemed no matter what Jessica did lately she wound up in trouble. There were so many rules, and it was as if they were hoping she'd mess up so they could banish her to her room. She was an embarrassment to the Kauffman family.

So then why did they insist she stay?

She just wanted to go home—home to Virginia Beach. The disappointment in Rebecca's eyes had haunted her dreams all night and her thoughts all day. Misery and grief surged through her constantly. She didn't belong here. She wanted to go back to her friends and Trisha. She wasn't cut out for the Plain life. She could see why her mother had left—the life here was too repressive and too depressing.

Groaning to herself, Jessica slumped over, allowing her forehead to smack the ledger on the desk. Daniel had said that his father, Eli, would take her home, since he'd decided to bring his buggy today, but Eli was busy trying to finish a project. Turning toward the desk, she lifted her cellular phone and examined the display.

No calls.

It had been a few days since she'd heard from anyone back home. She wondered if they'd forgotten about her.

"What are you still doing here?" a voice behind her asked.

Jessica sat up and turned toward Jake leaning against the door frame with his arms folded across his broad chest.

"Hi." She straightened her blouse and finger-combed her hair while her cheeks burned with embarrassment. "I didn't know anyone was here besides me and Mr. Kauffman."

"I was trying to finish up a few things before tomorrow. The orders have really picked up." He stepped toward her. "So, you didn't answer my question. Why are you here? Daniel left hours ago."

"He had to run some errands, so I'm supposed to ride back with Eli." She tried to force a smile but it came out more a grimace. "How are you? I didn't get to see you all day."

"Busy." He stood next to her and leaned against the desk. "You?"

She shrugged.

His eyes studied her. "What's wrong?"

Jessica gave him a sarcastic smirk. "How much time do you have?"

His expression remained serious. "All the time in the world, my friend."

His eyes were sincere. He really cared about her. She bit her lip while a lump swelled in her throat.

"Jess?" He touched her hand. "You know you can talk to me, right?"

She nodded, unable to speak due to the lump choking her throat.

"Hey, whatever it is, it'll be okay. I promise."

"I'm not so sure," she whispered, her voice trembling. "Things have gotten much worse."

Keeping her voice soft to avoid Eli overhearing her, she summarized the events from yesterday. Jake listened, hanging on every word and shaking his head in sympathy. When she finished her story, he frowned.

"I'm so sorry," he said, taking her hands in his. "They never should've treated you that way. You had no way of knowing that work on Sunday is forbidden."

"Exactly," she said. "I was just trying to do something good, and it blew up in my face like everything else. No matter what I do it's wrong. I really gotta get outta here before I suffocate to death from all of these rules."

He squeezed her hand and leaned in close. "It will get better, I promise."

She stared into his eyes and her heart thumped. He was so close that she could feel his breath on her lips. When he moved closer, her pulse raced at hyper speed. She licked her lips in anticipation.

He closed his eyes, and before she could react, his lips brushed hers, causing her knees to buckle and her heart to skip a beat.

"Jessica," a voice behind her boomed.

She jumped back and gasped. Turning, she spotted Eli scowling in the doorway.

"It's time to go," he said. "Now." He stalked to the front door, locked it, and then marched toward the back of the shop.

Jessica quickly packed up her bag. "I better go." She popped up and started for the door, but a strong hand pulled her back.

"I'm sorry," Jake said, his brows knitted in an apologetic expression.

"It's okay." She shrugged. "The Kauffmans will just add this to the list of rules I've broken."

"No." He shook his head. "This was my fault. I never should've kissed you. I'll tell Eli it was my idea. You're not to blame."

"No." She gave him a weak smile. "Really, it's okay. I don't care what they think. She touched his arm. "I'll see you tomorrow." She trotted through the shop and out the back door.

Jessica climbed into the buggy and held her breath, waiting for the lecture from Eli about her inappropriate behavior. However, he was silent the whole ride to Rebecca's house. She stared out the window, contemplating how the silence was much worse than a lecture would be. She almost wished he would scream and yell and get it over with.

When they arrived at Rebecca's house, Jessica gathered up her bag and turned to him. "Are you coming in?"

"*Nee.*" He stared straight ahead. "I shall see you tomorrow."

"Right," she said, staring at him. "Have a nice evening." She climbed down from the buggy and watched as it clip-clopped toward the main road.

20

"How was your day?" Rebecca asked as she sat down to supper with her nieces and Daniel later that evening.

"Fine," Jessica said with a shrug. "Busy."

"The bakery was busy too." Rebecca glanced at her husband and found him staring at his bowl of soup. She'd give anything for him to speak to her. Whenever his eyes met hers, he showed no emotion at all. The only word he'd spoken all evening was a grunt when he came in the door.

Rebecca cleared her throat and glanced down at her stew. The silence was deafening. She hoped someone would speak soon.

"I learned a new recipe today," Lindsay announced with a wide smile. "I made Shoo-Fly Pie." She then went into an elaborate explanation of the recipe and how delicious it was.

Jessica remained silent and nodded occasionally during her sister's discussion of the dish. However, Daniel kept his eyes focused on his plate as if it were the most fascinating sight he'd ever seen.

Rebecca squelched the urge to smack him and scream at him, asking him why he was making this situation more difficult than it needed to be. She wondered if he were punishing her for agreeing to be their guardian or for not being able to give him a family of his own. Did he resent that the only children they'd ever raise weren't his blood relations?

She closed her eyes and inhaled the aroma of the potato soup while pushing the painful thoughts away. She couldn't change the past. All she could do was make the best of it and hope for a better future. Her faith would see her through this.

"Aunt Rebecca?" Jessica asked, wrenching her from her thoughts.

"*Ya?*" Rebecca glanced across the table to her niece.

"You okay?" Jessica tilted her head in question. "Do you have a headache or something?"

"*Ya,*" she said, rubbing her throbbing temples. "As a matter of fact, I do."

"You can go lie down if you'd like," Lindsay said. "We'll do the dishes."

"*Nee.*" Rebecca waved off the thought. "That won't be necessary."

"We don't mind," Jessica said. Standing, she gathered the empty dishes. "Go relax."

Rebecca glanced across the table as Daniel rose and retreated to the living room. She knew where he was headed—to sit in his favorite chair and pick out Bible verses to read during their devotion time.

Last night, he'd hurried through the verses without much emotion. Prayer time was shorter than she'd ever experienced. His passion for their nightly devotions was gone. Her stomach twisted at the thought.

For a split second she felt as if it were her fault, but she pushed the thought away. No, it wasn't her fault. It was God's will that the girls live here.

Or was it?

Frowning, she wondered if Daniel would sleep on the sofa again tonight. She absently wondered if he'd ever sleep in their bed with her or speak to her again.

"Aunt Rebecca?" Lindsay asked.

"Hmm?" Rebecca turned to see her niece studying her.

"Jessica's right. You don't look too good."

"I'm just tired." Rebecca patted her niece's hands. "Thank you for asking."

"Please go lie down," Lindsay said, steering Rebecca toward the back staircase. "We've got it under control here."

Rebecca nodded and turned her attention to her older niece. "I went in to talk to you last night, but you were already asleep. Are you okay?"

"I'm fine, thanks." Jessica gave her an uneasy smile and then turned her gaze toward the sink. "I just listened to some music and fell asleep."

Rebecca wondered why her niece couldn't look at her. She wondered if it was too painful to talk about what happened yesterday. She contemplated pushing the issue, but she worried she'd push her niece further away.

"If you want to talk—" Rebecca began.

"I'm okay. Really." Jessica waved off the thought with a wet dishrag. "Don't worry about me."

"But I am worried." Rebecca touched her arm. "You and your sister mean a lot to me."

"Just go lie down." Jessica's eyes met Rebecca's. "Really, it's okay."

Rebecca studied her for a moment and then touched her arm.

Jessica turned, her eyes full of question.

"I know that the adjustment has been difficult, but I'd like to ask you again to respect our rules," Rebecca began softly.

Jessica scowled. She opened her mouth to speak, and Rebecca held up her hand.

"Before you get defensive, please listen. I know you didn't mean to upset Daniel yesterday, but I need you to be more mindful of your actions." She rubbed Jessica's arm. "It also might make things a little easier for everyone if you curbed your temper."

Jessica stared at her for a moment. Then she nodded and turned back to the dishes.

Stunned at her silence, Rebecca was speechless for a moment. "Thank you for helping," Rebecca said.

She stepped into the living room where Daniel sat in his favorite chair reading his Bible. She waited for him to look up, but his eyes never left the page before him.

"I'm heading upstairs to lie down for a few minutes," she said. "The girls are doing the dishes."

He nodded without meeting her gaze.

"Call me when you're ready for devotions," she said.

"Fine," he grumbled, still reading the Bible.

Hugging her arms to her chest, Rebecca made her way up the stairs and sank onto her bed. Staring at the ceiling, she prayed that somehow things would work out. There had to be a way that Daniel and Jessica would both accept each other so that they could all be a family.

❀

Jessica finished taking another order and hung up the phone the following afternoon. The phone rang nonstop all morning. Jake hadn't been kidding when he said the summers were busy at Kauffman & Yoder Amish Furniture. She'd gotten a short break at lunch to grab a sandwich before the customers flooded her with calls and visits in the store.

While she had the chance, she opened the ledger and began to update it. She was engrossed in the numbers when she heard someone call her name. She cut her eyes to the doorway where Jake stood.

"Hi," he said.

"Hi." She glanced back down at the ledger, trying in vain

to ignore the heat filling her cheeks at the memory of his lips brushing hers.

The kiss had been wonderful, but it hadn't felt right. She'd spent most of the night contemplating the kiss and Eli's silence, both of which boggled her mind. But she'd figured out one thing—she didn't want to move fast with Jake. Her life was too much of a mess to even consider a new boyfriend—that was if she and Brian were officially broken up.

His boots scraped across the floor as he stood beside her. "I owe you an apology."

"What for?" she said, her gaze colliding with his.

"I'm sorry for last night. I never should've kissed you." He sat on the desk and frowned. "I hope you can forgive me, and we can still be friends."

Stunned, she stared at him.

Frowning, he stood. "I guess that's a no. Well, I—"

"No, no!" She grabbed his hand and pulled him back. "I mean, not a no. No, wait." She shook her head and chuckled. "I'm all mixed up. Let me start over."

"It's nice to see you smile again," he said.

Her cheeks continued to burn. "Thank you. It's good to smile again. What I mean is that I'd love to still be friends, and I agree that the kiss was a little too fast for me. But I do forgive you."

"Good." He patted her arm. "I hope we can have lunch again soon. Just let me know when you want to charge your phone."

Jessica paused, considering the lunch invitation. Although it was tempting to spend time with Jake, she knew that it would only upset her uncle. The situation at home was tense enough.

"How about we skip lunch?" She handed him the phone. "Would you charge the phone and then bring it to Rebecca's house? I think the family would like to see you."

Taking the phone, he nodded. "That sounds like a good idea. I haven't seen Rebecca in a while."

"Cool." She grinned. "And I have to say it was the best kiss I've had in a long time."

"I agree." He winked and then disappeared through the door to the shop.

Jessica grinned while she glanced down at the book. It felt great to have a friend like Jake. Too bad he was her only friend in Lancaster County.

❀

"Elizabeth?" Lindsay called across the bakery later that afternoon.

"*Ya?*" Elizabeth padded over to her. "Do you need some help?"

"Does this look right?" Lindsay motioned to the walnut gingerbread. "It just doesn't look done to me."

The older woman leaned over and studied the bread. She slipped a toothpick in and pulled it out, examining how much of the filling stuck to it. "It looks perfect to me." She turned her glance to Lindsay. "Is something bothering you?"

Lindsay cut her gaze across the bakery, finding Beth Anne and Kathryn deep in conversation. Biting her lip, she debated sharing with Elizabeth.

"You can talk to me, child." Elizabeth touched her shoulder. "Your words are safe with me."

"I don't want Aunt Rebecca to hear."

"She's outside with Sarah and the *kinner.*"

Lindsay took a deep breath. "I heard her say that she and Uncle Daniel are having problems." A lump swelled in her throat. "I think it's because of my sister and me."

"No, no, no." Elizabeth gave a soft smile. "It's not because of you and Jessica. Married folk argue sometimes. Right now they are adjusting to a new life with you girls, but you aren't the cause of their problems." She squeezed Lindsay's hand. "They'll work it out. Don't you worry."

"Okay." Lindsay hoped she was right.

"How did you like the service?"

Lindsay smiled. "It was beautiful. I need to learn more Dutch so I can understand it and participate."

"You'll pick the language up in no time. You're a very bright girl." Elizabeth glanced down at Lindsay's Plain dress. "You look lovely in the dress you and Rebecca made."

"*Danki.*" Lindsay glanced down at the dress and then back at Elizabeth. "We're going to make more."

"That's *wunderbar.*" Elizabeth gave her a quick hug. "I'm so happy that you're here with us." She pulled back. "Now let's get that bread on the cooling rack. I want to show you how to make sand tarts."

"You caught her kissing Jake Miller?" Scowling, Daniel repeated the words his father had just said. He turned from the back door of the shop and stared over at the field.

Disappointment mixed with the anger boiling through his veins. He wondered why Jessica hadn't learned her lesson. What would it take for this child to realize her behavior was unacceptable and was bringing shame to the Kauffman family?

As if it weren't bad enough that she had been doing work on a Sunday in hardly any clothes, now she'd been caught kissing a boy in the shop at night. She was a bad influence on Jake and an embarrassment to the Kauffman name, and she had to be stopped—if he only knew a way to make her understand.

Shaking his head, Daniel's thoughts turned to his wife. Rebecca kept insisting the girls belonged with them. He wished he could make Rebecca see his concerns were not only for himself; they were also for her and her future.

Gaining negative attention from the bishop would bring problems that he didn't need for the family. The bishop would pressure Daniel to get the family in line. Daniel could lose customers if the problem persisted, and the community could ostracize him and Rebecca. Daniel knew he needed to get things under control before they got any worse.

But he didn't know how to get Rebecca to listen to him. He'd thought giving her the silent treatment would gain her attention, but she seemed just as stubborn as before. She was more determined than he'd ever known, acting as if everything were okay. He didn't know how to get her to listen to his concerns and trust in his judgment.

"What are you going to do, Daniel?" *Dat* asked, wrenching him from his mental tirade.

"I'm not sure," Daniel admitted with a frustrated sigh. He glanced over toward the field. "Nothing seems to be working. Rebecca insists the girls are part of the family. She won't see my side of it. I told her she had to choose between the girls and me, and she still says she can have both. She won't listen to me anymore. It's like she's a different woman."

"Jessica is a lost soul. She's been through a traumatic time after losing her parents and being uprooted from the only home she's ever known. She needs guidance in order to find her way now that her parents are gone."

"*Ya*," Daniel said. "I know."

"It seems that only Lindsay has found her way," *Dat* said. "She looked comfortable and at home during the service on Sunday."

Daniel nodded. He wasn't completely at ease seeing Lindsay in the Plain attire and attending service, but she seemed more genuine every day. Maybe the girl really did want to be a member of the community.

However, he couldn't help remembering how Grace had left. At one time she'd felt a part of the community too, but then she broke her father's and sister's hearts when she left. Daniel would hate to see Lindsay hurt Rebecca as Grace once had. Rebecca never fully recovered from losing her only sister; Grace had broken her heart.

But her pain didn't stop with losing her sister. He'd seen Rebecca go through more heartache when the doctor said she couldn't conceive children. If Lindsay suddenly changed her mind and left the community, it would seem as if Rebecca's own daughter were deserting her.

Daniel didn't want Rebecca to suffer through that pain and loss again. He couldn't allow someone to hurt her the way Grace had. He loved her more than life itself, and it was his job to protect her.

"We'd better get back inside." *Dat* smacked Daniel's shoulder. "Peter needs help with that bookshelf he was making."

Dat's expression softened. "Everything will work out. Remember Jessica is still trying to figure out where she belongs without her parents. Rebecca has a tremendous amount of pressure on her right now as their guardian. But, no matter what, she loves you. You and Rebecca have been through a lot, and your love will guide you through this. Together you'll figure it out. Your mother and I faced some tough times when we were building the bakery and the furniture store. At times we didn't agree, but we worked it out. Trust your love for each other. It's stronger than you think."

"*Ya.*" Daniel stared at the field.

"Oh, and everyone is invited to Robert's this Saturday," *Dat* said. "It's his turn to host us for Saturday evening." He then disappeared into the shop.

Daniel sighed while he contemplated the situation. How was he to convince Rebecca that he was asking for more than obedience to his will? He was asking her to trust that he knows what is best for their family. She had to accept that Jessica needed to respect their customs or return to Virginia. He couldn't risk losing his place in the community.

More importantly, he couldn't bear it if Rebecca was hurt again, when Jessica turned her back on her aunt.

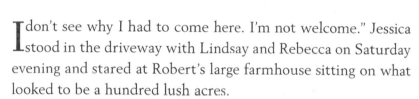
I don't see why I had to come here. I'm not welcome." Jessica stood in the driveway with Lindsay and Rebecca on Saturday evening and stared at Robert's large farmhouse sitting on what looked to be a hundred lush acres.

The dairy farm had been passed down through Sadie's family. The white clapboard house was larger than Rebecca's. Its vast three stories sprawled across the front of the property, while one large white barn and three smaller barns sat behind it, housing their livestock and farming supplies.

A newly painted white split-rail fence outlined the large pasture, and Sadie's gardens, her pride and joy, ran the length of the enormous house.

"You're a part of this family, Jessica." Rebecca touched her niece's shoulder. "I wasn't going to let you stay home alone while we went out visiting. That's just not right."

Jessica gave a sarcastic snort and folded her arms across her chest. "Yeah. I'm family. That's rich."

"Jessica." Rebecca stared into her eyes. "You're my family. You and Lindsay are precious to me. I know you don't believe it right now, but I love you both. I want you both to consider this your home. Please just give everyone a chance."

Jessica looked as if she was going to give a surly response, but then she closed her mouth. Rebecca wondered if she'd finally gotten through to her.

"We'll go visit for a while and then we'll head home. It'll be fine." Rebecca touched her older niece's shoulder. "Just be yourself. If you're uncomfortable, stay with me."

Jessica flipped her hair back from her shoulder. "I'm a big girl. I can handle it."

Lindsay grinned. "That's the sister I know and love."

Jessica snorted. "Whatever."

"Where's Uncle Daniel?" Lindsay scanned the property. "He disappeared awful quick."

"He ran inside to get away from me," Jessica muttered.

"Now, now." Rebecca patted Jessica's shoulder while their shoes crunched up the driveway toward the front porch. "Don't you worry about Daniel. Things will be just fine."

Jessica stopped and studied Rebecca. "He's not talking to you, is he?"

Rebecca sighed. She couldn't tell Jessica the truth and risk hurting her niece or making her feel guilty. "Everything is fine. Sometimes married couples argue. I would imagine your parents argued every once in a while too."

Jessica shook her head. "They did, but it wasn't like this. My father never stopped talking to my mother."

"Well, it's our way. Instead of yelling, some men stop talking." Rebecca shrugged as if his silence didn't hurt, even though the pain chipped away at her heart with every passing moment.

"But it's been a few days now." Jessica jammed her hands on her small hips. "It seems a bit extreme, don't you think?"

"Yeah," Lindsay chimed in. "I'd say he's being a bit of a jerk."

"That's disrespectful, Lindsay," Rebecca said.

Her younger niece frowned. "Sorry."

"Don't worry, girls." Rebecca balanced the plate of Whoopie Pies in her hands. "We'll get through this." She started for the door. "Let's go in and visit before they wonder if we walked home."

They stomped up the steps. When they entered the front door, they were greeted by a group of Kauffman children chasing each other around the living room and screeching.

"*Kinner!*" Robert bellowed from a nearby room. "Take it outside, please!"

The children filed through the living room toward the back door.

"I see it's a typical Kauffman family gathering," Rebecca said.

They padded to the kitchen, where the women were gathered around the table chatting. Rebecca's gaze moved to Sadie just as her sister-in-law frowned at Jessica. Irritation bubbled through Rebecca at her sister-in-law's expression. She wondered what it would take to get Daniel and his family to give her nieces the chance they deserved.

Pushing the thought aside, Rebecca placed the plate on the table. She then lowered herself into a chair near Elizabeth and patted the chair next to her for Jessica. Her older niece slowly sank into the chair, her expression illustrating that she'd rather be somewhere else.

Nancy and Katie stuck their heads in the back door, smiles spreading across their pretty, young faces.

"Lindsay!" Nancy called. "Come outside with us."

Lindsay glanced at Rebecca as if asking permission.

"Go on. Have fun." Rebecca waved her off. She then turned to Jessica, staring down at the table. She wished the women would speak in English in order for Jessica to participate in the conversation. However, they were gossiping about people Jessica didn't know, so the conversation wouldn't have been interesting to her anyway.

"Chocolate cake?" Elizabeth asked, pushing the plate toward Rebecca.

"*Danki.*" Rebecca cut two pieces, slapped them on two plates, and gave one to Jessica before forking a piece for herself.

Out of the corner of her eye, she spotted Jessica studying the cake while slowly eating it. She wondered what she could do to make her niece become a part of the family. If only she could get Jessica to feel like she fit in the way Lindsay did.

Rebecca savored the moist chocolate cake. When a hand touched her arm, she turned to Jessica.

"I'm going to go for a walk," Jessica said.

"You okay?" She studied Jessica's sad eyes, wondering how to reach out to her.

"I need to clear my head." Jessica pushed her chair back and rose. "I'll be back."

Watching her niece head out the back door, she sighed. She'd give anything to see Jessica smile.

"Is she doing okay?" Elizabeth asked.

Rebecca nodded and forked more cake. "She's fine."

Sadie frowned. "That's not what I heard."

"Oh?" Rebecca squelched the urge to tell her sister-in-law to worry about her own children and leave Jessica alone.

"I heard she was kissing Jake Miller at the store the other night. Apparently she thought the shop was empty, but Eli caught her." Sadie's smile was smug.

"No!" Kathryn gasped.

Rebecca sucked in a breath, hoping the rumor wasn't true. However, she couldn't imagine why Eli would make something like that up. "Maybe it was a misunderstanding," she said. "It's easy to assume the worst."

"She was kissing a boy, Rebecca." Sadie sliced her fork through the air like a sword, sending confetti made of crumbs and icing sprinkling down onto the table. "I think it's easy to assume what was going on. It seems to fit her after she was prancing around the yard in that little bikini top and shorts."

"Jessica is a good girl. She's just trying to find her place in our community." Rebecca kept her voice calm, despite the anger boiling within her.

Sadie snorted with sarcasm.

Rebecca narrowed her eyes. "I believe she needs our love and understanding instead of our judgment, Sadie. Didn't we discuss this? Remember—be faithful in prayer?"

Sadie's frown deepened. "*Ya*, I remember. But I'd say she's past praying. She's out of control and needs a stronger hand."

Glancing around the table, Rebecca found the expressions of all varying degrees of surprise.

"No one is past praying," Elizabeth said, her gaze fixed on Sadie. "Everyone deserves a chance. We all need to give each other patience and love. Remember the Scripture of Romans 3:23: 'For all have sinned and fall short of the glory of God.' "

"You're right, Elizabeth," Sadie said with a nod. She cleared her throat and then turned to Sarah. "Sarah, how have you been feeling? Did you go to the doctor yesterday?"

While Sarah discussed her latest doctor's appointment, Rebecca cut her eyes to Elizabeth and smiled. Elizabeth nodded. She was lucky to have her on her side. She hoped Elizabeth's words would break through Sadie's negative thoughts about her niece.

❁

Jessica hummed to Nickelback singing through her iPod while sauntering through the field behind Robert's house. She kicked a stone and wondered how long she was going to have to endure these tedious family gatherings.

She'd tried calling Trisha earlier, but she'd gotten voice-mail. She hoped Trisha had found a lawyer and initiated the paperwork to change the guardianship. Jessica wasn't sure how much longer she could stay sane under the microscope of the community.

Glancing across the field toward the four large, whitewashed barns, she spotted Lindsay talking and laughing with Nancy and Katie.

She frowned. Her sister looked so in her element and so comfortable in the traditional dress. She wondered why Lindsay fit in as if she'd been born here, but Jessica felt like an outsider.

"Jessica." A voice behind her startled her from her thoughts.

Turning, she faced Samuel, Robert's oldest son. His eyes twinkled in the late afternoon sun.

"Hi," she said, yanking the buds from her ears.

"Having fun?" He folded his arms across his wide chest.

"Yeah. Tons." She glanced over at her sister and sighed. At least her sister was having fun.

"You like kittens?" he asked.

Cutting her gaze to him, Jessica lifted her eyebrows in question. "Kittens?"

"*Ya*, you know, little cats. Haven't you ever seen a baby cat?" He smiled, and his handsome face lit up, accentuating that cute dimple in his right cheek. He had the trademark Kauffman powder blue eyes and fair skin.

She laughed, relieved to finally meet a Kauffman with a sense of humor. "Yeah, I've seen kittens before. Why do you ask?"

He nodded toward the barns. "One of our barn cats just had a litter a week go. Wanna see them?"

She studied him, wondering if his motive was to reach out to her or if she was being set up to make another mistake.

His smile faded. "I guess it was a dumb question. I thought maybe you were bored." He started toward the barn.

"Samuel!" She trotted after him. "Wait."

He stopped and faced her, his eyebrows raised in surprise. "Change your mind?"

"Yeah." She smiled. "I'd love to see the kittens."

"*Gut.*" He smiled, and the dimple reappeared in his cheek. He was adorable.

They fell in step on the way to the largest barn. The animal stench assaulted her senses while she followed him past a row of horse stalls. Horses snorted greetings as their shoes crunched the dry, yellow hay.

When they reached the back of the barn, tiny peeps and cries rang out. Samuel dropped onto the floor, folding his long legs under him. He moved a pile of hay, revealing a large black and white cat nursing six multicolored kittens. The peeping grew louder as the kittens staggered around their mother.

"It always amazes me how kittens sound like babies," Jessica said, sinking onto the floor next to him.

"*Ya.* They do." He gently lifted a tiny orange kitten and held it out to her. "Want to hold it?"

"Sure." She cradled the baby cat in her hands and rubbed its velvety soft fur. At the sight of this new life, a strange warmth and calm flowed through her. "What does life have in store for you, little one?"

"I would imagine he'll have a full life consisting of living in the barn and scrounging for food." Samuel nuzzled a multi-colored calico.

Jessica frowned. "Scrounging for food? That sounds so sad."

"Oh, don't worry. The cats all eat good around here. No one starves on this farm." He cut his eyes to the mother cat. "Right, Galilee?"

"Galilee?" she asked with a grin.

"Don't blame me," he said. "My little sister named her."

"I always love their pretty coats," she said, studying the peeping kitten. "When I was a kid, I used to say that God had fun with colors when He designed cats. As if they're His canvas, and He paints their coats with creative colors."

Samuel laughed. "I like that."

Jessica grinned and turned her attention back to the kitten. "I wonder if Aunt Rebecca would let me take a kitten home. I'd love to have a pet. My dad was allergic to cats, so we never had one."

"I bet you miss your *mamm* and *dat*."

"Yeah, I do." Jessica sighed, glancing over at him again.

"How do you like working in the shop with my grandfather?" He returned the kitten to its family. Then he bent his long legs, resting his elbows on his knees.

She shrugged. "It's okay, I guess."

"I wanted to go work for him, but my *dat* needs me here to help run the farm. There's always plenty of work to do." He gestured around the barn.

"That's a shame. You should be able to do what you want."

He shrugged. "Ack, it's okay. Farming is never boring."

Jessica lifted the kitten up and nuzzled its tiny head against her cheek. "So soft. Like velvet." She then gently put it back next to its siblings. "Be a good kitty and mind your mama."

Samuel snickered.

"Samuel!" a voice boomed.

Samuel jumped to his feet. "Sounds like my *dat*." Reaching out, he took Jessica's hand and lifted her to her feet.

"I need your help outside," the voice snapped.

Jessica turned to see Robert frowning at them. She let Samuel's hand go and brushed the hay from her jeans.

"Now," Robert said, his eyes boring into his son.

"Yes, sir." Samuel followed his father through the barn and out the door.

Jessica frowned and fished her iPod from her pocket. *So much for having someone to talk to.*

❧

"Did you have a nice time today?" Rebecca asked Jessica while they walked up their front steps later that evening.

Jessica shrugged. "It was okay. Not as bad as I expected."

Rebecca longed to ask Jessica about kissing Jake, but she

wasn't sure how to broach the subject without causing Jessica to shut down. Jessica wrenched open the storm door, and Rebecca reached out and clasped her arm.

"Can we chat for a minute on the swing?" Rebecca asked.

"Why?" Her niece eyed her with suspicion.

Rebecca shrugged. "We never get to talk. We're always so busy."

Her niece's brows knitted with suspicion.

"Please. Just for a moment." Rebecca motioned toward the swing. "Have a seat."

Jessica sank into the swing and stared out over the field.

"Pretty night," Rebecca said, lowering herself into the space next to Jessica. "At least the humidity broke a little."

"What is it that you want to talk about?" Jessica asked. "I'm sure it's not the weather."

"I wanted to ask you a question." Rebecca took a deep breath, wondering how to bring it up. She said a silent prayer that she wouldn't cause more distance between them.

"Please just spill it," her niece said.

"I heard something earlier, and I wanted to ask you if it was true."

Her niece frowned.

Rebecca touched Jessica's hand. "No matter what, I'm on your side."

"My side?" Her niece's frown deepened. "What have I done wrong now?"

"Don't get upset. I just wanted to talk to you about something that came up when I was talking with the other women." She glanced toward the door, hoping Daniel and Lindsay were out of earshot. She didn't want anyone to hear them or interrupt. "Sadie mentioned that Eli saw you kissing Jake. Is it true?"

Jessica clicked her tongue and made a sweeping gesture with her hand. "What is it with you people? Why is it that everything I do is the latest news?"

Rebecca reached for her, but Jessica moved out of range. "I'm not accusing you. I just want to know the truth."

"Well, the truth is that *Jake kissed me*." She scowled and smacked her thigh for emphasis. "There. Now you know. Are you happy?" Her tone cut Rebecca like a knife.

Speechless, Rebecca just nodded.

"And if you want to know the whole truth, we both decided it was a mistake. So, *nothing happened*. Got it?" Her niece rose. "I'm going to bed."

"Jessica! Wait." Rebecca followed her to the door. "I'm not accusing you of a crime. I just wanted to know if it was true."

Her niece faced her. "It is true. I'm a teenager. I'm going to make mistakes. Letting my good friend kiss me was a mistake, but I don't think I should be ripped apart in the latest Bird-in-Hand gossip."

"No one is ripping you apart." Rebecca touched Jessica's cheek. "I just wanted to know what really happened so I can set straight anyone who mentions it."

Jessica shook her head. "I don't get you people. You claim to be such wonderful Christians, yet you're the most two-faced people I've ever met."

Rebecca frowned. "We don't claim to be wonderful at anything. We all make mistakes, and we all need God's help to be better Christians. We strive to be like Jesus, and it's an impossible task."

Jessica shook her head. "I wish that everyone would just leave me alone to live my life. I can't wait to get out of here and go back home. I hate it here." She yanked the door open and stomped into the house.

Rebecca sank back into the chair and stared out over the dark field while regret washed over her. She should've kept the gossip to herself. She'd managed to push Jessica even farther away.

Elizabeth's words echoed in her mind. Rebecca was trying so

hard to listen. Why wasn't it working? What was she supposed to hear?

Closing her eyes, she prayed that God would help her find the way into Jessica Bedford's heart.

Anise Cookies

6 eggs, separated
3/4 cup powdered sugar
1 cup flour, sifted
3–1/2 tsp anise seed

Beat egg yolks until thick. Beat egg whites stiff and combine with egg yolks. Gradually add powdered sugar and mix lightly. Sift flour and add egg mixture together with anise seed. Drop from teaspoon onto greased cookie sheet, about 1 inch apart. Chill in refrigerator overnight. Bake at 300 degrees for 10 minutes.

22

Aunt Rebecca," Lindsay said, sidling up to her in the kitchen of the bakery the following Monday, "I have a great idea to share with you."

Rebecca smiled over at her niece while mixing up a gooey Shoo-Fly Pie. "Oh? What's that?"

"How about we plan a birthday get-together for Jessica for Sunday night? It's her sixteenth birthday."

Rebecca smiled. "That's a *wunderbar* idea! You can make your famous lemon meringue pie, and I'll make a chocolate cake."

"What are we planning?" Sarah leaned on the counter and lifted a glass of ice water. Her cheeks were pink from the heat of the kitchen.

"A birthday gathering for my sister." Lindsay grinned.

"A birthday?" Kathryn stepped over from the oven. "That will be wonderful *gut*! I love birthdays! I'll make apple fritters."

"It sounds like a great plan." Rebecca lifted her wooden spoon. "Should we make it a surprise?"

"No." Lindsay shook her head. "Jess hates surprises."

"Then we'll tell her tonight." Rebecca smiled. Maybe a birthday gathering was the way to get her niece to warm up to life in Lancaster County.

"Rebecca," Elizabeth whispered, tapping her shoulder. "I think it sounds like fun, but will Daniel agree?"

Rebecca met her mother-in-law's gaze, finding concern in her eyes. She scanned the kitchen and spotted her niece and sisters-in-law engrossed in their baking duties.

"Is he still not speaking to you?" her mother-in-law asked.

"*Ya.*" Rebecca wiped her hands on her apron. "How did you know?"

"I just know. Eli once was silent for a month."

Rebecca's eyes widened in shock. During her marriage, Rebecca had only seen her in-laws become cross with each other a few times. She couldn't imagine Eli being so angry with his wife that he would stop speaking to her for a month.

"You look surprised." Elizabeth smiled. "Eli is a very stubborn man, and his sons are very much like him."

"What did you do?" Rebecca asked.

Elizabeth poured mixture for bread into a pan. "I let him have his time. Finally, he came to me and asked if we could talk things out. I let him have his say and then told him how hurt I was that he could be silent for so long."

"What did he say?" Rebecca leaned in close to hear her mother-in-law over the chatter and noises of the kitchen.

Her mother-in-law gave a triumphant smile. "He never did it again."

Rebecca nodded, her thoughts turning to Daniel. She wondered how he would feel about a get-together for their niece. It had been nearly two weeks since he stopped speaking to her. Although he'd returned to their bed a few days ago, he climbed in without so much as a grunt.

She wondered what she could do to win his heart back. She'd considered begging him to talk to her, but she stood firm on her convictions that Jessica belonged with them. Rebecca was surprised to find she was almost as stubborn as her husband.

Or maybe she was as stubborn as Jessica? She pushed the thought aside.

Turning her gaze to Lindsay, Rebecca bit her bottom lip. Her niece laughed and talked to Sarah while cutting out cookies. Lindsay looked so happy and so comfortable dressed in Plain clothes and talking with Sarah. The girls did belong here, despite what Daniel thought. Rebecca knew in her heart that she was right.

It was God's will, wasn't it?

She glanced at Elizabeth, contemplating her words. Letting Daniel continue his silence might be the best way to handle him. She'd tell him about the gathering and leave it at that.

❀

Later that evening, Rebecca cleared the plates from the table and filled the sink.

"I'll get it," Lindsay said, adding a stack of plates to the sink.

"Don't be silly." Rebecca waved off the thought. "I'll do the dishes tonight. You can sweep the floor if you like." She glanced across the room to where Daniel rose from the chair and headed for the living room. If she was going to tell him about the plan, now was the time.

She cut her gaze across the room to Jessica, who was wiping the table with a rag. "Jessica," she said. "Lindsay and I wanted to celebrate your birthday Sunday."

Jessica met her glance and raised her eyebrows. "Oh?"

"Yeah, we want to give you a party," Lindsay chimed in with a wide grin. "We invited the rest of the family already, and I'm going to make you a lemon meringue pie."

"Wow." Jessica blinked, looking surprised. "Thanks."

"A party?" Daniel asked from the doorway, his scowl trained on Rebecca.

"*Ya*, just a gathering of friends and family." Rebecca folded her arms across her chest in defiance. Her body trembled with anticipation of his reaction. She wondered if he'd yell or simply remain reticent. She hoped for the former, since yelling would encourage a conversation, something they hadn't experienced in a long while.

"Can I invite Jake?" Jessica asked.

Rebecca nodded. "Of course." She looked over at Daniel, whose frown deepened. "You may invite anyone you like, Jessica," Rebecca said, still staring at Daniel. "It's your day."

"Cool!" Jessica said. "Thank you."

Daniel grunted and retreated into the living room.

Facing her nieces, Rebecca plastered a smile on her face, despite the hurt and disappointment surging through her. "I'll make a chocolate cake and get some ice cream," she said. "We'll make this day one to remember."

❋

Jessica stared at the calendar on the wall the following day. Two whole months had past, but it seemed like only yesterday that she had come to the store for the first time. Where had the last eight weeks gone?

She scanned the front of the store, studying the furniture pieces for sale. It may have been two months, but she still didn't feel as though she belonged. She wondered if she'd ever feel as though she belonged here.

Lindsay, on the other hand, went off dressed in her Plain clothes and laughing with Rebecca every morning. Jessica could hear Lindsay and Rebecca talking about recipes and gossiping about bakery customers late into the night. Lindsay participated in Daniel's evening devotions while Jessica stayed in her room listening to music. Jessica was still the outsider, and Lindsay became more and more a part of the Kauffman family every day.

Jessica sauntered across the front of the store and flipped the sign to "Open" and then retreated back behind the counter.

While she shuffled papers on the desk and prepared the ledger for the day, the door whooshed open.

"Good morning," Jessica said without looking up. "Welcome to Kauffman and Yoder."

Glancing up, her stomach twisted when she spotted Arnold Browne, a customer who'd recently demanded a corner curio cabinet built at light speed as a gift for his wife.

She forced a smile onto her face. "Mr. Browne. How are you today?"

"I'd be better if my curio cabinet was done." He slammed his hand on the counter. "My anniversary is tomorrow. If you people can't get it done in time, then you should've told me! I want a full refund, plus 10 percent for my inconvenience."

She stood and leaned forward on the counter. "Actually, Mr. Browne, I told you that this is our busiest time of year, and we're backed up with—"

"I don't want to hear about your summer orders." The middle-aged man tapped his finger on the counter. "I want to hear about *my* order!"

"I can tell you about your order if you stop yelling," a voice said.

Jessica glanced at Jake standing in the doorway clad in blue jeans and a black T-shirt. His eyes were brewing with confidence and determination as he folded his arms across his chest.

She smiled. How cool of him to come to her defense.

"Well, Jake?" The older man folded his arms over his flabby chest. "I'm waiting."

"I'm putting the final coat of stain on it." Jake stepped over to the counter, sidling up beside Jessica. "I'll finish it up and have it ready later today."

Mr. Browne eyed Jake for a moment and then nodded. "Fine then. I'll check back later."

"Sounds good." Jake motioned for the door. "I'll get right to work on it. You have a good day now."

Jessica gave Jake a sideways glance. He winked at her, and she grinned.

The door whooshed open and closed, and Jessica breathed a sigh of relief while sinking into her chair. "What a way to start off my day."

"I'm sorry about that." Jake shook his head. "I knew Mr. Browne was a jerk, but I never imagined he'd yell at you like that."

"I'm so glad you came out when you did." She nodded toward the door leading to the shop. "I was going to come back and get your grandpa to help me handle him."

"I was heading up to say good morning, and I heard him start in on you." He scowled. "That ticks me off. You didn't deserve that." His expression softened. "But don't let that cranky old man ruin your day."

"Thank you." She smiled. "Listen, do you have plans for Sunday night? My sister and Aunt Rebecca are throwing me a birthday party. Can you come?" She bit her bottom lip suddenly feeling self-conscious. "I understand if you're busy."

"Are you kidding?" he asked with a grin. "I wouldn't miss it for the world. I'd be happy to come."

"Jake Miller." His grandfather appeared in the doorway. "Every time I see you, you're chatting. Do I need to rethink making you a master carpenter?"

"No, Grandpa." Feigning a dramatic sigh, he faced his grandfather. "I was just making sure Jessica was okay up here. She's already had a run-in with Mr. Browne this morning."

"Old Arnie was at it again, huh?" Milton asked, shaking his head. "I hope he didn't get to you too much."

"Jake came to my rescue, so it was okay." Jessica smiled. "Jake is going to have the curio done before closing."

"Well then, Jacob, you'd best get to it." Milton gave a stern expression.

"Yes, sir." Jake's smirk faded. "I'll be right there." Milton disappeared through the door and Jake gave Jessica an apologetic expression. "I guess we'll chat later on."

"Get to work before you lose your job." She pushed her hair back from her shoulders. "I don't want to be responsible for your unemployment."

He chuckled. "I don't think my grandfather would fire me. My mom might have something to say about that."

"Go on." She waved him off. "If you keep talking we won't have anything to discuss later."

"I find that hard to believe." He pulled his keys from his pocket and tossed them to her. "Feel free to plug your phone in. The charger is still on the dash where you left it last week."

Jessica frowned, placing the keys on her counter. "What for? No one has called me in almost a week."

He raised his eyebrows. "Not Brian or Morgan?"

"Neither of them." She yanked her phone from her purse and glared down at the display. "It's like I don't exist to them anymore."

"It's their loss." His eyes mirrored her frustration.

"They promised they'd keep in touch, but I guess since school has ended they forgot about me." She shook her head. "Trisha hasn't called either, but I got a letter from her a few days ago."

"If they can forget you that easily, then they aren't your friends." He headed for the door. "I'll see you later. If you have problems with any more customers, yell for me. I'll set them straight."

Jessica stared at the doorway after he left, his words echoing in her mind. Was he right that Morgan and Brian weren't true friends? But they'd been through so much together in school—bad teachers, bullies, broken hearts. How could they just drop Jessica like yesterday's midterms?

The office phone rang and Jessica bounced back to reality. She had to push aside her heartache and concentrate on work. At least she could look forward to chatting with her true friend, Jake Miller.

Daniel's footsteps crunched across the gravel driveway while he headed from the barn to the house. He glanced up at the sky and blew out a frustrated sigh. The dark, threatening clouds overtaking the sky reflected his mood.

In less than an hour, he'd have to feign happiness while his family descended upon his farm to celebrate the birthday of a child who did not belong in his home.

He wondered how much longer he'd have to endure this façade. For two weeks he'd avoided any conversation with his wife in hopes that she would listen to him and consider sending the girls to live with Trisha. He knew in his heart that the girls belonged in Virginia in an English home with their English friends. Keeping them in Bird-in-Hand wasn't good for them or for the Kauffman family. They were just delaying the inevitable — when the girls left and broke Rebecca's heart.

Glancing at the house, Daniel's thoughts turned to his wife. Before the girls came to live with them, their lives were close to perfect. They were happy, despite their inability to have children. He and Rebecca rarely quarreled.

However, since the girls had arrived, their lives had been turned upside down. Of course he still loved his wife, but he missed the way things had been.

It didn't make sense that Grace, who had left the community

to marry and live among the English, would want her children raised here. She'd said she wanted them to experience her heritage. It would've made more sense to have the girls come and visit rather than send them here to live. Grace claimed in her letter that Philip prevented her from visiting. Daniel snorted with disagreement at the thought. He found that hard to believe, considering how headstrong and strong-willed Grace and Rebecca were.

The clip-clop of a horse slammed Daniel back to the present. Glancing up, he wondered who had arrived early. He met the buggy at the end of the driveway, and his stomach twisted as Abner Chupp emerged from the rig. When the bishop arrived unannounced it could never be good. Daniel's worst nightmare was playing out right before his eyes.

"*Wie geht's,*" Daniel said, hoping his stomach would ease.

"*Wie geht's,*" Abner echoed, tethering his horse to the post by the barn.

"What brings you out here this evening?" Daniel asked, leaning back on the fence.

"A situation has been brought to my attention that I need to discuss with you." Abner's expression was impassive.

"Oh." Daniel glanced toward the house and then met Abner's gaze, his shoulders tightening. "What seems to be the situation?" He took a deep breath, preparing for the tongue lashing.

"I've heard your niece's behavior is causing quite a bit of concern among the People." Abner folded his arms across his portly frame.

"My niece?" Daniel asked, even though he assumed he knew what the bishop was referring to. "I can't imagine what my nieces could have done to upset anyone."

"*Ya.* Jessica." Abner paused as if gathering his thoughts. "A few members of the community have told me that she is behaving like a harlot. She's forced her rock music and the Internet on your niece Katie. She was seen going out alone with Jake Miller and later kissing him. Plus, she was seen wearing hardly any clothes while working in Rebecca's garden on a Sunday."

Abner's expression transformed to a frown. "And she was caught alone in Robert's barn with Samuel. When Robert discovered them, Samuel was holding her hand and Jessica was covered in hay."

Daniel's body trembled while white-hot anger roared through him. Speechless, he grasped the fence post. How dare members of his community make such heinous accusations about an innocent child? He took a deep breath to gather his thoughts.

"Jessica is *not* a harlot!" he said through gritted teeth. "Maybe she doesn't understand our ways, and she does not belong here, but she's still a child. She's a good girl. She needs guidance and understanding while she learns her way around our community."

"As the head of the household, it's your duty to keep your family members in line," Abner continued. "The girl needs to learn boundaries. She must learn to respect our ways and obey our rules."

"I don't appreciate these cruel accusations about my niece," Daniel said, his voice quaking with ire. "This is nothing but cruel gossip. All children need to learn boundaries, but she also is still learning our culture. She can't be expected to learn our ways overnight."

"You must keep your family under control." Abner wagged his finger at him. "The community is very *concerned* about things that are going on in your house."

Daniel pursed his lips. He could read between the lines, and he knew what could happen. If the community turned against him, he'd be an outcast, possibly shunned. He couldn't risk that. If he were put under the ban, he could lose the rest of the Kauffman family and possibly his place in the shop.

If he lost his job, he and Rebecca would lose everything.

Daniel refused to let that happen. He'd worked too long and too hard to build this life for him and Rebecca. It was his job to take care of his family, and Rebecca was his family. She mattered most to him. She was his life.

Daniel folded his arms across his chest in the hopes of stopping his body from trembling with rage. How could his community turn on him over a teenager's actions? This was absurd!

"I understand your concerns," he whispered. "However, I'm offended that members of my church district would bring these horrible accusations to you without consulting me or giving my niece the benefit of the doubt. She's merely a child."

Abner sighed and rubbed his beard. "*Ya*, she's a child, but she's your responsibility. If the community is feeling threatened then they turn to me."

"Threatened?" Daniel's voice rose. He gestured wide with emphasis. "How can a sixteen-year-old girl threaten them? Our history is full of stories of persecution! We've survived religious genocide. We've met in secret and fled countries in order to keep our beliefs alive. Why on earth would a teenage girl cause the community grave concern?"

The bishop studied him, his eyes narrowing to slits and his expression becoming stony. "Daniel, it's your duty as the head of the household to keep your family in line. If you can't, then the community will have to handle this for you."

Daniel grimaced. He knew a veiled threat when he heard one. "I'll take care of it."

"*Gut*. See that you do. Quickly." Abner patted Daniel's arm, and Daniel bristled at the gesture.

Daniel scowled. "*Danki* for bringing it to my attention." His voice was void of emotion.

Abner untied his horse and opened the door to his rig. "You're a good man, Daniel. I'm sure the rest of the community would be happy to see your family back on track."

"*Danki*." Daniel held his breath while Abner climbed into his rig and his horse trotted down the driveway. Once the buggy was gone from his sight, he turned his gaze toward the house.

Thunder rumbled in the distance and a droplet of rain trickled from the brim of his straw hat. Irritation roared through him. Rebecca brought this onto the house. She was the one who refused to let the girls go back to Virginia.

Gritting his teeth, he stomped toward the back door. It was about time he made Rebecca know just what was at stake. It was time he took charge.

❖

Rebecca hummed while slathering icing on the cake. The smell of the chocolate permeated her senses. She couldn't wait to see Jessica's smile while they sang to her. She had a feeling tonight would be a turning point in her relationship with her niece.

Maybe things would get back on track and they could finally be a real family. She smiled at the thought. God had given her children. She was so blessed!

The back door slammed, and Rebecca jumped. She swiped more icing from the bowl and moved it across the last section of cake.

"Rebecca," her husband's voice boomed. "Rebecca!"

She spun, and her gaze collided with Daniel standing in the doorway, a furious scowl twisting his handsome face while droplets of rain streamed from his hat.

A shiver of panic raced through Rebecca. Something was wrong. "Daniel," she said. "Did someone arrive early? I thought I heard a horse."

"Someone was here but not for Jessica's birthday." His tone was laced with venom.

Her mouth dried. "Oh?"

"It was Abner Chupp." His gaze was unmoving, and his scowl deepened.

"The bishop," she whispered.

"*Ya.*" He took off his hat and stuck it on the peg by the door with a jerking motion. "We need to talk."

"We'll talk later," she said, turning back to the cake. "Your family will be here any moment, and I have a lot to—"

"Now, *Fraa!*" he shouted. "*Kumm.*" He stalked up the stairs.

"Aunt Rebecca?" Lindsay said, appearing the doorway from the living room. "Is everything okay?"

"*Ya.*" Rebecca placed the knife in the sink. "I'm going upstairs to talk to Uncle Daniel for a moment. Would you please finish the cake?" She wiped her hands on a rag. "And I believe your lemon meringue is done too. It looks *wunderbar.*"

"Sure." Lindsay gave her a confused expression.

"*Danki.*" Rebecca hurried up the stairs and down the hall to the bedroom, her stomach tied in knots. She could only imagine what Abner had said. It was probably about Jessica. Everything was going to come to a head right now, and she wasn't sure if she was ready for this.

Taking a deep breath, she stepped into the bedroom where her husband stood glaring at her. She shivered with trepidation.

"Close the door," he grumbled.

She pushed it closed with a quiet click. "What did he say?" she asked, her voice hushed and timid.

"What do you think he said?" Daniel stood near the window, his arms folded across his chest. "He said I need to get my household under control. Apparently gossip about her behavior was brought to Abner's attention, and now I'm the laughingstock of our district."

"No, you're not." She stepped toward him. "No one is laughing at you."

"Yes, they are." He made a sweeping gesture for emphasis. "Jessica has ruined my standing in the community. She's been seen alone in the barn with Samuel, out alone with Jake Miller, *kissing* Jake Miller, and out wearing nothing but a tiny top and shorts while weeding the garden on a Sunday. Do you know how this makes me look?"

Biting her lip, Rebecca prayed he'd open his heart and listen to her. "Those are all exaggerations," she began. "Jessica is a good girl. She's made a few unwise decisions, but she's not the person they think she is. She and Jake are only friends. She told me that they briefly kissed once but they—"

He smacked the top of the dresser, and she jumped. "It doesn't matter now, Rebecca! The damage is done. Jessica is considered a detriment to the People." He seethed with frustration vibrating in his voice. "It's time for you to listen to me." He raked his hand through his hair. "It's time that the girls go back to Virginia where they belong."

Rebecca stared at him for a moment. She'd never seen him so forceful or upset. But she would not give in. The girls meant too much to her, and it was time he respect her wishes and her feelings.

This was Grace's last wish.

This was God's will.

Her legs wobbled with the apprehension trickling through her as she took a deep breath from the depths of her toes. "No," she said.

"What did you say?" his voice rose.

"I said no, Daniel." She hugged herself in hopes of stopping her shivers. "I will not send them back, and I insist that *you* respect *my* wishes."

"Respect your wishes?" He shook his head. "You're talking foolish. It doesn't make sense for them to stay here. Jessica has caused enough trouble, and it's time for her to go. If it doesn't stop, I'll be shunned."

He slammed his hand on the dresser again for emphasis. "Do you want that for us? Do you want us to lose the community support? Do you want me to lose my job?"

Shaking her head with disbelief, she studied his eyes. "You're the one not making sense. No one is going to put you under the ban. You're very well respected in our district, and Jessica has done nothing wrong."

"What are you saying? She's done plenty wrong!" he exclaimed.

Rebecca frowned. "I won't allow you to send her back."

"You won't allow me?" He chuckled with sarcasm. "I don't think it's your decision."

"I think it is. For fifteen years I've kept my silence while you made all of the rules in this house, but I won't do it any longer. This is my house too. In fact, this was my parents' house. I have a say in who lives here, and I want the girls here. They need guidance and love, not judgment. They will stay here. God has sent them to us."

Daniel's eyes flashed with shock and then returned to cool frustration. "Are you sure it's God's will, Rebecca?" His voice was soft but trembling with emotion.

"*Ya*, I'm sure. I can feel it in my heart. That's my final word, Daniel Kauffman. The girls stay." With her body shaking like a leaf in a windstorm, Rebecca kept her stare fixed on his enraged eyes.

Silence engulfed the room while a steady rain beat on the windowpane and the roof.

A quiet knock sounded on the door, but Rebecca and Daniel continued to study each other.

"Aunt Rebecca?" a voice asked outside the door. "The company is here."

"Thank you," Rebecca said with her eyes focused on her husband. "I'll be right there."

Daniel continued to stare at her in silence.

She waited another moment for him to speak and then retreated toward the door, her heart overflowing with disappointment. She'd hoped Daniel would listen to her and finally understand her love for the girls.

But no, he'd kept his stubborn feelings and chose to follow the bishop over her.

Stepping into the hallway, she found Jessica leaning against the wall, frowning. Rebecca closed the door behind her and pushed thoughts of Daniel from her head.

She forced a smile on her lips and looped her arm around her niece's shoulders. "You ready to celebrate your birthday?"

"What was that about?" Jessica nodded toward the bedroom door.

"Daniel and I were having a discussion. It's nothing for you to worry about." She tugged Jessica toward the stairs. "Let's go downstairs and visit."

"No." Jessica stopped and studied Rebecca. "You were talking about me. What was he saying?"

Rebecca sighed. She didn't want to hurt her niece, especially tonight. "Daniel and I were having a disagreement, but it was nothing you should worry about. Sometimes married people disagree."

Suspicion sparkled in her niece's eyes. "But I heard my name. That tells me it has everything to do with me."

Rebecca rested her hands on her slight shoulders. "Jessica, today is your birthday. This is a happy day, and a special day. In fact, I have something for you." She nodded toward the end of the hallway. "Come with me." She led Jessica to the sewing room, where she picked up a folded quilt. "I want you to have this."

Jessica took the quilt and ran her hands over the intricate stitching in a lonestar pattern. She lifted a questioning gaze to Rebecca.

"Your mother made it a long time ago," Rebecca said. "I want you to have it."

Jessica's eyes filled with tears. "Thank you," she whispered.

"You're welcome. Happy birthday." Rebecca gave her a quick hug and then started for the door. "I have to go downstairs before our guests think we left. Put the quilt in your room and come down when you're ready."

Heading down the stairs, Rebecca prayed that the rest of the evening would somehow go smoothly.

24

Happy birthday!" Lindsay's voice rang out over the mutters of conversation that greeted Jessica when she entered the living room.

Jessica forced her lips to form a smile. She wished the party had been canceled. While taking the beautiful quilt to her room, a wave of memories and regret had crashed down on her.

She'd wished she could've spent a quiet birthday at home, since she couldn't shake thoughts of her parents from her mind all day. She'd awoken in a cold sweat at four this morning after having a nightmare about the night her parents had died. Celebrating her sixteenth birthday without them had only made the nightmare seem more horrible and real.

A pang of guilt roared through her as she replayed her conversation with her mother just minutes before the accident. Why had Jessica been so pigheaded? She sighed, knowing she couldn't change the past.

She scanned the sea of faces for Rebecca and Daniel, while the words she'd heard through the door haunted her. She'd only heard bits and pieces of the conversation.

However, Rebecca's words were loud and clear when she said that the girls would stay. Jessica couldn't help but wonder if Daniel wanted to get rid of her and her sister. If that were true, then everything would change. Jessica wondered what would happen to Lindsay now. She had found a home here—would she be as happy in Virginia? Had Jessica ruined everything for her?

But there was nothing she could do about it now as she stood before the Kauffman clan. She had no choice but to go along with the party.

A chorus of "Happy Birthday" broke out, and Rebecca weaved through the throng holding a large chocolate sheet cake decorated with flowers, "Happy Birthday Jessica" written in purple icing, and four burning candles.

"Oh wow," Jessica said when the singing ceased.

"Make a wish!" Lindsay hollered above the conversations breaking out around her.

Closing her eyes, Jessica blew out the candles, wishing she could somehow go home. She opened her eyes while the folks around her clapped.

"Happy birthday," Rebecca said. "Let's cut your cake."

"Happy birthday." Lindsay wrapped her arms around Jessica.

"Hey." A hand squeezed her shoulder. "Happy birthday."

Jessica turned to see Jake grinning at her. "Jake!"

He pulled her into a warm hug. "I got you a little something," he said.

She pulled back and stared up at him. "You didn't have to do that."

"Of course I did." He handed her a small purple gift bag. "Happy birthday."

"Thank you," she said, but before she opened it, a determined hand yanked her arm.

"Come have some cake," Lindsay said, tugging her toward the kitchen. "I made a lemon meringue pie just for you."

When they reached the kitchen, a plate with a heaping piece of lemon meringue and a fork were shoved into her hands. A swarm of Daniel's relatives engulfed Jessica in conversation, pinning her into a corner of the large room.

While the knot of relatives chatted, Jessica glanced at the doorway where Jake smiled at her. She wished she could sneak away and talk to Jake in a quiet, private room, away from the loud voices and meaningless conversation.

After finishing her pie, Jessica placed the plate on the counter and excused herself from the loud kitchen.

She felt her phone vibrating in her pocket on her way to the living room. She fished it out and found Trisha's name on the display. A hand on her arm stopped her from flipping it open.

"Are you going to open your gift from me?" Jake asked.

She breathed a sigh of relief. "I was so afraid you'd left."

"Are you kidding?" He shook his head. "I would never bail on you. I was just waiting for you to get away from the Kauffmans."

She scanned the room. "Let's go talk somewhere."

"How about the porch? We'll be safe from the rain under the roof as well as the prying eyes." He took her hand and steered her through the crowd and out the front door.

"Finally," she said, lowering herself into the swing. "Peace and quiet."

He chuckled and sat next to her. "You'd think they'd be quiet and reserved, but they can cut loose at times."

"You can say that again." She placed the gift bag on her lap.

"Please open it." His fingers brushed hers.

The tissue paper crinkled while she fished through and located a small box. Opening it, she gasped when she spotted a new cellular phone. "Jake," she said. "This must've cost you a fortune."

"Not really." He shrugged. "It's the newest model with the best battery. It'll keep a charge much longer than your current phone. We'll just take it down to the phone store in town, and they'll switch out the cards. Then you'll have a new phone with the same number."

"Wow." She opened it and examined the features. Then she frowned. "So, you're trying to prevent me from using your truck to charge my phone so often, huh?"

"Not at all." He grinned. "You don't need an excuse to ride in my truck. I just thought you might want a better battery so you can keep in touch with your friends." He pointed to a button. "It's got this really cool camera. Just push that." He grinned, and she took a photo of him. "Now you can take photos and send them to your buddies back in Virginia."

"Why?" she snapped. "They don't call me anymore."

He raised an eyebrow. "You're kidding, right?"

"Nope." She shook her head. "Brian and Morgan still haven't called me. It's been almost two weeks. They didn't even call to say happy birthday."

"They don't deserve to have you as a friend." He shook his head. "Not calling on your birthday is just plain terrible."

She sniffed back tears. Her old phone vibrated in her pocket, and she pulled it out. "Trisha again," she whispered, reading the screen.

"Go ahead and answer it." Jake nodded toward the front door. "I'll give you some privacy."

"No." She grabbed his sleeve. "You can stay. I won't be long."

He stood. "How about I go get you a drink?"

"That would be nice. Thanks." She flipped the phone open while he headed into the house. "Hello?"

"Happy birthday, Jessie!" Trisha sang into the phone. "How are you?"

"I'm okay." She leaned back in the swing, which swayed in the humid July air.

"I'm sorry I mailed your card late. You should have it by Tuesday."

"That's okay. How are things at the beach?" Jessica flicked a piece of lint off her jeans.

"It's been really busy. I'm sorry I haven't called or written in a while," her godmother said. "I think of you and Lindsay all the time. Business is picking up again with the construction company. We just got another condo deal. Pretty soon this place will be known for the condos and not the beach."

Jessica closed her eyes and frowned. Her father used to say those same words.

A surge of regret and sorrow slid through her. How she missed her parents—especially today. She should be home in her old house celebrating her birthday with them, not with this family she barely knew.

"Jessie? You still there?" Trisha asked.

"Yeah." Jessica's voice quavered, and she cleared her throat. "Have you talked to a lawyer?"

Silence greeted her on the other end of the phone, and Jessica's stomach soured. She knew the answer before her godmother spoke.

"Honey, I didn't get good news," Trisha said.

"What do you mean?" A lump swelled in Jessica's throat.

"I have no right to contest your mother's will."

"Why?" Jessica brushed away an errant tear with her palm.

The swing shifted, and she turned to see Jake sitting next to her, his eyes full of concern while he studied her. He placed two plastic cups on the porch railing.

"Because I'm not a blood relative, Jessie. I can't do anything."

"But you're my godmother, Aunt Trisha. Doesn't that count for anything?" Jessica swallowed a sob.

Jake rubbed her back, but she kept her focus on her lap.

"The lawyer said that's just a church ritual," Trisha said. "It means nothing in the eyes of the law. What matters is your parents wanted you and your sister with your aunt Rebecca. That's what the will said, so that's what the law sides with."

"But I don't want to be here. I want to be with you. I want to come home." Jessica couldn't stop the sobs wracking her body. When Jake pulled her into his arms, she pushed away and popped up from the swing. She padded to the other side of the porch without looking back.

"Jessica?" her godmother said. "Jessica, listen to me. Are you there?"

"Yeah," Jessica whispered. "I'm here."

"You have to make the best of this, honey. Two years from today you'll be eighteen, and you can do whatever you please. You just have to hang on for two years."

"That's impossible," Jessica said. "I can't stand another week working in that stupid furniture store. The days are long and boring, and one customer even yelled at me earlier this week. It's a nightmare." Jessica leaned on the railing, watching the rain pound down on the dirt driveway. "I just want to go home and finish high school. Then I can go to college."

"You can go to college in two years. You can get your GED and go to any school you want."

"I can't do it, Aunt Trisha. I have to get out of here before I go insane," she said. "I don't belong here."

"You're going to have to make the best of it. I've done all I can. I'm sorry it wasn't enough." Trisha sighed. "Look, Frank and I will get caught up at work and then we'll visit. Rebecca said we can come back any time to see you."

"I don't want you to visit," Jessica said, wiping her eyes again. "I want you to come get me and take me back to live with you. Nobody wants me here—especially Daniel."

The roar of an engine startled Jessica. Looking up, she spotted Jake's pickup rumbling down the dirt driveway toward the main road, and her stomach clenched.

"Oh no," she whispered. "Jake."

"What's wrong?" Trisha asked.

"Nothing." She shook her head as more regret bubbled through her. She'd hurt him. He'd been the one person who'd reached out to her and not judged what she said or did, and she managed to mess that up like everything else she'd done since she'd come here.

"Jessica, I tried the best I could," her godmother said. "I called three lawyers, and I got the same answer from each one. You just have to make the best of it and go out on your own when you're eighteen."

"I can't stand another two years here," Jessica said through gritted teeth despite the tears spilling from her eyes. "I'm sixteen. I'll have myself declared emancipated or whatever you call it."

"I don't think that's such a good idea," Trisha said. "You can't touch your parents' money for a few more years."

"I don't need money." She wiped her wet cheeks with the back of her hands. "I'm going to tell Aunt Rebecca that I want to leave. I've had enough."

"Jessica, you might not want to do that."

"I'll talk to you later." Jessica snapped the phone shut and stared out across the dark pasture while the large raindrops soaked her jeans and her blouse. She was ready to go. Nothing was keeping her in Lancaster County.

Except Jake.

But nothing could ever happen between them. They were just good friends. He was happy with his simple life of working in grandfather's furniture store, and Jessica wanted more. She wanted to go to college and get her degree. She wanted to see the world. She wasn't like these Plain People.

Glancing up at the sky, she thought of Jake's words. He'd said her being there was God's plan. But somehow it didn't seem right. She didn't know why her parents had died, but she didn't think God intended for her to be here. It didn't feel right.

No, this wasn't what He'd planned for her at all.

She fingered her mother's wedding ring dangling from the chain around her neck. Jessica was like her mother, and it was time she started acting like her. She was a Bedford, not a Kauffman.

Three-Layer Chocolate Cake

2 cups sifted cake flour
2 cups granulated sugar
3/4 tsp salt
1 – 1/4 tsp baking soda
1/2 cup soft shortening
3 squares unsweetened chocolate, melted
3/4 cup milk
1 tsp vanilla
1/2 tsp double-acting baking powder
1/2 cup milk
3 eggs

Grease, then line with waxed paper, the bottoms of three 1 – 1/4-inch deep 8-inch layer pans.

Sift together first four ingredients into large mixing bowl. Drop in shortening; pour in chocolate, 3/4 cup milk, and vanilla. With electric mixer, mix for 2 minutes at medium speed. Stir in baking powder. Add 1/2 cup milk and eggs; beat 2 minutes longer.

Turn into pans, bake at 350 degrees for 40 minutes or until done. Cool in pans on wire racks about 15 minutes. Remove from pans, peel off paper, cool on racks.

25

Daniel's harsh words echoed in her mind while Rebecca glanced around the crowded kitchen, scanning the sea of faces for Jessica. Lindsay emerged from the throng, and Rebecca pulled her over.

"Have you seen Jessica?" Rebecca asked.

"No." Lindsay shook her head. "I thought maybe she was with you. I wanted to give her the present I got her. I'll look upstairs. Maybe she got a call and went up to her room for privacy."

Rebecca glanced around the room. "I'll check outside." She weaved through the crowd of relatives and headed toward the front door. A rumble of thunder sounded in the distance, and the rain beat on the roof as she opened the door.

Jessica stood on the other side of the porch, leaning on the railing, her hair and blouse soaked as if she'd been standing in the falling rain.

"There you are," Rebecca said. "I've been looking all over for you."

Frowning, Jessica faced her. "I wanted to talk to you too."

Rebecca took a deep breath. "What's on your mind?"

"I want to leave," Jessica said. "I'm sixteen now, and I'm mature enough to be on my own." She stood up straight, her face exuding newfound confidence.

"Jessica, you're still a child." She took a step toward her. "Your parents wanted you and your sister to stay with me until you were eighteen, and we have to respect their wishes."

"I can't stand another day here, much less two more years." Jessica's pretty face transformed into a scowl. "I want to go now. Thanks for all you've done, but I don't belong here."

She gestured wildly. "I wasn't meant to live on a farm and work in a furniture store. I want to finish school with my friends. I want to be with my boyfriend. I want to go to college. This isn't my home."

"Honey, you're just upset." Rebecca reached for her niece, but Jessica yanked her hand away before she could touch it. "This is your first birthday without your parents."

"Just upset?" Jessica shook her head. "Well, I've been just upset for two months now. It's more than just upset." A gust of wind blew her hair back from her shoulders, and her mother's ring glittered in the dim light of the kerosene lamp on the little table by the swing. "I'm not like you or the Kauffmans. I'm like my mother. It's time for me to go and live my own life."

"Don't make a hasty decision. Let's talk about this." Rebecca rubbed her shoulder. "After everyone leaves, we'll sit down and talk about this calmly."

Jessica's brown eyes narrowed. "Don't you ever get upset? Don't you ever scream and yell? Don't you show any emotion at all?" A sour smile formed on her lips. "No, it's not your way, right?"

A cool mist of rain kissed Rebecca's face. "You need to calm down. We'll talk about this when everyone is gone."

"You're not listening!" Jessica said. "I want to leave. I want to go home."

"Jessica, please." Rebecca sighed, disappointment raining down on her like the drops hitting the roof above them. No matter what she did, she seemed to upset Daniel and Jessica. She was at a loss for what to say.

"I heard what you and Daniel were saying in your bedroom earlier," her niece said, her voice thick. "I know he wants us to leave."

"Don't worry about Daniel." Rebecca pushed a wet wisp of hair back from Jessica's face. "I'll get him to understand."

"You've said that before, but nothing has gotten better. I think it would be best for everyone if we left. Then you guys could get back to your normal life, and Lindsay and I could get back to ours."

The screen door slammed, and Lindsay sidled up to Rebecca. "You found her," she said. Her smile faded while she studied Jessica. "What's wrong? Did you have another fight with Brian?"

"No." Jessica glared at her. "Brian still hasn't called me. Neither has Morgan."

"So then what is it?" Lindsay asked. "Why aren't you enjoying the party Aunt Rebecca planned for you?"

Jessica folded her arms and moved away from Rebecca. "I was just telling Aunt Rebecca that I'm sixteen now and I want to leave."

Lindsay blinked her eyes, hurt radiating in them. "So, she planned this nice party and you decide to tell her that you want to leave? Do you have any feelings at all?"

"Why don't you just stay out of it?" Jessica took a step toward her sister. "You don't understand."

"Oh really?" Lindsay stood before her. "Why don't you explain it to me?"

"You're just a kid," Jessica said. "I'm a grown woman, and I'm going to make my own decisions."

"A grown woman?" Lindsay scoffed. "You're only eighteen months older than me. You're not legally an adult for two years." She held up two fingers for emphasis. "And your problem is your attitude. You don't see how much Aunt Rebecca has done for us. You're ungrateful!"

"Oh, and you're perfect, huh?" Jessica snapped. "I guess that's why you were always Mom's favorite."

While the steady rain beat on the porch steps, Rebecca looked back and forth between the girls. She placed a hand on each of their shoulders and gently nudged them away from each other.

"Girls, that's enough." Rebecca shook her head. "I don't think your parents would want you arguing like this. You're the only family you have left."

"That's right." Jessica glared at Rebecca. "Lindsay's my family, not you."

Rebecca gasped as if she'd just been shot in the heart. She stared at her niece, wondering how she could be so cold, so unfeeling. Was it simply the death of her parents or was it something more?

"I've only tried to be the best parent I can be," Rebecca said, lowering her voice. "I've never been a mother. I could never have children of my own. I'm only doing this because of your mother."

Jessica's eyes widened. "So, you're glad you finally got the opportunity to be a mother? You're glad she's dead?"

Rebecca sighed and shook her head. Talking to Jessica was even more frustrating than talking to Daniel. "That's not what I meant, and you know that, Jessica."

"But you just said that if my mother hadn't died then you never could've become a mother," Jessica said.

Rebecca folded her arms over her apron. For a brief moment she wondered if she should've let Trisha have custody of the girls. Maybe if Trisha had taken them, they would've been happy. However, it was God's plan for them to come to her and Daniel.

"I don't think there's anything I can say to show you how much I love you and Lindsay," Rebecca said. "I'm just doing my best."

"Well, I don't think your best is good enough," Jessica seethed.

"Jessica, how could you talk to our aunt that way?" Lindsay grabbed her sister's arm and shook it. "What's wrong with you?"

Rebecca closed her eyes and blew out a ragged breath. She couldn't take any more cruel words. The hurt was a deep ache in her soul. She turned to Lindsay. "I'm going to go inside and let you two talk this out." She headed back into the house before Lindsay could protest.

❀

Rebecca walked in the house, and the door slammed behind her.

Lindsay glared at her sister. "I just don't get you. Aunt Rebecca and Uncle Daniel have welcomed us into their home and into their lives, and you've done nothing but complain and upset Aunt Rebecca."

"They welcomed us?" Jessica shook her head. "You've got to be kidding me. I overheard Daniel telling Rebecca to send us back to Virginia. They haven't welcomed me. Daniel has seen me as nothing but a problem since I got here. That doesn't give me warm fuzzies about staying here."

"But Aunt Rebecca loves us," her sister said. "She wants us here, no matter what he says."

"She doesn't deserve the title aunt. She's a stranger to me," Jessica said. "And why are you taking her side anyway? You're my sister."

"She's our mother's sister." Lindsay blew out a frustrated sigh. "You really need to think about how you treat people. You only think of yourself. You're the most selfish person I know. We can learn from them."

"What are you saying?" Jessica shook her head in disbelief. "We're not Amish! Did you forget that?"

"Don't you get it?" Lindsay gestured wildly with her arms. "Rebecca is just like Mom. She's warm, she's sweet, and she's giving. We belong here, Jess. That's why Mom wanted us to come here."

Jessica stared at her younger sister. Dressed in the Plain clothing she looked just like the rest of the Kauffman clan. Jessica was officially alone.

Shaking her head, Jessica backed away from her. The cool rain splattered on the back of her shirt and soaked her hair.

"You don't mean that," Jessica said. "We belong in Virginia Beach. We were supposed to finish out the school year with our friends."

"With our friends?" Lindsay gave a sarcastic laugh. "Don't tell me you mean Brian and Morgan. When was the last time they called you?"

Jessica bit her quivering bottom lip. "Last week."

"So, they didn't call you and sing happy birthday to you today, huh?" Lindsay folded her arms. "Did they at least send you a card?"

Jessica shook her head.

"Has it ever occurred to you that maybe they aren't your friends?"

Jessica wiped the rain from her face. "You sound like Jake."

"Do I?" Lindsay gave a smug smile. "Maybe that's because Jake is your friend and Brian and Morgan aren't."

"How do you know?" Jessica yelled. "You have no idea how much Brian loves me. You never liked him, and you never gave him a chance."

"Oh really? Kinda like how you haven't given Aunt Rebecca a chance?"

"Don't throw that back in my face!" Jessica stepped toward her sister, wagging a finger at her. "You don't know anything about Brian."

"Ha." Lindsay shook her head. "That's a good one. I know

more than you think I do. I know things you don't want to know."

Jessica froze. "What's that supposed to mean?"

"Forget it." Her younger sister waved off the thought and started toward the house.

"Oh no." Grabbing her sister's arm, she yanked her back, causing her to stumble. "Not so fast. What did that comment mean?"

"Nothing." Lindsay shook her head, the ties to her prayer *Kapp* swinging back and forth. "It meant nothing."

"Tell me, Lindsay." She squeezed her sister's arm. "Tell me now."

Lindsay sighed. "Forget I said anything. You've already managed to ruin your own birthday party. I don't want to make it worse."

"Just tell me." She let go of her sister's arm. "Please, Linds."

Her younger sister frowned. "I shouldn't have brought it up."

"Lindsay ..."

"Brian's been cheating on you."

Jessica's gut twisted. "What?"

"I caught him with Morgan a week before Mom and Dad died." Lindsay touched Jessica's arm. "I'm sorry."

"Wait." Jessica held her hands up. "What do you mean you caught them?"

"You invited them over one night to watch a movie, and you'd gone to the kitchen to get drinks or something. I came into the den to ask you a question and caught them kissing."

"Oh no." Jessica clasped her hands and her body shook. "I was right all along."

"You knew?" Lindsay's eyes rounded. "Why didn't you tell me?"

"Because I hoped I was wrong." Jessica shook her head. "I can't believe this."

"Jessica, just forget them." Lindsay grabbed her arm, her eyes apologetic. "Forget Virginia and concentrate on building a life here."

Jessica ran her hand down her hot cheeks. Anger pulsated through her veins while she contemplated her sister's words. She refused to let Brian and Morgan make a fool of her.

"Come inside and enjoy the party," Lindsay said, tugging her toward the door. "You can apologize to Aunt Rebecca later."

Jessica followed Lindsay back into the house, where the crowd of Kauffman relatives were still talking, laughing, and eating snacks. Pennsylvania Dutch whirled through the air, making Jessica feel as if she'd stepped into another country.

"You're soaked," Sarah said, sidling up to Jessica. "I guess it's still raining."

"Yeah." Jessica plastered a smile on her face. "It's pouring."

"You should go get changed before you catch a cold," Sarah said, absently rubbing her small belly.

"Right." Jessica weaved through the crowd and up to her room. She stripped off her wet clothes and pulled on dry jeans and a dry blouse. While standing in front of her closet and closing her eyes, the conversations with Jake, Trisha, Aunt Rebecca, and Lindsay swirled in her head.

Jessica was trapped in a life she didn't want. No one understood her. They accused her of being a bad influence. Her only friends, Brian and Morgan, were lying and cheating behind her back.

But her sister could be wrong. There was a chance that they weren't betraying her. She had to know the truth. She just had to.

Jessica glanced across the room, her eyes focusing on a small duffel bag by the dresser. She could pack up a few things and leave. Maybe she could ask Jake to drive her to the bus station. She could trust Jake to keep her leaving a secret. That was if he could forgive her for giving him the cold shoulder earlier. But Jake was just a friend, so why would he care if she wanted to go?

Rebecca had said it was God's will for Jessica and Lindsay to be here. But was it God's will for Jessica to be so unhappy?

Jessica bit her lip, contemplating if she were strong enough to run away. She fingered her mother's wedding ring on the chain around her neck. Sure she was—her mother had done it twenty years ago.

After packing up some clothes and toiletries in her duffel bag, she pulled on a light jacket and padded down the back stairs and out the back door into the rain.

Picking up her pace, she sloshed through the mud and trotted down the road toward Jake's two-family house.

26

Rebecca moved through the knot of people in the kitchen and stood by the counter. A wave of disappointment and regret crashed down on her as she watched her sisters-in-law talk and laugh at the table while polishing off the rest of the cakes and pastries.

Leaning against the counter, her conversation with Jessica weighed heavily on her heart. She was at a loss as to what to do. Jessica wanted to leave, and Daniel wanted her to go too. It seemed as if there was nothing she could do.

"Rebecca," a voice behind her said. "Come."

Rebecca followed her mother-in-law through the living room and out the front door to the porch, where they sank onto the swing and faced the pouring rain.

"What happened?" Elizabeth asked.

"What makes you think something happened?" Rebecca kept her gaze on the sheets of rain falling on the field.

"Please, Rebecca." Her mother-in-law gave a little snort. "I'm more observant than you think. Daniel just came down from upstairs, and he's hardly spoken. You look as if you've just lost your best friend."

"Ya, I believe I have." Rebecca sighed. "I don't know how everything got to be such a mess." She blinked back threatening tears. "Abner Chupp was here earlier."

Her mother-in-law gasped. *"Nee."*

"Ya, he was." Rebecca leaned back in the swing. "It was about Jessica. Abner listed all of Jessica's transgressions, and he said Daniel must get his household in line. Daniel was furious. He told me that I must listen to him, and he said he wants the girls to leave."

Elizabeth shook her head and touched Rebecca's hand. "Oh, Rebecca. What did you say?"

"I told him I'd been letting him run things for fifteen years, and it was time for me to speak up. I reminded him that this is my family's house, and I have a say in who lives here. I said the girls would stay."

Her mother-in-law grimaced. "How did he respond?"

Rebecca brushed away a tear. "He's not speaking to me at all."

Elizabeth looped her arm around Rebecca and pulled her close. "I know you feel you're doing the right thing, but have you really listened?"

"What do you mean?" Rebecca glanced up at her with surprise.

Her mother-in-law smiled. "Have you listened to what God has been telling you? Have you really listened—with your heart?"

Rebecca studied Elizabeth's wise eyes, contemplating her words. What was Rebecca missing? What was Elizabeth trying to say?

She pushed the questions away. Elizabeth wasn't listening to her.

"There's more." Rebecca sat up, wiped her cheeks, and took a deep breath. "Jessica overheard some of the conversation between Daniel and me. I told her she has nothing to worry about, but I can tell she doesn't believe me. I talked to her earlier on the porch, and she was more upset than ever. Now she really wants to leave. I could see a determination in her eyes that wasn't there before. She really scared me."

Breathing in a trembling breath, Rebecca felt a new rush of tears forming in her eyes. "What am I going to do, Elizabeth? I think I've lost Daniel and Jessica. How can I get them to see that I only want what's best?" She looked over at her mother-in-law and prayed she had the answers.

"Rebecca," Elizabeth began, taking her hand, "I love you like a daughter. You're a wonderful wife to my Daniel. However, you don't see what's right before your eyes."

"I don't understand." Rebecca wiped her eyes.

"You haven't heard what I've said. I told you to listen, to open your heart to God's Word. I don't think you've been listening to anyone except your own heart."

Rebecca shifted uncomfortably on the swing. "What are you trying to say?"

Elizabeth stared off across the field, a faraway look gleaming in her eyes. "Remember two years ago when Miriam Lapp broke Timothy's heart?"

Rebecca nodded, recalling how a girl from Gordonville left her brother-in-law a week before their nuptials. "Of course. Timothy was heartbroken. Daniel was beside himself over the hurt it caused his brother."

"It was so hard for me to keep my opinions to myself, but I could see his relationship with that girl unraveling before he could."

"Why do you say that?"

"The signs were there all along, but Timothy chose to ignore them. Miriam dragged her feet accepting his proposal. She didn't want to rush to set a date, and then she came up with every excuse under the sun when he wanted to discuss building the house on my farm."

Elizabeth met Rebecca's gaze and gave her a soft smile. "Timothy wasn't listening to God. He had made up his mind that Miriam Lapp would be his bride even though she had her heart set on leaving the community. She left to go to medical school, and he lives in that house all alone now."

Rebecca nodded slowly, letting the words soak in. "So, you're saying I'm not listening to God."

Elizabeth sighed. "Jessica is unhappy here. She's been trying to tell you that since she arrived. Daniel has felt it all along too, but you were so focused on being their mother that you missed what was right before your eyes all along."

Tears stung Rebecca's eyes. "But the girls were the children I could never have. Grace wanted them here."

Elizabeth pulled Rebecca into a warm hug. "I know you want them to be the children you've always prayed for, but it's not meant to be. Jessica is not meant to live here."

Closing her eyes, Rebecca succumbed to her sobs. She shook her head in disagreement with Elizabeth. She had to be wrong. She just had to!

❋

With the rain splattering on the hood of her windbreaker, Jessica studied the small, two-family house with Jake's dark blue Chevrolet pickup truck parked out front.

Thunder rumbled in the distance, and Jessica shivered. She had run across two mud-soaked fields and then sprinted down Beechdale Road before finding the house.

"This must be the place," she whispered. Sucking in a deep breath, she sauntered up the front steps and knocked on the door.

After a few moments, locks clicked and the door creaked open revealing Jake in tight blue jeans and a dark blue T-shirt. His eyes widened when they met hers.

"Jessica?" His eyes moved down her body. "You're soaked to the bone! Get in here. I'll get you a towel." He took her arm and tugged her through the door.

"No, that's okay. I'm fine." She stepped back into the doorway. "I was just wondering if I could get a ride somewhere." She opened her purse and fished out her wallet. "I'll give you some gas money."

"Get a ride?" Jake peeked over her shoulder toward her bag. "Where are you going?"

"The bus station." She placed her hand flat against his hard chest and felt her expression soften. "I'm sorry about before. I didn't mean to hurt your feelings."

"Don't mention it." He waved off the thought and then gazed at her for a moment. "Now, let me get this straight. You're blowing off your birthday party, which I assume is still going on, to go to the bus station? Are you meeting someone there? Is your boyfriend coming in for a surprise visit or something?"

She shook her head. "No. I'm going to the bus station to catch a bus."

He rubbed his chin. "Does this have something to do with your conversation with Trisha?"

"Maybe." She pulled out a ten and held it out for him to take. "Will you please take me? I'd walk, but it's raining pretty hard."

"Keep your money." He leaned back against the wall and studied her, his face accusing. "You're running away."

Jessica shoved the bill into her pocket and jammed her hand on her hip. "I'm not running away. I'm sixteen now. I'm old enough to go wherever I please."

"Do your aunt and sister know where you're going?"

She narrowed her eyes to slits. "They don't need to know what I do."

"Really? So, when they wake up in the morning and can't find you, you'll be okay with them worrying themselves sick about you?"

She sighed, the guilt nipping at her. "If you're not going to give me a ride, that's fine. I'll just walk." She turned to go, but a strong hand grabbed her bicep and spun her around to face him.

"You're not thinking this through," he said, frowning. "Why are you running away? What could possibly be so bad?"

"What could be so bad?" Jessica dropped her bag with a thud. "I was forced to quit high school in my sophomore year, leave my friends, and move to a place where I don't belong and am not welcome."

"You don't belong here?" He shook his head. "Wasn't I at your birthday party tonight? From what I saw, the house was packed with people eager to sing happy birthday to you."

"They were there because Rebecca invited them."

"Right." He nodded with emphasis. "She invited them for *you*, Jessica. Don't you get it? Your aunt loves you."

"She says she loves me, but her husband doesn't want me there. I heard them arguing, and he said I had to go. Why would I stay in a place where I'm not wanted?" Jessica shook her head. "You just don't get it. Virginia is my home. That's where I need to be."

"With the boyfriend who doesn't call you on your birthday, right?" he asked. "Can't you see the people who love you are *here?*"

Overwhelmed with regret, tears flooded Jessica's eyes. "But why do I feel like an outsider?"

"Hey." Jake's expression softened. "Come here."

Tears spilled from her eyes. He pulled her into his arms, and she buried her face into his shoulder while he rubbed her back. She inhaled the spicy scent of his cologne.

"It's okay." His whisper was soft and soothing in her ear. "You're just upset because this is your first birthday without your parents. I know how that feels. Just go back home and be with your family. That's the only thing that will help."

"You keep saying that you know how it feels, but you haven't told me why." Looking up at him, she wiped her eyes. "How can you possibly understand how I feel?"

"I told you that I lost my brother," he said. "He was my twin."

Jessica cupped her hand over her mouth in shock. "I'm so sorry."

"He died when we were sixteen, and I blamed myself for a long time." Jake touched her arm. "But I realized it wasn't my fault that he went out partying that night. I'd warned him about the guys he was hanging out with, but he wouldn't listen. I couldn't control what he did, even though I wished I could."

"But I argued with my mom that night—just moments before the accident." Her voice quavered. "I called her on her cell phone and yelled at her. I told her I was upset that she wouldn't let me invite my boyfriend over. I told her she didn't treat me like an adult. Then I stomped upstairs in a huff and never said good-bye." Tears rained down from her eyes while the memories drowned her.

He rubbed her arm. "I know what you mean. I argued with Jeremy that night too. My last words to him were that he was a loser for partying with those guys. That was the last thing he heard me say." He frowned. "I know how it feels not to get to say good-bye."

"It's so unfair." Her voice cracked. "They shouldn't have died."

"You're right, but there's nothing you can do." He continued to caress her arm; the touch was comforting and warm. "I had to just let it go and realize that for some reason it was God's will."

"Why would God want my parents to die?" Jessica sniffed back the tears. "I don't understand."

"I know it doesn't make sense sometimes." He shrugged. "I just know that we must trust in Him. You will come out of this a stronger person. There's a Bible verse that gets me through the rough times when I find myself drowning in grief. It's Nahum 1:7. It says—'The Lord is good, a refuge in times of trouble. He cares for those who trust in Him.'"

She shook her head and swiped her hot cheeks with her hands. "You sound like Aunt Rebecca."

He gave her a gentle smile. "That's because she's right."

Jessica glared at him. "I thought you'd understand, but you're like everyone else in that house."

"Jess, give it time, and you'll feel like you belong."

"I'll never feel like I belong here." She hefted her bag onto her shoulder. "Are you going to take me to the bus station, or should I walk?"

"Let me take you home."

"Great. Then drive me to Virginia." She yanked out her wallet again. "I'll pay for the gas."

"No." He shook his head. "You belong here where there are people who love you. Home is here."

She shook her head in disgust. "You're just as bad as the Kauffmans."

"Jessica, I do understand. I understand you more than you'll admit." He rested his forearms on her shoulders. "Let me take you home to your aunt Rebecca's house."

"No." She stepped back from his reach. "I'll walk."

"Don't be silly." His eyes pleaded with her. "I'll drive you."

"No. I need time to think."

Jake reached for her, but she backed away. He gave her a pained expression, and she swallowed more guilt.

"I guess I'll see you at work tomorrow," he said.

"Yeah, sure. I'll see you then." She stepped onto the porch. "Thanks again for the phone."

"You're welcome." He leaned on the doorway. "We'll take it to the store and get it hooked up tomorrow."

"Fine," she said. "Good night."

"Night." He waved.

Jessica trotted out into the rain. She hated lying to him, but he'd never understand why she had to leave. It was a long walk to the bus station, but she figured she could make it in forty-five minutes if she jogged.

The drops pounded harder on her head, and she groaned. She was soaked to the bone. She pondered the conversation with Jake as she splashed through the mud. Jessica wondered if he was right. Maybe she should just go back to Rebecca's house. Trisha had told her to stick it out until she turned eighteen. However, that felt like a lifetime. And Daniel was so angry with her right now.

If Jessica had learned one thing after losing her parents it was that life was short and precious. She had to live in the now and not wait for things to get better.

Jessica picked up her pace and trotted until she lost her breath and then power-walked for a block. When she felt as if she were going to collapse, she leaned against a post and raised her thumb. Even though her parents had warned her never to hitchhike, she knew she couldn't make it to Lancaster on foot.

When a minivan slowed, Jessica's heart skipped a beat. A middle-aged woman asked Jessica where she was headed and offered to take her to the bus station in downtown Lancaster. During the short ride, Jessica and Mrs. Reynolds made small talk about the rainy weather.

When they reached the bus station, Jessica thanked Mrs. Reynolds for the ride and hurried to the ticket booth.

"May I help you?" a woman asked.

"I'd like a ticket to Virginia Beach, Virginia, please." Jessica yanked her wallet from her purse.

"Just one?" the woman asked, a keyboard clicking while she typed.

Jessica nodded and tapped her finger on the counter.

"I have a bus leaving in five minutes," the woman said.

"Great." Jessica paid cash for the ticket, grabbed the paperwork, and rushed over to the bus bay.

She climbed on and found her seat near the back. She sank down and peeled off her soaked jacket.

Closing her eyes, she settled in the seat. In approximately fourteen hours (thanks to the long layovers), she'd be at the bus station in Virginia Beach. She could finally learn the truth about Morgan and Brian. She dug through her purse and found the phone from Trisha.

No calls.

She fished out her new phone and fingered it. Jake must have spent a lot of money on it. Flipping it open, she stared at the photo of him she'd taken at the party. He was so handsome staring back at her and smiling. He'd seemed upset when she said she was leaving. He was a good friend, and she would miss him.

Jessica closed her eyes. Her head hurt from all of the questions running through her mind. She felt so lost, so alone. Whom could she trust? Did she belong in Lancaster with Jake or in Virginia with Brian?

She hoped this trip would help her solve that puzzle. At that moment, all she knew was she was exhausted.

The bus roared to life and soon pulled out of the bay. She stared out the window at the rain and then closed her eyes. The Bible verse Jake had shared echoed through her mind.

"The Lord is good, a refuge in times of trouble. He cares for those who trust in Him."

She concentrated on it, letting the meaning seep through her like the rain that soaked her clothes.

Within moments, she was asleep.

27

This is the last of it," Lindsay said, placing a stack of forks on the counter. "I already cleaned up the plates and napkins."

"Thank you." Rebecca wiped off the table. "Have you found your sister?"

"No." Lindsay shook her head. "I guess she must've gone for a walk or something." She lowered herself onto a chair and grimaced. "I guess I was too hard on her on the porch."

"It's not your fault." Rebecca sat across from her and placed her hands on Lindsay's. "She was really upset, and she has some things to work through. I don't think you or I can help her. She needs to open her heart to God for help."

Lindsay sniffed. "I just feel like I shouldn't have been so mean to her. I said some awful things. I told her she's selfish, and she needed to think about how she treats people." She wiped her eyes. "And I told her Brian's cheating on her."

"Is he?" Rebecca asked.

"I caught him kissing Morgan one night at our house. I just never told Jessica because I was afraid she wouldn't believe me." She wiped her eyes.

Rebecca patted her shoulder. "Don't worry. You did the right thing. You're just looking out for your sister, and that's honorable. Someday she'll realize you did it because you love her and want what's best for her."

Lindsay gave a smile that didn't reach her eyes. "I hope you're right."

"You're a good person, Lindsay." Rebecca leaned over and hugged her. "Don't ever doubt your heart."

"I don't know what we'd do without you." Her niece pulled back.

"Thank you." Rebecca touched her hair, her heart swelling with love for the girls. Elizabeth's words invaded in her mind. Was she wrong not to let Jessica go? Was she ignoring what Daniel, Jessica, and God were trying to tell her?

Lindsay gazed down at the table. "Do you think we should get in the buggy and search for her?"

Standing, Rebecca considered the question. Part of her wanted to organize a search, but the other part of her felt that she needed to give Jessica her space to come back when she was ready. "I think we should wait. I'm sure Jessica will realize she acted in haste and come back."

"Can I ask you something?" Lindsay bit her bottom lip.

"You can ask me anything." Rebecca leaned against the counter.

"Jessica said she heard you and Uncle Daniel arguing earlier." Her niece's eyes glittered with the question. "Is it true Uncle Daniel wants us to leave, but you want us to stay?"

Rebecca's stomach twisted. Telling her niece the truth would hurt her, which was the last thing she wanted to do. She glanced toward the door leading to the living room and hoped Daniel wasn't within earshot.

"It's true, but you have to understand Daniel's point of view." Rebecca took a deep breath. "The bishop came to see him tonight."

"What does that mean?" Lindsay looked confused.

"It means some people in the district have said they're concerned Jessica's behavior isn't good for our community." Rebecca glanced toward the doorway and then back at her niece.

"Daniel is worried the community may start treating us differently because of Jessica. He feels she belongs back in Virginia, but your mother wanted you both with me. I want you here."

"What's going to happen to us?" Lindsay sniffed and wiped her eyes.

"You're going to stay here with me." Rebecca hugged her. "Don't worry about anything."

"Is Uncle Daniel mad?"

Rebecca nodded. "He's angry with me. But it's something I have to deal with and nothing you have to worry about. Understand?"

"*Ya.*" Lindsay cupped her hand over her mouth and yawned. "I guess I'll head to bed. We're leaving early in the morning for work." She touched Rebecca's shoulder. "Good night."

"See you in the morning," Rebecca said.

Lindsay disappeared through the doorway, and Rebecca finished cleaning up the kitchen. She stepped into the living room and found Daniel sitting in his favorite chair while reading the Bible. His eyes met hers and a frown creased his face. He stood and headed up the stairs without saying a word.

Rebecca lowered herself onto the sofa. Her heart ached for him to speak to her, but she knew she couldn't change his mind about the situation. Her main focus was seeing Jessica come home. She'd handle Daniel later.

While rain pounded on the roof and splattered the windows, she leafed through the Bible and waited for the sound of Jessica coming through the door. After an hour, she fell asleep.

❁

Rebecca rolled over. Her first thought was that her neck ached. Sitting up, she glanced around the room. She was on the sofa in the living room. Why had she slept there?

Rubbing her eyes, she recalled that she had fallen asleep waiting for Jessica to return. Jessica had never come back in last night! She popped up and rushed up the stairs. Padding down the hallway, she spotted the door to Jessica's room open. Standing in the doorway, she found the bed still made, untouched since the day before. Panic coursed through Rebecca's veins.

Where's Jessica?

"She didn't come home?" Lindsay's voice sounded behind her as if reading Rebecca's thoughts.

Rebecca turned to see Lindsay standing in the doorway clad in her dress and apron. "I guess not," Rebecca said.

Her niece folded her arms across her chest, her eyes glittering with distress. "Do you think something happened to her?"

"I don't know." Rebecca shook her head. She scanned Jessica's room looking for clues, and her heart raced with question and worry. "Maybe she and Daniel left for work without waiting for Barry Holden. I'll go check." She peeked in her bedroom and found it empty and the bed made.

"They must've gone to work," Lindsay said, sidling up to her. "But I'd feel better if I knew for sure."

"I'll get changed," Rebecca said. "Let's go by the shop to make sure she's there."

"Sounds like a good plan." Her niece nodded, wiping her eyes.

❁

Jessica awoke when the bus pulled into the station in Virginia Beach. She'd endured a restless night, sleeping little between bus connections. Her brief dreams consisted of a mishmash of memories centering around her parents.

Anxiety and doubt filled her while she gathered up her belongings and climbed off the bus. She worried she'd made a mistake coming back to Virginia. What if Brian wasn't happy to see her? Would Lindsay ever forgive her for leaving without telling her where she was going?

Jessica pushed the uncertainty aside and approached a taxi

idling at the corner outside of the bus station. She opened the door and gave the driver Brian's address. She then loaded her bag into the backseat and climbed in.

A gentle sprinkle of rain peppered the windows while the taxi weaved through the busy roads. She glanced up at the dark clouds, which seemed to mirror her mood.

Yanking out her phone, she studied it. No missed calls or messages. She wondered if Lindsay had discovered she'd left yet.

A pang of guilt radiated through her. She should've told Lindsay she was leaving, but she knew her sister would never have understood. Now she had no way of reaching her, unless she called the bakery.

Jessica scrolled through to the bakery's number but snapped it closed before hitting Send. She couldn't call just yet, especially since the battery was almost dead. She wanted to talk to Brian first and then she'd call Lindsay.

Flipping the phone open again, she powered it off. She didn't want Lindsay trying to call her before she accomplished her mission.

The taxi steered down Brian's street and Jessica's stomach clenched. She hoped he was home and not at work. Cutting her eyes to her watch, she found it was almost eleven.

The taxi pulled up in front of Brian's house and stopped. Jessica's stomach soured when her eyes fell on Morgan's SUV parked in the driveway next to his pickup. She wondered why Morgan was there on a Monday morning when they should both have been working.

"This is the address, ma'am," the driver said.

"Thank you." Jessica fished her wallet from her purse, counted out the fare and a tip, and handed it to him.

"Would you like me to wait?" the driver asked.

"No, thank you," she said. "This may take awhile."

Gathering her duffle bag and purse, Jessica opened the door. She thanked the driver again and dashed through the rain to

Brian's parents' two-story brick colonial. She climbed the front steps and rang the bell.

After a few moments, the door opened slowly. Brian stood in the doorway clad in a T-shirt and boxers. His eyes widened with shock. "Jessica. What are you doing here?"

Confidence surged through her despite the hurt and disappointment rioting within her. "I thought I'd come and see why you stopped calling me." She dropped her bags on the wet cement porch. "Did you know yesterday was my birthday?"

"Yes, I did." He nodded. "Your gift's in the mail."

"Sure it is," she deadpanned, folding her arms.

"Brian?" a feminine voice called. "Who is it?"

Craning her neck to see past him, Jessica gasped when she spotted Morgan leaning in the doorway to the den wearing only one of Brian's T-shirts.

Morgan met her stare and shrieked. "Jessica? Oh no!"

"Jess," he said, grabbing her forearms. "It's not what you think."

"It's not what I think?" Jessica stepped out of his grip and shook her head. "Do you think I'm an idiot?"

"No." He gave her an apologetic expression. "I'm so sorry. We were planning to tell—"

"Save it, Brian." Jessica held her hands up. "You know, on second thought, I *am* stupid. My sister had already figured out you were cheating on me with Morgan. I guess I knew all along in my heart, but I was too stupid to admit it."

"I'm really sorry." He reached for her again, but she backed away. "Really, I am."

"Don't touch me," she warned. "I'll just leave."

"Jessica!" Morgan stood beside Brian. "This wasn't planned. It just happened. I'm sorry we didn't call you for your birthday. We were out all day, and the time just got away from us."

"Whatever." Jessica shook her head, her sour stomach making

her feel as if she were going to be sick. "Just leave me alone. Don't call me. Don't write me."

She heaved her bag onto her shoulder and started for the street, the rain splattering her blouse and pelting her hair. She absently wished she'd worn her windbreaker instead of shoving it in her duffel bag when she boarded the bus last night.

"Jessica!" Brian ran after her. "Just wait."

"No." She faced him. "There's nothing more to say. I've been a fool, and it's my own fault."

"Jess, I want to be friends." He gave a weak smile. "You were my first love."

Jessica laughed with sarcasm. "Like that means anything."

Morgan trotted down the front steps. "You're my best friend, Jess. Please forgive me."

Jessica glared at her, contemplating if she'd actually known her so-called best friend at all. "Go put on some clothes. The neighbors will talk." She cut her eyes to Brian. "I hope your parents aren't home. They might not be happy to find hanky-panky going on in their house."

"Jess, wait." He grabbed her arm again.

"Go back in the house and finish whatever it is you were doing." She backed away from them toward the street, not taking her glare off the two people who'd hurt her most of all.

A lump lodged in her throat with the realization she'd now lost everyone in her life — Lindsay, Trisha, Aunt Rebecca, Morgan, and Brian. She was utterly *alone*.

"Jessica! Wait!" Morgan yelled.

Without listening, Jessica stepped into the street. By the time she saw the truck speeding toward her and hydroplaning on the wet pavement, it was too late to get out of the way.

Brakes squealed, and something heavy knocked her backward. She felt her head hit the pavement and then everything went black.

❀

Rebecca rushed in through the back door of the shop.

"Rebecca?" Jake Miller rushed over to her. "Good morning."

Rebecca scanned the room behind him, searching for her niece. "Have you seen Jessica?"

He frowned. "She didn't come home last night?"

"No." Rebecca glanced over at her husband. His eyes met hers and he scowled. She pushed aside her disappointment in him and concentrated on Jessica.

"We thought maybe she came to work early," Lindsay said, standing beside Rebecca. "She's not here?"

Rebecca shook her head while her stomach twisted with icy fear. "I have a bad feeling."

Eli approached them. "What's going on?" he asked.

Daniel's younger brother Timothy also joined the group, a concerned expression clouding his face.

"Jessica is missing," Lindsay said. Her voice quavered as tears filled her eyes.

"She's missing?" Eli's eyes widened.

"I don't understand it," Jake said. "I thought she went home last night."

"Jessica was with you?" Eli's eyes narrowed. "Do you have something to tell us, Jacob?"

Jake's eyes widened. "What?" Recognition flashed through his eyes. "No, no!" He waved his hands. "Not like you mean. Jessica was upset last night. She walked to my house and asked me for a ride to the bus station."

"The bus station?" Eli asked.

"Oh no." Rebecca covered her mouth and groaned as panic gripped her. She did it! She ran away!

Daniel sidled up to his father, his eyes not moving from Rebecca. She met his stare, and intensity flashed between them.

She wished he'd speak, say anything. But he remained silent, breaking her heart into tiny pieces.

Lindsay shook her head. "Why didn't you stop her, Jake?" Her question wrenched Rebecca from her thoughts.

"I tried!" Jake said, gesturing with his hands for emphasis. "We talked, and I thought I had convinced her to go home. I offered to drive her back to the house, but she insisted on walking to clear her head."

"She never came home." Lindsay leaned on the counter behind her. "She went back to Virginia Beach." Her eyes filled with anxiety while she gazed over at Jake. "What do we do now?"

"We wait," Eli said. "We can't do anything until we hear for sure that she's in Virginia."

"*Ya*, you're right." Rebecca sighed. "I should've talked to her more last night. Maybe if I had listened to her, she wouldn't have run away."

"It's not your fault." Jake touched Rebecca's arm. "There's nothing that any of us could've said to make her stay. Her mind was made up." He pulled out his phone. "Why hasn't she called us?"

"Rebecca," a voice called from the other end of the shop.

Rebecca glanced over at Peter standing in the doorway.

"The phone is for you and Lindsay. It's someone named Morgan," her brother-in-law said.

"Morgan!" Lindsay yelled. "That's Jessica's best friend in Virginia."

Rebecca and Lindsay maneuvered through the workers in the shop toward the front. Rebecca snatched the receiver from Peter. "Hello?" she asked. "This is Rebecca Kauffman."

"Mrs. Kauffman," a young feminine voice said. "My name is Morgan. I'm Jessica's best—" She paused. "I'm Jessica's friend."

"Yes," Rebecca said, her stare fixed on the desk next to her.

"Jessica's mentioned you. Please tell me what's going on." Her heart pounded with anticipation.

"There's been an accident," the girl said.

"What?" Rebecca trembled, and Lindsay touched her arm. "What happened?"

"Jessica got hit by a truck." Morgan's voice was thick. "She's in the hospital."

"Oh no." Rebecca cupped her hand to her mouth, tears spilling from her eyes. Worry and guilt surged through her. She should've searched for Jessica last night. Maybe then she'd be okay. She should have stopped Jessica from running off!

Lindsay wrapped her arms around Rebecca. "What happened? Where's my sister? Please tell me!"

Jake lunged for the phone and held it to his ear. "Morgan?" he asked. "My name is Jake. I'm friends with Jessica. Can you tell me what's going on?"

He was silent while he listened on the phone. "I see," he finally said. "We'll be there as soon as we can. Thank you." Jake glanced over at Rebecca. "Whenever you're ready, we'll leave."

"What's going on?" Daniel asked as he stood in the doorway.

"Jessica's in the hospital in Virginia Beach," Jake said. "She was hit by a truck this morning."

Lindsay gasped.

Jake touched her arm. "Go pack a few things. I'll drive us all there."

Jessica moaned. Her head felt like it was stuck in a tightening vise. Pain radiated from her right ankle to her knee. She opened her eyes and stared up at a long fluorescent light, which was buzzing so loud that it echoed in her aching head.

Where am I?

She opened her mouth to speak and a moan escaped.

"Jessie?" a familiar voice asked. "Are you awake?"

Moving to her side, more pain shot up Jessica's leg, and she moaned again. *What's going on? Why do I hurt so badly?*

"Jessie, honey." Trisha stood over her. "Don't move. I'll get the nurse."

"Nurse?" The question came from Jessica's lips in a hoarse whisper.

"You're in the hospital." Trisha pushed a button.

"May I help you?" a nurse appeared in the doorway.

"Miss Bedford needs some pain medication, please," Trisha said.

"I'll get it right away," the nurse said, stepping back through the door. "I'll be right back."

Trisha leaned over Jessica and pushed her sweaty hair back from her face. "You really scared your family."

"What do you mean?" Jessica asked.

"You don't remember what happened?"

A wave of pain surged through her foot and stole her breath for a moment. Once the pain subsided, she shook her head.

"You were hit by a pickup truck in front of Brian's house." Trisha rubbed Jessica's arm.

Memories flashed through Jessica's mind like lightning. It all came back to her—her arguments with Lindsay and Aunt Rebecca, walking to Jake's house in the rain, boarding the bus, and finding Brian and Morgan together.

Jessica licked her dry lips and rubbed her throbbing temple. "How'd you find out I was here?" Her voice croaked.

"Morgan called your aunt at the furniture store. Before they left Lancaster County, Rebecca called me and asked me to come to the hospital and stay with you until she can get here." Trisha held her hand. "Your family is worried sick about you."

Jessica closed her eyes while regret rained down on her. She shouldn't have left without telling them. She was wrong to do that to Lindsay—and also to Rebecca.

"Brian and Morgan are in the waiting room," Trisha said. "Do you want to see them?"

Jessica shook her head. The last thing she needed was to see those two liars. How dare they make a fool of her by saying they were her best friends and then cheating behind her back!

"I didn't think so." Trisha gave a weak smile. "Morgan told me what happened and admitted they've been seeing each other behind your back." She shook her head with a disgusted expression. "They should be ashamed of themselves."

"Can you help me sit up?" Jessica asked.

"Sure." Her aunt pushed a button, and the bed creaked while lifting Jessica to a sitting position.

A nurse stepped into the room. "How are you feeling?"

"I'm sore," Jessica whispered. "My head feels like it's going to explode."

"This should take the edge off." The woman handed Jessica a small plastic cup with two pills in it.

Jessica swallowed the pills and sipped some water. "Why does my foot hurt so badly?"

"You broke your ankle in three places." The nurse took the cup. "You're going to be sore for quite a while."

Jessica leaned back in the bed and moaned. A broken ankle. She wondered how she was going to get around. What a nightmare. She should've just stayed in Bird-in-Hand. No, she didn't belong there.

Where *did* she belong?

"If you need anything else, just let me know." The nurse smiled. "My name is Kelley."

"Thanks," Jessica said.

"Why don't you close your eyes for a while? Lindsay and Rebecca won't be here for a few more hours." Trisha rubbed her arm again. "I'll be here with you."

"How are they getting here?" Jessica asked. "Are you picking them up at the bus station?"

Trisha shook her head. "Jake is driving them."

"Jake?" Jessica asked.

"Yes." Trisha raised her eyebrows. "Who's Jake?"

"A friend." Jessica's cheeks heated. "We work together at the furniture store."

"I guess he isn't Amish if he drives a car, huh?" Trisha's grin widened.

"No, but his grandfather is. His grandfather and Aunt Rebecca's father-in-law own the store." Jessica scanned the room for her purse. "If you can find my purse, I can show you a photo of him."

"You carry a photo of him?" Trisha opened the closet and pulled out her purse.

"Not exactly." Jessica took the purse and pulled out the new phone. "Jake gave me this for my birthday, and it has a camera in it." She pulled up his photo and handed the phone to Trisha. "I took his picture at my party the other night."

"Wow." Trisha grinned. "He's very handsome." She glanced at Jessica. "He bought you this phone for your birthday? He must really like you."

"I told you we're just friends." Taking the phone from Trisha, she glanced at Jake's image. She missed him already. How silly was that?

"Jake seems like a very nice young man," Trisha said, putting the purse back in the closet. "That means a lot that he'd drop everything and drive your aunt and sister here to be with you."

Nodding, Jessica closed her eyes.

"I bet he'd treat you better than Brian," her godmother said.

"We're just friends." Jessica yawned. "I think the pills are working. I'm so tired."

"You get some sleep," Trisha said.

Fading off to sleep, Jessica wondered when Jake would be there.

❈

Rebecca stared out the window while Jake steered his pickup truck through the streets of Virginia Beach. Her mind raced during the long ride from Lancaster County. She contemplated the situation over and over again with Daniel's and Jessica's words echoing in her mind.

Guilt mixed with regret poured down over her like the big, sloppy drops hitting the windshield and windows of the truck.

Rebecca wished she'd stopped Jessica from leaving. She never should've left Jessica on the porch with Lindsay. If Rebecca had paid more attention during the gathering, she could've gotten Jessica to talk to her instead of running away.

She glanced over as Jake steered onto another busy highway. Virginia Beach was the complete opposite of Bird-in-Hand. Instead of beautiful rolling farmlands and lush pastures, the area was overgrown with close-knit neighborhoods and businesses. Claustrophobia gripped Rebecca at the thought of living in such a densely populated area.

The wet pavement glistened under the bright streetlights. According to what Morgan had told Jake, rain had played a part in the accident. If it hadn't been raining, the truck wouldn't have swerved to avoid that fallen branch, and it wouldn't have hit Jessica after she'd stumbled into the street.

Her stomach twisted at the thought of Jessica in a hospital bed and injured from the accident. Rebecca hoped Jessica wasn't in pain, and she prayed Jessica wouldn't require surgery. She'd sent up multiple prayers that her niece would recover well and be able to come home soon.

Home. Sighing, she wondered where home should be for Jessica.

If Daniel had his way, Jessica's home would be here in Virginia Beach. Daniel hadn't said a word to Rebecca before they departed for Virginia.

Although she was angry with Daniel, his last words to her still haunted her. She couldn't help but wonder if he were right. While she was disappointed in her husband as well as in the rest of the community for not giving Jessica the patience she needed to adjust to their culture, she also wondered if it was time to let her go.

The thought caused her eyes to fill with tears and her heart to ache. Grace had relied on Rebecca to give the girls a good home. However, the home only seemed to agree with Lindsay.

Rebecca reflected on Jessica. The girl had said she was like her mother, and she needed to go back to her English life. Perhaps she was right, and making her stay to endure a life she hated was a mistake. She wondered if Jessica should leave as Grace had.

Elizabeth's words rang through her mind. Rebecca needed

to open her heart and listen to God. She needed to hear her husband. She needed to listen to Jessica.

Had Jessica been telling her the answer all along? Had Rebecca been too focused on her own needs to listen?

Closing her eyes, Rebecca sent up a prayer. She asked God to give her the answer. What had He been trying to tell her? Her heart and her ears were finally open to His Word.

Should she let Jessica live the life she yearned for in Virginia Beach or force her to live where she would be unhappy?

"This is it. Turn here," Lindsay said, breaking through Rebecca's thoughts.

The truck bounced into the parking lot of Sentara Princess Anne Hospital, and Rebecca's stomach twisted. She hoped Jessica was okay. She couldn't wait to give her a hug and tell her how much she loved her. All that mattered was that she was going to be fine, despite running away and the accident.

"Just park anywhere," Lindsay said. "The lot is always full."

"You used to come here often?" Jake steered into a space near the back of the lot.

"I've been here a few times," Lindsay said, leaning over into the front seat. "It seemed like I always had a friend in the hospital for something a while back. My one friend had her appendix out, and another friend's older sister had a baby here. It's a nice hospital. Good doctors."

"That's good to know," Rebecca said.

They navigated through the lot, parked, and walked into the hospital lobby. A nurse at the front desk directed them to Jessica's room.

Rebecca's stomach churned while they moved through the bustling hallway to the room. She trailed behind Lindsay and Jake, feeling uncomfortable in this strange environment. Rebecca hadn't been to a hospital since her father passed away ten years ago.

They approached the door, and Jake knocked.

Trisha opened the door, and gasped as her eyes fell on Lindsay. "Lindsay!" She wrapped her arms around her. "It's so good to see you."

"You too." Lindsay hugged her neck.

"Let me look at you." Trisha held Lindsay at arm's length, her eyes wild with surprise. "You've become Amish?"

Lindsay smiled, her cheeks turning a bright pink. "It helps me feel close to my mom."

Rebecca smiled, tears filling her eyes. She was so proud of Lindsay. She hoped Jessica would find where she belonged just as Lindsay had managed to do.

Trisha hugged Lindsay again. "You look lovely." Trisha glanced beyond Lindsay. "You must be Jake."

"Hi." He nodded. "How is she?"

"She's okay." Trisha nodded. "She took a little nap, and she's feeling better. They're going to release her tomorrow."

"That's wonderful." Rebecca breathed a sigh of relief.

Trisha gestured for them to come into the room. "She'd love to see you."

Jake and Lindsay entered the room, while Rebecca stayed behind.

"Rebecca?" Trisha asked, her eyebrows knitting in question. "Is something wrong?"

"I was wondering if we could go somewhere and talk." Rebecca fingered her apron while taking a deep breath.

"Sure. There's a waiting room just down the hallway." Trisha nodded and closed the door to Jessica's room.

Rebecca followed her down the short hallway to a small, empty room filled with chairs. A woman on the flat screen television screen hanging in the corner announced that the temperature would reach a sweltering one hundred and four degrees tomorrow.

"Can I get you a drink?" Trisha offered. "There are snack machines just around the corner."

"No, thank you. We stopped for a drink when we got to town." Rebecca lowered herself into a chair near the back corner of the room.

Trisha sat across from her. "So, what's on your mind?"

Rebecca took another deep breath, mustering all the strength she had left after the long, draining six-hour ride. "I've been doing some thinking about the girls."

"Oh?" Trisha asked, raising her eyebrows.

"While Lindsay has adjusted well to our lifestyle, Jessica has struggled. I love them both dearly, but I'm starting to wonder if what's best for Lindsay isn't the same as what's best for Jessica." Rebecca paused and glanced at the television, which featured a commercial for a car.

"Are you saying that Jessica should stay here?" Trisha asked.

"*Ya.*" Rebecca cleared her throat in hopes of stopping the lump swelling within it. "I want you to know that I haven't come to this decision easily. Jessica is having a difficult time fitting in. She's broken a few rules, and unfortunately some in our community have gone to our bishop to complain about her."

"What did she do that was so awful?" Trisha asked with a scowl.

"She shared her music with my niece Katie, and music isn't allowed in our community. She weeded my garden on a Sunday. Work isn't allowed on Sundays, and she was wearing a bikini top and shorts."

Trisha covered her mouth to stifle a laugh. "I'm sorry," she said. "I know that isn't funny."

"It's okay." Rebecca gave a weak smile. "She was seen kissing Jake and was caught alone with my nephew Samuel in a barn. I'm sure the encounters were innocent, but our community requires scrupulous adherence to the rules. The complaints were brought to Jessica's attention, and I know it has hurt her. Jessica has always felt alone, even though I've assured her that she has my support and love."

Rebecca paused to wipe her eyes and swallow the sobs caught in her throat. Saying the words out loud hurt more than she expected.

"I've tried to tell Jessica that I want her to stay no matter what. But even if she obeyed all the rules and the community accepted her, she would not be happy. She is so like my sister, Grace—so full of life and adventure. She needs more than we can offer her at home. With her running away, I see that forcing her to stay was very selfish of me." She wiped more tears. "I know that you had tried to get custody of the girls."

"I did, but the lawyers told me I had no rights to them." Trisha's smile faded. "I'm sorry I did that behind your back."

"It's okay. Your reason for doing it was understandable." Rebecca absently clasped her hands. "Would you consider allowing Jessica to stay with you?"

Trisha gasped, and Rebecca met her shocked expression.

"Yes," Trisha whispered. "I would be honored. I'll take good care of her."

Rebecca forced a smile, even though her heart was crying with the regret in her soul. "I want you to promise to have Jessica come visit us."

"Of course." Trisha nodded with emphasis. A concerned look overtook her face. "What about Lindsay?"

Rebecca sighed. "I'd prefer to keep her with me, but I'll let her make that decision. I don't want to separate the girls if they prefer to stay together."

"Of course." Trisha nodded.

"I guess we better tell them." Rebecca stood. "Thank you."

"No." Trisha rose and hugged her. "Thank you."

Closing her eyes, Rebecca prayed she'd made the right decision.

29

Rebecca stood in the doorway of the hospital room and watched Jessica smile at her sister. Jessica's skin was pale, and her dark hair framed her face, making her look like a china doll she'd seen in the gift shops back home.

"Go on," Trisha whispered. "I'm sure she'll be happy to see you."

Jessica met her gaze, and the girl's eyes welled with tears. "Hi."

When Rebecca stepped into the room, Jake rose from his chair next to the bed and gestured for Rebecca to sit.

"Thank you." Rebecca sank into the seat. "Hi," she said to her niece. "How are you feeling?"

"Kinda sore." Jessica licked her lips. "I'm sorry for running off. It was thoughtless and stupid."

"I'm sorry too," Rebecca said. "I was wrong to not listen to you and see what you really needed." She clasped Jessica's hand. "I'm just glad you're okay. You gave us quite a scare." She squeezed her hand. "Trisha and I wanted to talk to you about something." She cut her gaze to Trisha, who nodded.

"Lindsay." Trisha fished her wallet from her purse and handed Lindsay a few bills. "How about you and Jake go get a snack?"

"Oh. Okay." Lindsay shot Jake a confused expression.

Amy Clipston

Trisha walked Lindsay and Jake to the door and explained how to find the snack machines. After they left, she closed the door behind them.

"Are you guys having an intervention or something?" Jessica asked, looking between Rebecca and Trisha.

"No, not an intervention, but we need to talk." Trisha sank into a chair on the other side of the bed from Rebecca.

"I'm in trouble, right?" Jessica sighed. "Look, I'm really sorry. Running away was immature and stupid. I never should've—"

"It's okay." Rebecca patted her niece's arm. "That's not what we want to discuss with you."

"Oh." Jessica's eyes simmered with confusion. "So, what's going on?"

"I spoke with Trisha, and she said that she'd be happy to have you live with her." Rebecca held her breath, again praying she was making the right decision.

"What did you say?" Jessica whispered, an expression of disbelief overtaking her pretty face.

"I've been doing a lot of thinking about you and how unhappy you've been." Rebecca sucked in a breath as tears again threatened her eyes. "I want what's best for you and your sister, and forcing you to live somewhere that makes you unhappy is not what's best for you."

Tears shimmered in Jessica's eyes. "You're going to let me move in with Trisha?" she asked, her voice thick with emotion.

"If that's what you want, then that's what I want." Rebecca rubbed her arm. "I love you, Jessica. All I ever wanted was what was best for you and what would make your mother happy. I don't think Grace would want you to be unhappy. And I don't think that's what God wants either. I haven't been listening to what's really His will. Daniel has been trying to tell me that it isn't right to force you to live by our rules, and I wasn't listening. I've only heard what I wanted."

Rebecca pushed a dark lock of hair back from Jessica's face. "Besides, you look just like your mother. I need to let you go like I had to let her go."

"Thank you," Jessica whispered, tears spilling over her pink cheeks. "Thank you so much."

Rebecca nodded as her own tears began to fall.

"I'm so sorry for all the trouble I caused," Jessica said, swiping her tears from her cheek.

"Don't you worry about anything," Rebecca said. "Just promise to be good and also visit me as often as you can. I'll send you a bus ticket."

"Thank you, Aunt Rebecca." Jessica squeezed her hand. "I love you."

Rebecca's heart warmed. Jessica had finally called her "aunt," and she finally said that she loved her. Leaning down, she gave her niece a warm hug.

Jessica then turned to Trisha. "Thank you too."

"You just get better." Trisha rubbed her shoulder. "Then we'll get your new room set up."

"Will you send my things?" Jessica asked Rebecca. "I really want my quilt that you gave me."

"Of course," Rebecca said.

The door clicked open, and Lindsay and Jake walked in carrying cans of soda and small bags of chips.

"Is everything okay?" Lindsay asked, lowering herself into a chair.

"Yeah." Jessica wiped her eyes. "I'm staying here. I'm going to live with Trisha."

Lindsay gasped. "What?" She gave Rebecca a questioning glance.

Rebecca nodded. "It's true. I decided it would be best for Jessica to stay and finish high school. You can stay too, if that's what you want. All I want is for you girls to be happy." She held her breath. Losing Jessica would be difficult, but losing them both would be devastating.

Lindsay turned her gaze to her sister. "If it's okay with you, I'd like to stay with Aunt Rebecca. I'm happy there."

Jessica gave her a weak smile. "I understand. But we'll visit each other as often as we can. I'll even leave you the phone so we can text each other."

Lindsay nodded. "How about you learn how to write a letter?" She popped up and hugged her sister. "I'll miss you."

"I'll miss you too." Jessica wiped more tears.

Jake placed his drink on the floor and moved over to her bed. "You're leaving me, huh?"

Jessica nodded, wiping more tears. "But we'll still be friends."

"Of course we will." He kissed her cheek. "I expect you to use that new phone and call me at least once a week."

Rebecca hugged her arms to her chest and smiled. Although it hurt to see Jessica leave Lancaster County, she knew in her heart that she'd made the right decision.

❁

Rebecca stepped into the guest room at Trisha's home later that evening. After placing her clothes on the dresser, she turned to find Lindsay standing in the doorway.

"Hi," Lindsay said. "Can we talk for a minute?"

"Come in." Rebecca motioned for her to enter the room. "I was just heading to bed."

"Me too." Her niece sat on the edge of the double bed. "It's been a long day. Jake already went to bed. I heard Trisha say that Jessica is coming home, I mean here, tomorrow."

"That's what I heard too." Rebecca ran a brush through her long hair.

"I'm going to miss her, but I'm glad that she'll finally be

happy. She's been so miserable since Mom and Dad died." Lindsay bit her bottom lip. "Have you called Uncle Daniel?"

Rebecca sighed. "No. I was thinking about leaving a message at the shop."

"You should." Her niece nodded toward the phone. "Do you want me to dial?"

"I guess so." Rebecca sat on the bed.

Lindsay dialed the phone and handed it to her.

Rebecca cleared her throat while the answering machine picked up and Eli spoke, telling the caller to leave a message after the beep. Once the beep sounded, Rebecca spoke.

"Hello. This is Rebecca. I wanted to tell Daniel that Jessica is fine." She closed her eyes and searched for the right words. "We're planning on leaving to come home tomorrow. We'll see you sometime tomorrow night." She then disconnected and replaced the phone in the cradle.

When she turned to her niece, she found the girl staring at her with her eyes wide with confusion.

"Why didn't you tell him that Jessica is staying here?" Lindsay asked.

"I'll tell him when the time is right." Rebecca turned the covers down on the bed.

"Why are you afraid to tell him?" her niece asked.

"I'm not afraid." Rebecca lowered herself onto the bed. "I just feel it would be best to tell him in person."

Lindsay fingered the cuff on her plain white gown. "Can I stay in here?"

"Of course." Rebecca patted the space next to her. "Turn off the light and get in."

Her niece flipped off the light switch, climbed into the bed next to her, and snuggled down.

Rebecca shifted in the bed until she found a comfortable spot. Her thoughts swirled, wondering if she'd made the right decision and how Daniel would react when he learned that Jessica wasn't returning with them. She pondered if he'd ever open up to her and accept her back into his heart. She prayed their marriage would heal and their family would return to normal.

Her thoughts then turned to Lindsay and her happiness. Would Lindsay regret her decision to stay in Bird-in-Hand? She wondered if separating the girls was what Grace would truly want.

Rebecca sighed as confusion and doubt overtook her. She needed her husband's support. Making these decisions alone was a mistake.

"Aunt Rebecca," Lindsay whispered through the dark.

"*Ya?*" Rebecca asked.

"I want you to know I think you did the right thing by letting Jessica stay."

Rebecca was speechless for a moment while she considered if her niece had read her thoughts. "*Danki,*" she finally said. "I appreciate that."

"I'll miss my sister, but I think it's best for her to stay here."

"What about you?" Rebecca turned toward her, wishing she could see the girl's expression through the darkness. "Are you certain you want to come back to Bird-in-Hand with me?"

"*Ya.*" Lindsay said. "I'm sure. I want to be with you. I feel like the Kauffmans are my family now. Besides, I'll see my sister plenty. I'm sure she'll come to visit to see Jake. I think they belong together, but they haven't figured it out yet."

Rebecca smiled and touched Lindsay's arm through the dark. "I think you're right. You're wise beyond your years, young lady. Now, get some sleep. We have a long ride home tomorrow after your sister is settled here."

"Good night."

"Good night." Rebecca closed her eyes and smiled. She looked forward to getting Jessica settled and then heading home. Turning her thoughts to prayer, she thanked God for helping her see the answers that had been there all along.

Scripture Cake

1/2 cup butter (Judges 5:25)
2 cups flour (1 Kings 4:22)
1/4 tsp salt (Leviticus 2:13)
1 cup figs (1 Samuel 30:12)
1 – 1/2 cups sugar (Jeremiah 6:20)
2 tsp baking powder (Luke 13:21)
1/2 cup water (Genesis 24:11)
1 cup raisins (1 Samuel 30:12)
3 eggs, separated (Isaiah 10:14)
1/4 tsp each — cinnamon, nutmeg, cloves (1 Kings 10:10)
1 Tbsp honey (Proverbs 24:13)
3/4 cup almonds (Genesis 43:11)

Blend butter, sugar, spices, and salt. Add beaten egg yolks. Sift in baking powder and flour then add the water and honey. Chop fruit and nuts and flour well. Fold in stiffly beaten egg whites. Bake 50 minutes at 375 degrees.

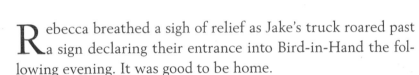

30

Rebecca breathed a sigh of relief as Jake's truck roared past a sign declaring their entrance into Bird-in-Hand the following evening. It was good to be home.

The day had been long, beginning with getting Jessica settled in Trisha's house. Although she was sore from the accident, Jessica looked well. Rebecca's heart ached at the thought of leaving her niece in Virginia Beach. However, despite the pain, she knew it was the right choice.

Jake and Lindsay had been quiet most of the six-hour ride to Lancaster. After asking Rebecca's permission, Jake had turned on a country music station and hummed most of the way back. Rebecca assumed Jake missed Jessica almost as much as she did. A smile crept across Rebecca's lips at the memory of Lindsay's words last night. Maybe Jessica and Jake did belong together. They'd promised to keep in touch, so only time would tell.

Lindsay and Jessica had cried when they said good-bye. Rebecca hoped that the separation wouldn't be too hard on the sisters. Rebecca had asked Lindsay several times if she was sure she wanted to remain in Pennsylvania. Each time, Lindsay had said yes. Rebecca was happy to have her niece with her; however, she wanted to be certain it was Lindsay's decision.

Rebecca's stomach clenched as Jake's truck bounced up Beechdale Road toward her homestead. A mixture of panic and anger surged through her at the thought of seeing Daniel and telling him that Jessica had stayed in Virginia. She was nervous about his reaction and also angry that he'd been right about Jessica. She'd desperately wanted him to be wrong. She'd wanted Jessica to adjust to living in Lancaster County, and she'd hoped that the community would give her the love and patience she'd needed.

Now she was arriving home with only Lindsay, and she wondered if she and Daniel could work things out. The truck merged onto Gibbons Road, and Rebecca sucked in a deep breath. Anticipation of seeing Daniel surged through Rebecca when Jake steered into the dirt lane leading to her home.

"Well, here we are," Jake said, nosing his truck to the end of the driveway. "Home again, home again, as my grandmother always says."

As Rebecca glanced at Jake, he gave her a wide grin.

"Corny, I know." His smile faded while he drummed his fingers on the steering wheel.

"You miss her already?" Rebecca asked, touching his hand.

"Yeah." He leaned back, letting his head smack the headrest on the seat. "Who's going to sponge a charge for her phone off my truck battery?"

"It's okay." Lindsay leaned over the seat and touched his shoulder. "I made her promise she'd visit before school starts in August, so we'll see her before the summer is over."

He gave her a weak smile. "Good." He held up his phone. "I'll call her in a few days. Let me know if you want to talk to her too."

"I will. Thanks." Lindsay grabbed her bag. "Well, I'm tired. I'm ready to grab a bite to eat and then call it a night." She cut her eyes to Rebecca. "How about you?"

"*Ya.*" Rebecca wrenched open the door on the truck. "I'm tired too." Her stomach twisted as her eyes fell on the back door. She assumed Daniel was sitting in his favorite chair reading the Bible. She absently wondered if he'd missed her and if he'd worried about their safe arrival home.

Rebecca climbed down, and Jake met her at the back of the truck with her bag over his shoulder. "Thank you for driving us. You're very generous." She pulled her money from the pocket deep within her apron. "This should cover the gas."

"No, no." He waved off the offer. "It was my pleasure."

"Please take it." She put the money in his palm and closed his fingers over it. "I insist."

"All right." He slipped the money into his pocket. "Thank you." He nodded toward the house. "I'll walk you in."

"Would you like something to eat?" Lindsay asked while they walked toward the back door.

"No, thanks," Jake said. "I want to get home and get to bed. Work comes early in the morning."

Rebecca led them in the back door. Her body trembled at the thought of seeing Daniel. She wondered if he'd be happy to see her. Would he even speak to her?

Jake placed her bag on the floor and scanned the kitchen. "I'll say hi to Daniel and then head out."

"I bet he's in the living room." Lindsay gestured for him to follow her. "Hi, Uncle Daniel. We're home."

Rebecca remained cemented in the doorway while Daniel stood from his favorite chair and shook Jake's hand.

"I'm glad to see you made it home safely," Daniel said, idly pulling on his beard. "Thank you for your help. You've had an exhausting couple of days, no?"

"Yes, we have." Jake chuckled. "You sure can say that."

"I'm going to head upstairs," Lindsay said. "Thanks for the ride, Jake. I'll see you around."

"Good night." Jake waved. He turned back to Daniel. "I guess I'll see you at the shop tomorrow. Have a nice evening."

"You too, Jake. Thank you for bringing the girls home safely." Daniel shook his hand again. "Good night."

"Good night, sir." Jake smiled at Rebecca as he passed through the doorway. "Good night."

"Thank you, Jake." Rebecca watched him disappear through the back door. When the door clicked shut, she cleared her throat and faced her husband. She hoped he would greet her with a hug and kiss and then welcome her home.

However, he frowned and the tension radiated through her. Part of her wanted to rush over and kiss him in an effort to change his mood. Instead, she stood glued to the same spot, her pride holding her back from making amends. They studied each other in silence for what felt like an eternity.

"Where is Jessica?" he finally asked, folding his arms across his chest.

"You got your wish," she whispered, her voice wavering.

His eyebrows careened toward his hairline. "What do you mean?"

"You won," she whispered, heaving her bag on her shoulder.

He stepped toward her. "I don't understand."

"She stayed in Virginia Beach." A tear trickled down her hot cheek, and she impatiently swiped it away. "You won, Daniel."

He stared at her, his expression impassive. "That is probably for the best."

Disappointment twisted around her heart. He hadn't changed. He was still the cold, stubborn man she'd left at the shop yesterday. Their marital problems remained despite everything.

"Good night," she whispered before she turned and slowly made her way upstairs. Closing the door, she dropped onto the bed and sobbed. She'd lost her niece and her husband.

She'd listened to God and let her niece go. However, the distance between her and Daniel remained.

"Please God, guide me in how to save my marriage," she whispered. "Show me how to reach Daniel's heart."

❊

Lindsay rushed into the kitchen of the bakery a week later. "Are we out of molasses cookies? A woman came in and requested two dozen."

"Two dozen?" Sarah's eyes widened with shock. "I've got a dozen in the oven, but I haven't even started rolling out the next dozen. Can she come back in a couple of hours or does she need them right now?"

"I'll ask." Lindsay dashed back to the front, the ties of her prayer *Kapp* bouncing with her fast pace.

"It's amazing how quickly Lindsay has become a part of our family," Sarah said with a grin.

"*Ya*, I know," Rebecca said, standing by her youngest sister-in-law. "I feel as if she's always lived with Daniel and me." She rolled out the dough.

"How are things?" Sarah asked, studying Rebecca as if she could see into her soul. "I mean, how are things really?"

"Not much has changed. Daniel still refuses to speak to me unless he's reading to us during our devotions, asking what's for supper, or asking if I've checked the mailbox." Rebecca bit her bottom lip, hoping to stop the threatening tears. His silence cut into her soul like a razor.

"Rebecca." Sarah touched her arm and gave her a sympathetic frown. "I know my brother is stubborn. He's the spitting image of our father, both physically and emotionally. Have you tried speaking to him?"

Rebecca wiped her hands on her apron. "I've made a few attempts to make conversation by asking about his day, but I only get one-word answers. He's been like this since the bishop came to see him about Jessica."

"Just give him time," Sarah said. "You two will get through this. It's just a bump in the road as *Mamm* says."

"But if I wait too long I'm afraid I'll lose him." Rebecca blew out a frustrated sigh. "I told him that he got his wish since Jessica stayed in Virginia. I don't know what else to do."

"It's because of us, isn't it?" Lindsay's voice was meek behind Rebecca. "Me and my sister ruined your life with Daniel."

"No, no!" Rebecca spun and hugged her niece. "It's not you. The problems Daniel and I have are of our own making. You and Jessica did nothing wrong."

Her niece nodded, but her eyes glimmered with evidence that she wasn't convinced.

"Listen to me, Lindsay." Rebecca cupped her niece's face in her hands. "You and your sister are two of the most important people in my life. I love you both dearly. Daniel is just being stubborn. This is about Daniel and me, and you don't have anything to worry about. Do you understand?"

"*Ya.*" Lindsay nodded. "I understand."

"What did the woman say about the cookies?" Sarah asked.

"She said this afternoon was fine." Lindsay snatched a knife. "Can I help you cut out the cookies?"

"*Ya.*" Sarah smiled. "I'd like that."

Rebecca stepped over to the counter and stopped short when a wave of nausea suddenly crashed over her. Groaning, she lowered herself onto a stool.

"You okay?" Sarah asked, rushing to her side. "You look a bit green."

"*Ya.*" Rebecca placed a hand on her clammy forehead. "I suddenly don't feel too great."

Sarah raised her eyebrows. "What's wrong?"

"I don't know." Rebecca hugged her queasy stomach. "I feel kind of uneasy. It came on quickly."

Lindsay filled a glass with water and brought it to Rebecca. "You look like you could use this."

"*Danki.*" Rebecca took a long drink.

"You sit." Her niece rubbed her shoulder. "Me and Sarah will take care of the cookies."

Rebecca contemplated Sarah's words while her sister-in-law and niece cut out cookies. Waiting for Daniel to open up to her didn't seem like a wise plan. She worried that if she waited too long, the distance between them would grow to an irreconcilable chasm. She craved the close marriage and friendship they'd once enjoyed.

Rebecca missed the intimacy, the comfortable camaraderie, the friendship. She prayed that somehow they would renew their love, but it seemed impossible. She'd never known Daniel to carry such a grudge. He was so cold to her that she wondered if any love for her remained in his heart.

Despair surged through her veins as another wave of nausea overtook her. She hoped God would give her the guidance she needed to reach out to her husband and find the love they once had.

Go to him. Apologize.

The words sang through her veins. She bit her lip and held her breath. Yes, she needed to apologize.

31

Daniel scanned the shop for his father while a table saw buzzed on a neighboring workbench. The stench of burning metal stung his nostrils. Glancing across the large room, he spotted Jake speaking to Peter and Timothy.

"Jake," Daniel bellowed, raising his voice over the bang of hammers and whizzing of the table saw behind him. "Have you seen my *dat?*"

"Yeah." Jake gestured toward the front of the store. "He's out front with a customer."

The scent worsened, and Daniel shook his head. Couldn't Silas smell that? He glared toward the older man. "Silas!" Daniel yelled.

The middle-aged man stopped sawing and gave Daniel a confused look.

"Can't you smell that?" Daniel asked, raising his arms in question.

Silas sniffed and then nodded.

"Turn that saw off before you burn down the shop." Daniel gestured toward his workbench. "Use mine if you like."

"*Danki*, Daniel." Silas schlepped over to Daniel's work area and snatched his saw.

Daniel blew out a frustrated sigh on his way to the front of the shop. He sometimes wondered how aware of their surroundings his coworkers were. Their disregard for safety often made his stomach sick.

Stepping into the front of the shop, Daniel found his father helping a customer while the phone rang. He rushed over and answered the call, quoting prices and product information before disconnecting.

"*Danki*, Daniel," his father said after the customer left the store. "It's been like that all morning." He wiped his brow. "I don't know how Jessica kept up with the customers and stayed sane."

A tidal wave of guilt crashed over Daniel at the mention of his niece's name. He frowned and cut his eyes to the desk, hoping to avoid his father's questioning glance.

Daniel had been struggling with how to apologize to his wife ever since she and Lindsay had arrived back in Lancaster a week ago.

He blamed himself for how badly Jessica's short stay in Lancaster County had unfolded. Over and over, he wished he had stood up to his brother and the bishop on Jessica's behalf. However, he still believed that Jessica belonged back with the English. She wasn't happy here and never would be despite Rebecca's best efforts to show the girl love and support.

He hadn't realized, though, how much he'd hurt Rebecca until the night she returned from Virginia. His heart had broken into a million pieces when she uttered the words, "You got your wish." The pain on her beautiful face and the hurt in her gorgeous eyes stung him deep in his soul.

He'd wanted to beg for her forgiveness, and he longed to tell her that he loved her. He needed her to know that he supported her decision to let Jessica stay in Virginia and he only wanted what was best for the girls. Yet, the realization of how much he'd hurt her rendered him speechless. The words never formed in his mouth; they were stuck in his throat.

He'd continued to spend each night on the sofa. He never

slept; he simply stared at the shadows on the ceiling and turned over ways to express how much he loved her and wanted to start over.

Now, a week later, the pain was so deep and so raw in her eyes that he feared he'd lost her forever. If only he could form the words to apologize.

"Daniel?" his father's voice wrenched him back to the present.

"*Ya?*" He glanced at his father.

"You okay?" *Dat* asked.

Daniel paused, gathering his thoughts. "*Dat*, have you and *Mamm* ever disagreed on things? I mean *really* disagreed to the point where it affected your relationship?"

Dat chortled as he sank onto the desk chair. "Are you joking? Of course we have. Why do you ask?" His expression became solemn. "Are you and Rebecca still having problems?"

Daniel nodded. "I guess you could say that. I've hurt her, and I'm not sure how to fix things between us. I'm worried I may have lost her forever."

Dat stood and patted Daniel's shoulder. "Son, I doubt you lost her forever."

"*Nee*, I think I have." Daniel sat on the desk, absently pulling on his beard. "You should see how she looks at me. It's like her love for me is dead. She despises me."

"Rebecca loves you. If you can't see that, tell her you're sorry. Tell her how you feel." *Dat* gave him a weak smile. "Your mother and I have had our ups and downs. We were always careful to keep our problems to ourselves, so that you and your siblings never worried about us. I learned over the years to always remind her that no matter what, I loved her. Saying those words got us through the tough times."

Daniel contemplated *Dat's* words, resting his chin on his hand. "That makes sense. I need to find the right words."

"Speak what's in here." *Dat* pointed to his chest. "The words will come to you if you listen to your heart."

Daniel smacked his father's shoulder. *"Danki."*

"But that's not it." His father waved a finger in the air for emphasis. "If you remember one thing, remember this—marriage is a compromise."

"A compromise?" Daniel folded his arms across his chest.

"Ya, that's right. A compromise." *Dat* rubbed his long beard. "As the Bible says, a woman should submit to her husband—but I think the man should submit to his wife as well."

Daniel stared at *Dat's* tired eyes. He felt as if a light had been awakened within him. Never before had he thought of marriage as a compromise.

Now he understood what he needed to do to win her back—he needed to listen to her, respect her opinions, and love her with all of his heart.

A scream from the shop startled Daniel. He stuck his head in the doorway just as an explosion shook the building. Daniel fell backward, slamming his back into the desk. He turned to his father and found him staring wild-eyed at the door.

Smoke filled Daniel's lungs and he choked on his words for a moment. "Call nine-one-one," Daniel yelled through the smoke quickly filling the room. "Call now!"

Standing, Daniel staggered toward the door while smoke stung his eyes. He cupped his hands over his mouth and made his way into the shop.

Smoke blurring his vision, he dropped to his knees and crawled toward the silhouette of a body on the floor. "Hello?" he called. "Is anyone there? If you can hear me, get out of the building! Get out now!"

❈

Rebecca removed another Shoo-Fly pie from the oven and set it on the cooling rack. Wiping her hands on her apron, she closed her eyes while another wave of nausea gripped her.

"You okay?" Beth Anne asked, rushing over and taking Rebecca's arm. "Have a seat." She steered Rebecca to a stool and helped her sit.

Rebecca took deep breaths and fanned her face with her hands. "I don't understand it. This is the second time this morning I've felt like I was going to be sick."

A grin formed on her sister-in-law's lips.

"What?" Rebecca asked. She took deep breaths until the feeling subsided.

"Are you expecting?" Kathryn asked with a grin.

"Rebecca?" Sarah rushed over. "You're pregnant?"

"*Nee!*" Rebecca held her hands up. "Please. I just have a stomach flu. No one said anything about me being pregnant. Please don't say that." A frown turned down her lips. "Daniel and I have tried for fifteen years. I doubt that it could happen now."

"They say that it happens when you stop expecting it," Kathryn said with a coy smirk.

"*Ya*, but we stopped hoping for it years ago when the doctor told us that it was impossible." Rebecca started to stand and stopped when a dizzy spell overcame her. Groaning, she put her hands to her face and shut her eyes, hoping that the horrible dizzy and queasy feelings would subside.

"She's pregnant," Beth Anne whispered.

"*Ya*," Kathryn chimed in. "I think so."

"I'm not pregnant," Rebecca said. "It's not possible. I just have the flu."

Kathryn turned to her youngest sister. "How are you feeling, Sarah? Has your morning sickness gotten any better?"

Sarah shrugged. "*Ya*. It's not so bad. I still feel sick but not as often."

The muffled sound of a ringing phone sounded from the front of the store.

"How are things with Peter?" Rebecca asked. "You'd told your mom that he was acting strangely and cold."

Sarah frowned. "He's the same. It's like he's a different person. I'm really concerned."

"Girls!" Elizabeth's urgent voice interrupted Rebecca's thoughts. "We must leave at once!"

Rebecca spun, facing her mother-in-law's panicked expression.

"I just got a call from Irma Zimmerman," she said. "The furniture store is on fire."

"What?" Beth Anne gasped.

"On fire?" Kathryn asked. "Is *Dat* okay?"

Feeling lightheaded, Rebecca's stomach dropped. "Daniel," she whispered.

"Peter!" Sarah cried.

"I've already locked up. Nina Janitz, one of our regular English customers, is going to drive us over there. Let's go!" Elizabeth hollered, rushing out the back door.

32

The thick black smoke billowed into the air as the van sped closer to the furniture store. When the sight of the building engulfed in flames came into view, Rebecca gasped. Terror and panic rioted within her while the flashing lights from the half-dozen fire trucks blinded her.

The van screeched to a stop, and Rebecca and Sarah leaped to the sidewalk. They rushed into the knot of people standing near a line of police officers.

"Daniel!" Rebecca shouted. "Daniel!" She searched the sea of faces for her husband.

"Ma'am," a police officer took her arm and pulled her back. "You need to stay back here. You can't get any closer to the building."

"My husband's in there!" Rebecca's body trembled and tears threatened. "I have to find him. I have to see him. I have to—" Her voice cracked as tears trickled from her eyes.

"Shh." A strong arm pulled her close. "The firefighters will get him out."

She glanced up into Jake's eyes. "Jake," she whispered. "I'm so frightened."

"I know." He rubbed her arm. "Me too."

"Is he still inside?" She wiped her eyes while she stood

before him. The scent of burning wood filled her nostrils, and her body trembled with fear.

He nodded. "I think so. I saw Mr. Kauffman, Timothy, and a few of the guys, but I haven't seen Daniel, Silas, or Peter."

"Where's Peter!" Sarah grabbed Jake's sleeve and shook him. Her eyes were wild with panic. "Where is he? I can't find him."

"The firefighters are working to get everyone out," Jake said. His voice quavered, and he cleared his throat. He looked as worried as Rebecca felt.

"He's inside?" Sarah bit her lip and tears streamed down her cheeks. "He has to be okay! He has to. He just has to." She sobbed, hugging Rebecca.

Rebecca held on to her sister-in-law and closed her eyes. She prayed for her husband and the rest of the men to be delivered from the fire safely.

Gazing toward the building, Rebecca watched in horror as the roof on the back of the building collapsed, shaking the ground beneath her feet. She screamed.

"Daniel!" She pushed past Sarah and rushed toward the building. "Daniel! No!"

"Rebecca! Rebecca wait!" A strong arm held her back and Jake gazed down at her. "He'll be fine. I promise you."

"No." She shook her head while tears poured from her eyes. "This can't be happening. He can't die. We have too much to work out. I need to tell him I'm sorry for being so stubborn and not listening to him. I need to tell him that no matter what, I love him and how much our life together means to me. He can't die. He just can't!"

She sobbed into Jake's chest while memories of how she and Daniel courted and then married poured down over her. She loved him so much that her heart ached for him. She longed to feel his arms around her and hear his voice in her ear while they snuggled in bed at night.

"Aunt Rebecca." Lindsay's timid voice yanked her back from her thoughts. "Aunt Rebecca. Is Uncle Daniel in there?"

Unable to speak, Rebecca studied her niece's eyes and nodded.

"Oh no." Tears spilled down Lindsay's pale cheeks. She hugged Rebecca, and they cried while holding onto each other.

"Rebecca," a voice in her ear said. "Rebecca. It's Daniel."

Rebecca spun and wiped her cheeks while Daniel walked toward her, a firefighter on each side of him, holding onto his arms. His dark blue shirt was tattered and black with soot. His blond hair and beard were peppered with dirt and black streaks lined his handsome face.

His gaze met hers, and his expression softened. He opened his arms to her, his eyes glistening with tears.

"Daniel!" She ran toward him and wrapped her arms around his neck. "Oh Daniel," she whispered in his ear. "I was so scared!"

"Oh, *mei Fraa*," he whispered, holding her close to his lean body. "*Mei* Becky. I'm so sorry. I love you more than words can express. I'm so sorry for everything."

"No, I'm sorry," she said, her voice quavering with the love and relief surging through her. "I was so wrong not to listen to you. I was wrong not to listen to Jessica and realize what was best for her."

He gazed down at her, his fingers tracing her face. "I'm sorry for forcing you to let Jessica go. I never realized how it hurt you."

"But I was wrong, not you. I wasn't listening to what you and Jessica were trying to tell me. I wasn't listening to God. I was so, so wrong. It wasn't God's will for her to stay here and be unhappy. I was so very wrong. I'm sorry for hurting you." She ran her hand down his cheek, wiping away the soot. "I love you, Daniel. I want to start over."

"*Ya*." He cupped her face with his hands. "Me too." Leaning down, he brushed his lips across hers, sending warmth and hope surging through her body.

Rebecca glanced around, silently counting the men who were gathered near the ambulances. They were all covered in soot, their faces and beards blackened with evidence of the fire. Biting her lip, Rebecca realized who was missing.

"Peter," she whispered, staring at her husband. "Where is he?"

Daniel shook his head. "I don't know. I didn't see him."

"Excuse me," a voice behind her said. "We need to make sure you're okay, sir." An Emergency Medical Technician nodded toward the ambulance.

"But where is Peter?" she asked, her heart hammering in her chest.

"We'll find him." He touched her cheek. "I'll be right back." Daniel glanced down at Rebecca. "You go make sure *Mamm* and Sarah are okay."

"Okay." She brushed her lips to his. She then watched him walk over to the ambulance, silently praying and thanking God for delivering him safely from the fire.

A scream sounded behind them, and Rebecca spun to see Sarah sobbing and holding onto her mother. Her father stood nearby rubbing Sarah's back. Rebecca rushed over and touched her mother-in-law's arm. Elizabeth glanced up and Rebecca gasped at the pain in her eyes.

"Peter perished in the fire," her mother-in-law whispered. "The firefighters found his body. He's gone."

"No," Rebecca said, shaking her head. "No, no! It can't be!"

"What happened?" Timothy asked, stomping up to Rebecca and looking from her to his mother and sister. He was covered in soot like Daniel.

"Peter died in the fire," his *mamm* said, her eyes filling with tears.

"Peter?" Timothy grimaced. "Peter's gone?"

"*Ya,*" Elizabeth said, wiping her cheek.

Timothy embraced Rebecca and they sobbed together. Closing her eyes, Rebecca prayed for her lost brother-in-law and his family.

❄

Rebecca pulled on her nightgown and lowered herself into the chair in her bedroom. She pulled the pins out of her bun, letting her hair fall to her waist. While running the brush through it, she silently prayed Sarah would find strength and hope in the coming days.

The funeral earlier today had been draining. Sarah had been so distraught that Rebecca's heart broke for her. She wished somehow the hands of time would turn back, and Peter would be saved. But Rebecca knew that wasn't how life worked.

The door creaked open and Daniel stepped in, clad in his nightclothes. His eyes met hers, and his stern expression softened, causing her heart to pound in her chest. She was so thankful to have her husband back.

Biting her lower lip with anticipation, she idly ran her hand over her stomach and wondered if now was the appropriate time to share her news. Perhaps some good news would be welcome in light of the tragedy that had unfolded.

At the insistence of Beth Anne, Rebecca had used a pregnancy test yesterday after she'd returned from visiting Sarah. When the plus sign appeared, Rebecca was filled with a radiating joy like she'd never felt in her life.

However, she immediately felt guilty for harboring such happiness while Sarah was experiencing such pain. Guiltily, she'd kept the secret between her and Beth Anne.

Now that the funeral was over, she longed to tell her husband the news. Still, she worried he was too upset about Peter to focus on their blessing.

"I can't believe I buried Peter today," Daniel said, crossing the room and standing beside Rebecca. "It just doesn't seem real somehow." He ran his fingers over her shoulders, sending warmth down her back.

"*Ya*, I know." She pressed her cheek against his hand and sighed. She was so thankful that he'd survived the fire with nothing more than bruises and minor burns. She only wished Sarah had experienced the same blessing.

"I'm worried about Sarah," he said, moving his fingers to her cheek. "She's so fragile now. I wish there was something we could do for her."

"I'm glad she's staying with your parents," Rebecca said, gazing up in his eyes. "She needs your *mamm* right now."

"*Ya*." He sighed and shook his head. "It's like some bad dream. We'll begin cleaning the debris tomorrow. The shop is a total loss. It will take several months to rebuild. My father is very distraught over it."

"Have they determined the cause?" she asked.

"*Ya*." He sighed. "Silas's table saw caught fire. When he tried to stop it, he panicked and knocked over a kerosene lamp. The lamp hit the floor, ignited an oily rag, and caused the explosion. Peter was trying to help Silas." His voice was thick.

He cleared his throat and shook his head. "It's all so unreal. *Dat* and Milton built that place with their bare hands before I was even born."

"I'm so sorry." She took his hands in hers and squeezed them. "With God's help, we'll get through this."

He squatted before her, lowering his face to hers, and the corners of his mouth turned up in a sad smile. "*Ya*, Becky. You're right. It's been a crazy couple of months, no?"

"*Ya*," Rebecca said. "But Lindsay is doing well. She's a blessing at the bakery."

"Have you heard from Jessica?" he asked.

"*Ya*. I talked to Trisha yesterday. Jessica's foot is healing well, and she's connected with some old friends. She's very happy. We made the right decision letting her stay in Virginia."

"*Gut.*" He pushed a lock of her hair behind her ear and then leaned forward. His warm lips brushed hers, sending the pit of her belly into a wild swirl. He suddenly broke the kiss. Sitting back on his heels, he studied her, the intensity in his eyes making her mouth dry.

"You're beautiful," he whispered.

"Beauty is vanity," she whispered.

"*Ya.*" He laughed. "But you still are."

She sucked in breath, wondering if now was the time to share the news.

"What's on your mind, Becky?" He squeezed her hands. "You need to open up to me, not let things fester. We both know what silence can bring."

She nodded and licked her lips. "I have something to tell you, but I'm not sure if now is the time." Self-doubt robbed her confidence. She looked down and fingered her nightgown to avoid his probing stare.

"Please tell me. I promise I'll listen." He pushed another lock of hair back, and she breathed in his fresh scent when she met his gaze.

"We're going to have a baby, Daniel. We're going to have our own *baby.*"

His eyes widened. "What did you say?"

"I'm pregnant," she whispered.

Gasping, he stood, took her hands, and lifted her to her feet. "We're going to have a baby?"

"*Ya.* It's a miracle!" She laughed as he picked her up and spun her around.

"This is a *wunderbar* miracle! A blessing!" His grin glowed in the flicker of the kerosene lamp. "How long have you known?" he asked, still keeping his hands around her waist.

"Beth Anne insisted I take a test yesterday, and it was

positive. I plan to see the midwife next week." Her smile faded. "I was afraid to tell you since the funeral was today. I didn't feel right celebrating our news when Sarah has so much sorrow." She drew imaginary circles on his hard chest.

He lifted her chin so their eyes met. "*Mei Fraa*, you should never be afraid to tell me anything. I'll always listen. Always."

His lips met hers again, and she closed her eyes, losing herself in his touch.

Epilogue

Sarah moved back and forth on the porch swing and stared out over her father's vast fields while idly caressing her rounded belly with her hand. The past few days had been a nightmarish blur.

In a less than a week, the life she'd known and loved had been turned upside down. She'd cried so much that her body was now a hollow shell of the woman she'd once been.

She used to dream of the future with her husband, Peter. Now she wondered how she'd get through tomorrow without even a thought for next week.

Glancing up at the sky, she studied the gray clouds forming in the distance.

The screen door opened and slammed against the house with a loud bang, causing her to jump. Sarah kept her eyes locked on the fields while a light breeze kissed her face. Footsteps clomped across the porch, and the swing shook as her *mamm* lowered herself down beside her. The swing moved in silence for several minutes.

"Sarah Rose," her mother whispered, squeezing her hand. "Your father and I are glad you agreed to stay here."

Sucking in a breath, Sarah nodded and continued to rub her belly. "It seems the only way we'll make it."

"We'll get through this, Sarah Rose," *Mamm* said, squeezing her hand again. "I promise you."

"I just don't see how."

Mamm continued to hold her hand. "I know it's hard to accept that he's gone. It doesn't seem real. But the Lord will be our strength. Like the verse the minister read from Isaiah 60 last week—'The Lord will be your everlasting light, and your days of sorrow will end.'"

A lump swelled in Sarah's throat. "All I know is that Peter didn't deserve to die. He was good and sweet and loving." She hugged her belly in her hands. "He would've been a wonderful father. Now we're alone."

"You're not alone. You have your family. We'll all take care of you and the baby."

"It's not the same." Sarah stared down at her lap. "My baby won't have a father. How is that fair?"

"We'll do the best we can to be there for you," her mother whispered, her voice trembling. "I promise you that."

"I can't believe I'm going to be a *mamm* and a widow at the same time," Sarah said. She cupped her hands over her mouth hoping to stifle a sob.

"Shh," her mother pulled her close. "It's okay, Sarah Rose. We'll all help you through this."

Closing her eyes, Sarah let her tears fall. While her *mamm* held her and rocked her, she wondered how she would find the strength to raise her baby without her beloved Peter.

Discussion Questions

1. Rebecca's interpretation of "God's will" changes through-
    out the book. She is so set on what she wants (having chil-
    dren) that she doesn't look to God for further guidance.
    The answers to prayers are not always what we want or
    expect. Think about a time in your life when you misun-
    derstood God's will.

2. Rebecca and Daniel's relationship is strained when the girls
    join their family. Is she listening to her husband? Are they
    partners in the decisions that are best for the household?
    Does their relationship grow and change throughout the
    book? If so, how?

3. Think about a time when you and your spouse or partner
    didn't agree or listen to each other. What kind of strain did
    that put on your relationship? How did you work through
    it?

4. Is Jessica wrong to argue with Rebecca about her future? Is
    she a petulant teen, or a determined young girl?

5. Gossip, even in a community that is supposed to be Christ-
    like, can hurt and lead to misunderstanding. Have you
    judged someone recently based on gossip or spread a rumor
    without knowing all the facts?

6. Read and reflect on Hebrews 11:1 (print out the verse).
    How does this verse relate to the story? Are you able to
    relate this verse to your life and experiences?

7. Which character can you identify with the most? Which character seemed to carry the most emotional stake in the story?

8. What did you know about the Amish before reading this book? What did you learn?

9. Reflect on Elizabeth's favorite verse, Romans 12:12, "Be joyful in hope, patient in affliction, faithful in prayer." What does this verse mean to you? How does it apply to your life?

10. What role does the bakery play in the family unit and community? Can you relate this to your life and your family traditions?

Smoke filled Sarah Troyer's lungs and stung her watering eyes. Covering her mouth with her trembling hand, she fell to her knees while flames engulfed the large carpentry area of the Amish furniture store.

"Peter!" Her attempt to scream her husband's name came out in a strangled cough, inaudible over the noise of the roaring fire surrounding her.

Peter was somewhere in the fire. She had to get to him. But how would she find her way through the flames? Had someone called 9 – 1 – 1? Where was the fire department?

A thunderous boom shook the floor beneath Sarah's feet, causing her body to shake with fear. The roof must've collapsed!

"Sarah!" Peter's voice echoed, hoarse and weak within the flames.

"I'm coming!" Sobs wracked Sarah's body as she crawled toward the back of the shop. She would find him. She had to!

317

Turning her face toward the ceiling, Sarah begged God to spare her husband's life. He had to live. She needed him. He was everything to her. They were going to be parents.

Their baby needed a father.

Standing, she threw her body into the flames, rushing toward the crumpled silhouette on the floor as the remaining ceiling came crashing down on top of them.

Sarah's eyes flew open, and she gasped. She touched her sweat-drenched nightgown with her trembling hands. Closing her eyes, she breathed a sigh of relief.

It was a dream!

Stretching her arm through the dark, she reached for Peter. Instead, her hand brushed only the cool sheets next to her in the double bed.

Empty.

Sarah cupped a hand to her hot cheek while reality swept over her. Peter had died in the fire in her father's furniture store three months ago. He was gone, and she was staying in her parents' house.

Taking a deep, ragged breath, she swallowed a sob. She'd had the fire dream again, the fourth time this week.

When were the nightmares going to cease? When was life going to get easier?

She rested her hands on her swelling belly while tears streamed down her burning cheeks. It seemed like only yesterday Sarah was sharing the news of their blessing with Peter and he was smiling, his hazel eyes twinkling, while he pulled her close and kissed her.

It had been their dream to have a big family like most of the Amish couples in their church district. Sarah and Peter had spent many late nights snuggling in each other's arms while talking about names. She'd wanted to name a daughter after her grandmother Rachel and a boy after Peter.

However, Sarah had buried those dreams along with her

husband, and she still felt as bewildered as the day his body was laid to rest. She wondered how she'd ever find the emotional strength to raise her baby without the love and support of her beloved Peter.

She had believed since the day she married Peter that they would raise a large family and grow old together. But that ghastly fire stole everything from Sarah and her baby—their future and their stability.

Closing her eyes, she mentally repeated her mother's favorite Scripture, Romans 12:12: "Be joyful in hope, patient in affliction, faithful in prayer."

However, the verse offered no comfort. She tried to pray, but the words didn't form in her heart.

Sarah was numb.

She stared up through the dark until a light tap on her door roused her from her thoughts.

"Sarah Rose." Her mother's soft voice sounded through the closed door. "It's time to get up."

"*Ya.*" Wiping errant tears from her cheeks, Sarah rose and slowly dressed, pulling on her black dress, apron, and shoes. She then parted her golden hair and twirled long strands back from her face before winding the rest into a bun. Once her hair was tightly secured, she placed her white prayer *Kapp* over it, anchoring it with straight pins.

Sarah hurried down the stairs and met her mother in the front hall of the old farmhouse in which she'd been raised.

"I'm ready," she said.

Mamm's blue eyes studied her. "Aren't you going to eat?"

"*Nee.*" Sarah headed for the back door. "Let's go. I'll eat later."

"Sarah Rose. You must eat for the baby." *Mamm* trotted after her.

"I'll eat later. I'm not hungry." Sarah headed to the family bakery adjacent to the big old house.

"Did you have the dream again?" *Mamm's* voice was filled with concern.

Sarah sucked in a breath, hoping to curb the tears rising within her throat. "I'm just tired." She started down the dirt driveway toward the bakery.

Mamm caught up with her. Taking Sarah's hand in hers, she gave her a bereaved expression. "Sarah Rose, *mei Lieb*, how it breaks my heart to see you hurting. I want to help you through this. Please let me."

Swallowing her threatening tears, Sarah stared down at her mother's warm hand cradling hers. Grief crashed down on her, memories of Peter and their last quiet evening together flooding her. He had held her close while they discussed their future as parents.

Rehashing those memories was too painful for Sarah to bear. She missed him with every fiber of her being. She had to change the subject before she wound up sobbing in her mother's arms.

"We best get to work before the girls think we overslept," Sarah whispered, quickening her steps.

"Don't forget this afternoon is your ultrasound appointment," *Mamm* said. "Maybe we'll find out if you're having a boy or a girl. Nina Janitz is going to pick us up at two so we're at the clinic on time."

Sarah swallowed a groan at her mother's words. The thought of facing this doctor's appointment without Peter sharpened the pain that pulsated in her heart.

Pushing the thought aside, Sarah stared at the bakery *Mamm* had opened more than twenty years ago. *Mamm* prattled on about the weather and how busy the bakery had been since tourist season descended upon Bird-in-Hand. Sarah nodded.

After climbing the steps, Sarah and *Mamm* headed in through the back door of the bakery. The sweet aroma of freshly baked bread filled Sarah's senses while the Pennsylvania Dutch chatter of her sisters swirled around her.

Nodding a greeting to her sisters, Sarah washed her hands before pulling out ingredients to begin mixing a batch of her favorite sugar cookies. She engrossed herself in the task and shut out the conversations around her.

"How are you?" Lindsay, her sister-in-law's young niece, asked.

"*Gut,*" Sarah said, forcing a smile. "How are you today?"

"*Gut, danki.*" The fourteen-year-old smiled and her ivory complexion glowed. Although she'd been raised by non-Amish parents, Lindsay had adjusted well to the lifestyle.

When her parents had died in a car accident, Lindsay and her older sister had been left in the custody of her aunt Rebecca, Sarah's sister-in-law. Lindsay had quickly adapted to the Amish way of life and was learning the Pennsylvania Dutch language as if she'd been born into the community.

Lindsay tilted her head in question and wrinkled her freckled nose. "You don't look *gut,* Aunt Sarah. Is everything okay?"

"I'm fine, but *danki.*" Sarah stirred the Anise cookie batter and racked her brain for something to change the subject. "You and Rebecca got here early this morning, no?"

"*Ya.*" Lindsay began cutting out cookies. "Aunt Rebecca was having some tummy problems this morning." She nodded toward her stomach, and Sarah knew the girl was referring to morning sickness. "She was up early, and I was too. So, we just headed out. We had a couple of loaves of bread in the oven before Aunt Beth Anne and Aunt Kathryn got here."

Sarah nodded and glanced across the kitchen to where *Mamm* was speaking softly to Sarah's older sisters. When *Mamm's* gaze met Sarah's, her mother quickly looked away, causing Sarah's stomach to churn.

She hoped her mother wasn't talking to them about her again. She was in no mood for another well-meaning lecture from her sisters. They were constantly insisting Sarah must accept Peter's death and concentrate on the blessing of her pregnancy.

What did they know about loss? They both had their husbands and children living and healthy.

"I best go check on the children," Lindsay said, wiping her hands on her apron. "Aunt Kathryn must need a break since she came back in from outside."

Sarah snatched the cookie cutter. "I'll finish cutting out your cookies."

"*Danki.*" Smiling, Lindsay crossed the kitchen and disappeared out the back door toward the playground set up for Sarah's young nieces and nephews.

"Sarah," a voice behind her said. "How are you today? *Mamm* mentioned that you had a rough night."

Sarah glanced over at Beth Anne and swallowed a groan. "I'm fine." *I wish you all would stop worrying about me.*

Beth Anne's blue eyes narrowed with disbelief, and Sarah braced herself for the coming lecture.

"You can talk to me. I'll always listen." Her older sister squeezed her hand.

"I appreciate that, but there's nothing to say. I didn't get much sleep last night, but I'm *gut.* Really." Sarah turned back to her cookies in the hopes Beth Anne would return to work and leave her alone to her thoughts.

"I know you're hurting," Beth Anne began, moving closer and lowering her voice. "However, you must let Peter's memory rest in peace. You need your strength for your baby."

Sarah gritted her teeth and took a deep breath, trying in vain to curb her rising aggravation. Facing her older sister, she narrowed her eyes. "I know you mean well, but you can't possibly know what I'm thinking or what I'm feeling. I lost my husband, and you have no idea how that feels. I know I need to let go, but how can I when Peter's baby is growing inside me?"

Beth Anne's expression softened. "I just want what's best for you."

"Then leave me alone and let me work." Sarah faced the counter. "I have a lot of cookies to make. We sold out yesterday."

"Okay," Beth Anne's voice was soft. "If you need to talk, I'm here."

"*Ya. Danki.*" Sarah closed her eyes and prayed for strength to make it through the day.

❁

Late that afternoon, Sarah lay on the cold, metal table at the clinic and stared at the computer screen while a young woman moved the cool probe through the jelly spread on her belly.

Sarah stared at the screen and sucked in a breath while the ultrasound technician pointed out anatomy on the screen. Sarah wondered how many years of schooling it took for the young woman to figure out which was the spinal cord and which was the heart when it all resembled a bunch of squiggly lines.

Miranda Coleman, Sarah's midwife, interrupted the technician and moved over to the screen. "Do you see that?" Miranda asked the young girl in a hushed whisper. "I believe that's ..."

"Yes, you're right," the technician said with a grin. "I think so."

"This is something." Miranda folded her arms and shook her head. "Well, that explains her sudden weight gain."

"What?" Sarah started to sit up, her heart racing with worry. "What's wrong with my baby?"

Her eyes full of worry, *Mamm* squeezed Sarah's shoulder.

Miranda chuckled. "Nothing's wrong, Sarah."

Sarah held her breath and wished Peter was by her side to help her shoulder the news. "Please tell me what's going on."

"Sarah Troyer, you're doubly blessed," Miranda began with a smirk. "You're having twins. I guess one was blocking the other when we did the last ultrasound."

"Twins?" Sarah gasped. Lightheaded, she put her hand to her forehead.

How would she ever raise twins alone?

Share Your Thoughts

With the Author: Your comments will be forwarded to the author when you send them to *zauthor@zondervan.com*.

With Zondervan: Submit your review of this book by writing to *zreview@zondervan.com*.

Free Online Resources at
www.zondervan.com

Zondervan AuthorTracker: Be notified whenever your favorite authors publish new books, go on tour, or post an update about what's happening in their lives.

Daily Bible Verses and Devotions: Enrich your life with daily Bible verses or devotions that help you start every morning focused on God.

Free Email Publications: Sign up for newsletters on fiction, Christian living, church ministry, parenting, and more.

Zondervan Bible Search: Find and compare Bible passages in a variety of translations at www.zondervanbiblesearch.com.

Other Benefits: Register yourself to receive online benefits like coupons and special offers, or to participate in research.